OTHER BOOKS BY T.J. KELLY

THE ARMAGEDDON'S WARD SERIES

Armageddon's Ward
Irregular Magic
Darkness Wins
Praelia Nox

T.J. KELLY

GATEWAY JUMPERS
THE NAVIGATOR

PERSISTENCE PUBLISHING

Fort Worth, Texas

Library of Congress Control Number: 2021942830

ISBN: 978-1-948744-14-0 (paperback)
ISBN: 978-1-948744-15-7 (eBook)

Any references to historical events, real people, or real places are used fictitiously. Names, characters, and places are products of the author's imagination.

Manufactured in the United States of America

First Edition 2021

Cover Art by Designs By Persistence
Copyright © 2021 Daniele Jennings

For more information regarding reproductions of works by Designs By Persistence, please contact artist care of Persistence Publishing, addressed "Attention: Permissions Coordinator," at the address below.

Persistence Publishing, LLC
P.O. Box 6663
Fort Worth, Texas 76115
info@persistencepublishing.com
www.persistencepublishing.com

www.tjkellybooks.com

For my husband, with thanks for his support.

CHAPTER ONE
The Fifth Journey

WE WERE GETTING READY for my fifth journey when I met him. Our team needed a new strategist, and I guess the boss thought he'd fit the bill. He certainly looked the part.

This guy was definitely a throwback - he was brawny, muscles bulging yet streamlined, his skin a dark tan, brown hair streaked with blond highlights from spending days on end out in the sun and long enough to touch the collar of his shirt. Not that his shirt really had a collar.

Instead, he wore a black t-shirt that he had tucked into his dusty gray jeans since he wasn't wearing his standard issue clothing yet. His weapons were affixed to his back using wide leather straps. He had a sword and a bow with arrows since we were going into a backwater no-tech rube of a dimension.

The kind we call a Mention. As in, don't mention it. Not worth a mention. Wouldn't be mentioned in the top five hundred planets to visit. And so on.

Maybe things would go well. But then he introduced

himself. And he said his name was Bain.

"Really? Your name is actually Bain? Or is that what you like to call yourself to strike terror in the hearts of our enemies?"

Oh, no. Why did I say that? Was I really incapable of saying something funny or at the very least keeping my mouth shut around an attractive guy so I'd look mysterious? I only wished what came out of it was something sexy or intriguing. Instead, I had just mocked the new guy five seconds after we met, ruining my chances.

"Mason Bain," he corrected. He didn't hold out his hand for a shake and he glared, eyes scorching me with his scorn as he sneered, then turned away. So much for my amazing interpersonal skills that saved our collective butts time and again out in the Mentions.

I was actually making a name for myself by that point, too. I'd been courted by several other units before my last two journeys, but teams that stuck together were more likely to strike it rich, so I stayed where I was. Odds were that we'd hit the big-time sooner rather than later and I didn't want to start over. Most explorers in the Corps averaged about ten trips before they retired. I optimistically ignored the fact that "retired" usually meant "dead" instead of "rich."

But whatever, I had nothing left to lose. Like most of my other teammates.

I heard Ginger let out a sultry laugh, grabbing my attention. She always did that - made some kind of show that drew all eyes to her, even mine. And I spent most my time trying to avoid her.

Ginger was barely older than me, but for some reason her twenty-five years screamed "I'm an experienced sex goddess who will rock your world," while my twenty-three years said, "no, really, I'm standing here too, please just give me a chance big fella."

Not like I was trying to attract anyone's attention, of course. Especially this new guy. So I guess it didn't really matter that I screwed up the first time I opened my mouth. Shaking my head, I turned my attention back to my preparations.

I couldn't help it. I looked over to where Ginger stood sorting through her gear. Mason, who I swore to myself I would never call Bain, was leaning in to murmur something in her ear. I gritted my teeth as I jerked a strap on my pack. She had on the same standard issue pullover and vest that I did, but she still managed to give him a peep show. Straight-up cleavage from heaven. Damn, that girl had moves.

It had to be the hair. I wished I had smooth chestnut locks and dark smoldering eyes the way Ginger did. She should be the one stuck with my strawberry blond hair with a name like Ginger, not me. That and my mud brown eyes could never compete with what she had, and there was nothing sleek or sexy about me. Ah, well, Bain obviously already hated me so no big loss. And I'd keep telling myself that until I meant it, too.

Another sexy laugh floated my way. I suspected that she was deliberately taunting me, especially when I saw what she did next.

Ginger "accidentally" lost her balance, her shaky stance

forcing her to lay her hand against Mason's beefy arm. His muscles tightened under her touch, a line of tension making its way up his forearm to his shoulder, stiffening his chest as he reached out to steady her. His hands were large, probably big enough to wrap around her entire body. Or almost. She wasn't as little around the waist as I was. I bet if he put those hands out to hold on to me, his fingers would touch. The thought made me feel little and delicate, sending a shiver up my spine. Usually my small stature put me at a disadvantage, but something about his large body only made me feel like he would have my back. And that felt good, too.

"Bailey, quit daydreaming and get your butt over here," our group leader, Nash, called. His dark brown skin had a sheen of sweat from the midday heat. Well, no wonder he was so irritable.

Ginger and Mason looked up, startled out of their little love-fest when Nash yelled at me. They looked right at me and caught me staring. Sometimes I wished I could drop into a hole in the ground. I recognized that triumphant look in Ginger's eye, which sent heat into my cheeks and my stomach clenched. I couldn't get a read on good old Mason, though. He probably thought I was an idiot and the weak link on the team.

I tried to act natural. I hopped to and did a little jog over to Nash and gave him a mocking salute and a jaunty bow, but I thought it might have looked as stiff and awkward as I felt instead of confident.

"Lieutenant Bailey Hawke at your service, oh mighty one," I responded, chipper as hell to show everyone that nothing bothered me.

I caught Mason jerking into an upright position out of the corner of my eye. Now he would have plenty to say about my last name. I hoped he didn't make the connection, anyway. I guess I shouldn't have saluted, though. It was a dead giveaway.

"Quit your crap girl, the Corps don't have ranks, and if they did, you'd be a lowly private mopping my floor, not leading my team through the Mentions. Tell me your read on this one. We need to get out soon as we can."

Good old Nash. He was all business on the trail but wasn't above insulting a fellow explorer for kicks. I loved that in a man.

I pulled out my compass. It worked just fine as a standard compass. Most worlds had a magnetic field like Earth-prime, but there were all sorts of hidden buttons on mine and it had its own energy source. It took me three years to master it, and that was fast. Faster than anyone else coming out of the Nav School. Most trackers studied at least five years, if they passed at all. I was actually kind of amazing. At some things.

"We can go in ten minutes, but if you wait twenty-nine exactly, we'll land only a few clicks away from the nearest population center. It'll save us a week of hiking," I told Nash. The whole point was to drop through the portal close enough to suss out the indigenous people and categorize the threat, but far enough away that we didn't land on their heads. The locals always ended up complying with what the Corps wanted, which usually included them providing free labor, but it could take a few dead bodies to do it. Our goal was to limit the number of deaths while also finding the best way to exploit the planet. The more people, the more workers. If this earth-copy was mineral-rich, our percentage would make us all millionaires and we could retire. It was better to get the people part out of the way before we looked for the loot.

"Good job, Bailey."

Nash stole my heart when I realized he never called me by my last name like he did to everyone else. I think he saw me wince the only time he called me Hawke, and that was all he needed. If he wasn't older than my dad, I'd probably have tried to marry him. He wasn't a bad-looking man, and he had a command about him I admired.

He turned to the others and spewed out a few orders. "Listen up, team. You need to be ready to jump in twenty-eight minutes. Bailey will get us to an empty space, but you never know who might show up that close to home. The initial report shows they're likely to be hostile and you should know that because you better have read it already. If not, no time like the present - but don't let me catch you. Prepare sooner and don't make me tell you again."

I noticed Ginger pulling out a reader from her pack. Ha. Of course she hadn't read anything yet. She always acted like she was too good to need advance preparation. If she wasn't such a talented medic, I would have refused to work with her. But she saved my life a dozen times. I owed her - I kept quiet.

Will and Logan continued taking inventory, so they must have done the reading. Tyler stretched and jogged in place, did a few push-ups, basically showing off his hot body for anyone in the crowd at Base Camp, the usual collection of riffraff and travelers bored and standing around watching us prepare to jump. I couldn't blame him. He had the typical dark black hair and amber-brown skin of his Hispanic ancestors and practically glowed with vitality and health. Tyler was also sweet as hell, but he had as much bad luck with guys as I did. We bonded over that on the last trip. He winked at me and jerked his chin towards Mason with a little grin, indicating something was happening in that direction.

I turned and looked.

Yeah, Mason was definitely checking me out. But Tyler didn't know enough about me to know why that might be the case. He thought Mason thought I was hot. I wish.

I cringed as Mason walked over to where I had set my bags, apparently to talk to me. Hell. *Don't react, don't react, don't react.*

"Hawke. That's not a common name. You related to General Atticus Hawke?"

Damn. I wished I could lie. But our group motto was "Never Lie" and that really meant "You Lie You Die" and Nash himself would knife me in the back if he heard me deny it. Trust was the only way to stay alive.

"Yeah. What of it?" Not everybody knew all the details, but those that heard the rumors usually had quite a few hateful things to say to me.

"I've seen his daughter, and you aren't her." His hazel eyes searched mine.

I couldn't tell what he was thinking. I was so good at reading people, I could usually communicate out in the

Mentions before anyone else. It came in real handy. But Mason was like trying to read a brick wall.

"I'm his other daughter," I grudgingly admitted.

I braced myself. Everyone compared me to my sister, and they always found me lacking. She was ten years older than me and looked like her mom. I looked like mine. That meant her blond hair didn't have any strawberry to ruin it, and she had icy platinum eyes. Some people called her the Golden Goddess. She married the President's son twelve years before and everyone worshipped her. She never even sent me a wedding announcement, much less invited me to the reception. But whatever.

"You anything like him?" he asked.

Ask, not assume? That was a first. A feather could've knocked me down. "I hope not."

Mason studied me, his eyes taking their time as they measured me. "How old were you when he got caught?"

Don't react, don't react, don't react. I kept my hands pressed firmly to my sides. People think they've stumbled onto something important once I've crossed my arms over my chest. Of course, they were usually right. And he really had gotten to me. Not that I wanted him to know it.

"Eight."

"Must be why I didn't see you on the vids. Had to be tough."

Holy hell. I couldn't believe I was actually having an actual conversation about my dad that didn't start with calling me names. Or worse, with that hopeful look that told me they wanted to use me as a ticket to meeting the man himself. But Mason even sounded a tad sympathetic.

And after I made fun of him, too. Maybe Nash made another good choice with this one.

"Yeah. It wasn't a picnic." Good. I sounded tough, like it didn't still hit me like it was yesterday. As if I didn't still have nightmares about it. At least I learned to stop screaming with night terrors or else I would have been a huge liability out in the Mentions. And I passed the psych evaluation. That counted for a lot.

"You're the tracker, right?" Mason kept talking to me. I wondered why. I frantically thought about what to do to keep him talking, although I wasn't even sure why I cared. Maybe it was Tyler's look as he winked at me from behind Mason's back. Was he right? Was Mason interested after all? Should I try that move of Ginger's so I could accidentally show him my cleavage? My chest was actually really nice looking, even if it wasn't triple-d like hers.

What the hell was I thinking? Get it together, girl. "Yeah. This is my sixth trip." *Just keep it simple. Don't talk too much.* "I also help with linguistics. I don't learn their language, but they seem to understand me pretty well until Will's training kicks in. He's the one with the language implant."

Will was born with a silver spoon in his mouth, but he knew how to work hard and paid to get the implant with his family money instead of wasting it on a life of luxury. I met him on my third journey. He was one of the ones who joined the Corps for the adventure. Crazy bastard.

"I guess I'll find out how good you are when we get there," Mason growled.

"Wow, thanks." As if he had the right to judge me? Yet I

had done the same. We all did. Until we see our teammates out in the Mentions, there was no telling how good they really were. Or if they would turn and run right when we needed them to stay and fight.

Instead of arguing, or worse, saying something to make me look more like an idiot, I gave him a snappy salute and hightailed it out of there. Time was running out to get ready for the jump, anyway.

For some reason, Mason made me want to smack him. I had a strict non-violence policy with my teammates, since physical contact - even while joking around - could lead to worse things. Images of him laying his hands on me flooded my mind. I gulped, walking stiffly to a shaded area to cool off. Despite the heat, goosebumps rose on my arms, pricking at the back of my neck. My entire body felt ultra-sensitive, the tough fabric of my uniform rubbing against my skin, setting off spikes and tingles all over.

Flustered, unsure how to feel or know what I wanted, I focused as hard as I could on my equipment. Distraction was dangerous, and I needed to get it together.

Another image of me hitting his arm, more a caress than anything else, flitted across my mind. No. I had to stop before I went into a tailspin. My team was counting on me. Besides, I didn't know what wanting to strike him was all about, but I didn't have the time to figure it out. Not with the clock counting down.

We all had a pre-jump routine. I noticed that on the second trip. It was systematic and nobody else seemed to realize it. At least, nobody ever said anything about it to me.

Ginger checked her pouch with the meds five times. Not in a row, but still, five times exactly. Will patted his right front pocket twice. Then he rubbed his right ear, and then the pocket again. I didn't think there was actually anything in there, either. He just patted an empty pocket. Logan and Tyler checked each other's packs. They always tugged three times on the right, and four on the left. Nash ran his hands across the scar on his chin a few times. He did that at other times too, not only before a jump, so he looked more natural than anyone else.

I wasn't sure what my routine was. Probably people-watching. I also tapped the side of my compass a lot. It could be that. But I didn't know what Mason would do. He changed into his standard issue clothing, stomping his boots a few times to break them in. Maybe that was it. Maybe he lumbered around like an angry giant. He must have seen me looking because he winked at me.

Oh, boy. A thrill shot through me and somewhere inside, a decision was made. I liked it. So maybe this would turn out better than I originally thought.

Then, Ginger. Damn. She didn't have to brush up against him like that, diverting his attention from me again. She did it on purpose, and it pissed me off.

"Line up!" Nash yelled. We all fell into pecking order, Nash in the front, then me since I navigated. Mason had my back because he was the main fighter and strategist, then Ginger and Will, Logan and Tyler. We were all trained to fight, but the strategist had skills like nobody's business. At least the good ones did. Once we arrived in the Mention, he would walk in front of me. He and I would collaborate sometimes. I decided to keep my eye on Mason whenever I could so I could see if he was any good at his job, too.

I ignored the clenching of my stomach at that thought. Watching him wouldn't be a problem. Keeping my focus out where the danger was would be if I didn't cut it out.

Nash clenched his fist in the air near his shoulder. I flipped the compass open and started the sequence. It was the first thing we learned - how to open a door on this side. It was specific to Earth-prime, so it wouldn't work on any other world in any other dimension no matter how much they looked alike. If they looked alike.

It would be up to me to figure out how to get back once we were on the other side. We were stuck there until I figured out the other sequence. That was why I was so important. I was the way back home. All I needed to do was watch the stars for a few nights and we were golden. It was simple once I had the method beaten into my brain after the entire first year of school. Now, I could calculate our way home half-conscious with rebar pinning my shoulder to a wall. That wasn't an exaggeration, either, that was the test navigators had to pass to make it into the second year.

"Engaged," I announced.

Nash started the countdown from ten, trusting I lined him up at the right moment to plant us in the right place. I had natural timing, which was a huge help. On one, Nash raised his fist into the air and swung it forward. Then he jumped. We all followed immediately. If a jumper took too long, we ended up half a mile away, all alone. And if our luck didn't hold, that would get us killed. We lost Abilene that way. That was why we had to replace her with Mason.

It was like hopping from one foot to the other. The only way we could tell we made it through was that it was night on the other side. Portals were invisible and we all jump blind. Coming and going. Usually the terrain looks just like where we left, but on my second trip, we landed right next to a tar pit instead of on subcutaneous rock. Something had altered that dimension to change the very nature of the earth, the way something had disrupted the orbit of the copy-earth we were about to explore.

I started taking environmental calculation classes after that. It was advanced material and most people never used it, but I wanted to get it right. I wanted to earn my place, but I also wanted to exceed everyone's expectations and shine. It was my strategy to stay alive. That way when people like Tyler found out who my father was, they would remember how much I did for them and they wouldn't hate me.

I wanted a chance for once. I wanted people to like me no matter who I was related to.

It didn't matter how pathetic that made me, either. Not after being the eight-year-old daughter of a man like my father, trying to figure out what to do when people weren't nice to me, even though I was barely older than a baby myself.

They weren't nice to me, even when I was the one who found the dead bodies and called the police.

Even though I lost everything doing what was right.

The experts, and the journalists, and the therapists weren't nice to me, either, not once they realized they couldn't gain access to him through me. It may have been temporary, but that was the only reason people played nice after that awful day. They wanted to see him, touch him, study him, worship him, or hate him. They didn't get what they wanted, so they turned on me. The daughter of an infamous father.

Three-Star General Atticus Hawke.

Baby-killer.

And I was his spawn.

CHAPTER TWO
Arrival

IT WAS A PRETTY good landing, even if I said so myself. A clearing surrounded by trees giving us space to land without obstacles to hurt ourselves yet cover from potential prying eyes. Not sure what kind of foliage was out there - we would have to wait for daylight for that, which was about two hours away if I had my calculations right. And so far, I always had.

Mason peeled off from his position behind me and started his circuit to ensure we weren't observed or in immediate danger. Logan and Tyler would split up and went in different directions to help cover the area. They were the support fighters and deadly when needed.

My eyes searched Logan's face before he took off. It was too dark to see his expression, but I could already tell he was going to love the place. There were plants and weeds everywhere around us, and it would cheer his little botanist heart right up.

He'd be doubly happy since he was also our geologist and there were large piles of rocks, embedded in the soil that rose sharply to one side of the clearing, all lumpy and bumpy and ridged and pockmarked and smooth. It had taken a while for Logan to warm up to me, but once I realized all I needed to do was keep him in the know about the readouts on my compass so he knew exactly where to search, things worked better.

"Perfect landing, Bailey," Nash said. He was good about that, dishing out the praise when deserved. The flip side was his searing reprimands, but I avoided those like the plague.

"Thanks, boss." I grinned, knowing full well there was a sour look on his face in response to my flippancy.

"Don't get used to it. Your head's getting too big as it is." His gruff voice soothed me, as did the mild rebuke. He wouldn't have said it that way if my ego really was large enough to unbalance the team. But it showed he cared.

Until we received the all-clear, we would stay where we were, at the ready. I took the time to take in our surroundings, straining my eyes to draw even more input.

There was no way to tell what the world would look like until we got there, but it was the best thing when I jumped us into night. Unfortunately, it was just my luck it was overcast. I sighed. There were other ways to figure out the sequence to get back home, but nobody wanted to wait an entire year for me to mark the days on my compass before figuring it out.

We didn't even know how long a year was yet, although so far all the worlds seemed to be exactly like Earth-prime, three hundred and sixty-five long days around the sun. The scientists had announced these portals were taking us to planets that were really different versions of the same Earth, but I wasn't sure I believed them. The stars were all so different. How could another Earth be in a different place in the universe if we all started the same?

And Logan once told me that the mineral deposits were never in the same place as Earth, either. Maybe all those tiny, minute decisions that supposedly made all those alternate Earths into a Multiverse also changed the planet's position and where the platinum mines were located, but somehow I doubted it. But it didn't even really matter. All that mattered was we could go to other planets now and make lives better.

Whose lives, they never said. But I would end my tour of duty rich or dead, and I knew whose "Better Life" I was shooting for.

Mason got back from his search of the surrounding area and reported to Nash. I couldn't hear everything he said, but Nash looked satisfied by the news, the predawn helping define his face. He sent Ginger out with Logan and Tyler to test the nearby stream. Fresh water was top priority after safety was established, and Ginger would tell us if it was safe to drink. We all got the standard vaccines, but who knows if the bacteria that caused dysentery was the same everywhere? What if one of those earth-copies that split off into its own dimension had bred a different kind of disease that no vaccine would cover?

Shaking off those grim thoughts, I cleared my compass settings and took my first reading. Today was day one. As long as I tracked every day - even if I only tracked a day once every week or so, really - I'd know how to get home. Eventually. I couldn't stand the thought of failing my team. They were counting on me to get them home as soon as we got what we needed.

Nobody knew why some teams never made it back, but you could bet sometimes it was the tracker's fault. And I wouldn't do that. I might not have been able to save those babies from my father, but I sure as hell wasn't going to lose anyone else.

I yawned, suddenly drained of all energy. Sometimes working through the calculations did that to me.

"Sleep When You Can" was my personal rule number one on jump day. I cultivated the talent of taking a nap anytime, anywhere. An overcast sky freed up a lot of time for the navigator, so I pulled out my sleeping bag and wrapped up, sitting in the middle of the clearing.

It was because I hated the thought of bugs and snakes. I would never tell anyone that, but it was true. My sleeping position was in the center of a clearing because there were no trees or brush to hide nasty, creeping creatures. The sleeping bag was designed to stop anything from crawling in that wasn't human, but still. Why test it?

Everyone else was busy with their various tasks, but until they were done, I had free time. I was always too jazzed to sleep the night before a jump and was exhausted once I landed. With relief, I closed my eyes and drifted off.

Too bad I'd been dozing for only a little over an hour when the sounds of fighting woke me.

I burst out of my sleeping bag and was in fighting stance less than two seconds after the shouts woke me. We were all trained to respond that quickly, and it saved our butts many times out in the Mentions. In the home camp, too.

"Bain," Nash hissed, summoning Mason to where he had been standing near me. I hadn't expected to have anyone looking out for me like that, but it was a relief to know Nash would keep an eye out for me when I was asleep. I had really lucked out when I joined his team.

"I hear it," Mason murmured as he drew closer. He had already been walking the perimeter, but none of us had the chance to get to know him yet. I guess there were some things that are the same about all the strategists because he was all over it. "The others are still out."

If Ginger and the guys were still gone, that was a little long for checking water sources. Nash and Mason moved off closer to the direction of the noise, their voices too quiet to follow. All I could see was them exchanging a few gestures that would be impossible for an outsider to interpret. Which was the point when somebody might be coming. It might be our teammates fighting, but until we knew that for a fact, we weren't going to jump into anything, either.

Will walked over to where I was standing so we could partner up in case we needed to fight. He might have been a prep school boy, but he was also lethal. I was no slouch myself, so we had a pretty good chance against whatever was moving our way. And by the sound of it, trouble had almost arrived.

Mason grabbed the packs near his position and stuffed

them in a low depression behind some rocks. I collected mine and Will's packs, picking up the cooking implements and adding them to the same pile. It was better to keep as much of our supplies and equipment as hidden as possible. Meanwhile, Will kept his eyes peeled, his Nakamura steel katana at the ready. His family had made their riches from their steel, and then later the resurgence of less conventional weapons made them even richer. But as a Nakamura, he had also been trained to use their weapons since he was a toddler.

Maybe it wasn't a normal upbringing, especially when compared to the children of the slums, but at least he knew how to protect himself. That was better than what I learned a child, even when I lived with my father. He may have been a legendary military leader, but he thought nothing of leaving his daughters defenseless.

Mason also had a sword, although his had a wider straightedge. His bow and quiver were on the ground, propped against a rock in case they would work better to fight off what was coming our way. "You all right over there, navigator?" he asked gruffly.

"I'm good," I said. I had my knives if anyone came up on me. I was well-versed in throwing knives. Accurate aim and timing made them worthwhile weapons. Will had also been teaching me to use throwing stars, but I wasn't good enough to use them to defend myself. If the enemy broke through our main fighters, I would take as many out as possible and an unpracticed weapon did none of us any good.

Will and Mason were large men, strong and tall

yet light on their feet, which were good traits to have if forced to fight with a sword. The Corps didn't allow much technology on these trips because they didn't want it to fall into the wrong hands. We couldn't bring any light sticks or lasers or even guns since this Mention was so low-tech.

The Corps could always tell - they may not have a lot of visibility, but electricity, nuclear technology, and various other emanations were trackable outside the portal gate and gave fair warning which earth-copies to avoid. The pre-industrial copies were still explored, but the Corps allowed tech to help quell the more advanced capabilities.

My compass and Ginger's reader were the only true tech we had. It wasn't likely any primitive humanoid would understand more than the basics on my compass, and the technical features were keyed to my DNA print anyway, so an enemy could never access them. Ginger's reader was an important diagnostic tool, but if anyone tried to use it without her coding and print, it was a worthless piece of plastic. But we didn't want to lose or break them.

I clipped my compass to the chain I kept in my pack for just that purpose and slipped it around my neck, tucking it under my shirt. I scanned the edges of the clearing. We couldn't lose the compass. If we didn't make it back home, the Corps wouldn't come looking for us. They'd write us and this portal off. That was the risk we took as explorers, and we knew it.

It really was a free-for-all when it came to the Corps. Their training schools were run by sadistic veterans from the last war. Most people exalted them and called them heroes because they came back, and a lot of them were. But the ones who teach had special things wrong with them. The Corps has a test and the more psychotic they were, the more likely they would be hired. At least it seemed that way to me.

If we made it through training, and surprisingly most of us did, they gave us standard issue clothing and a pack, and we were on our own to find a team. When there were enough people to fill in the required skill sets to form one, then the team jumps into the next available portal and hopes for the best.

Besides our required tech, the Corps only provided communal housing and basic rations. It was almost worse than the slums, except there was a chance to strike it rich if we were brave enough to take the trip. It was the only opportunity most of us had, so there were plenty of volunteers despite the brutality. As in millions of volunteers. And there were still so many portals left to explore. The scientists said it could take another five hundred years at the current rate before they run out. Other scientists said they would never run out. That there were more alternates constantly being made, and we actually could never run out of copies.

As bad as it all was, there was one thing for sure. We were ready to take on the enemy. Mason may be new, but the rest of us had all been in some serious skirmishes and brawls and had learned to trust we would have each other's backs.

The slightest whistling sound floated in the air. I hit the ground. Good thing, too, because when I looked behind me, there was an arrow still vibrating from the force that plunged it several inches into a tree. Nash was across the clearing from where I was, and he gestured at me to disappear into the woods. I could pull my weight in a fight, but the compass is useless without me. In times like these, it was up to me to keep myself alive. Most of the time, that meant running away. A few last-chance throwing knives wouldn't keep me safe enough to get my team back home. I felt like crap every time I ran, but I did it anyway.

I left my pack behind. I hated to lose it, but I had my compass and my knives on me. Those were the only important things I owned. As I made my way to the edge of the clearing, I had my two knives strapped to my belt and a small, deadly blade wrapped against my shin under a bandage. It looked like I had hurt myself, not that I was concealing an instrument of death. I did it in hopes that if I got caught, anyone frisking me or stripping me down would ignore it.

Nash had determined I needed to run, not make a stand - I only needed my knives out when the enemy pushed through our tougher ranks. That had never happened on any of our trips, at least not when I was there. To them, my skills were untested. I had experience fighting in other areas of my life, though, because I've been attacked more times than I could count, at school and in the camps back on Earth.

Women were the favored targets. I guess some things never changed.

The sun was breaking over the horizon, but I lost all benefit from the light when I melted into the trees. There was a rustling coming from my right, so I dodged left and hightailed it as fast as I could.

I wasn't fast enough.

The man who came out from behind the trees wasn't as tall as Mason or Will, but he was intimidating enough for me, especially since he had his sword already drawn and I had no clue who he was or what he wanted. Although it wasn't hard to guess that he wasn't going to sit down for a cup of tea and chit-chat about all his plans while I braided his long brown hair.

I ducked below his arm when he swung his sword and rolled to the side. My pants were tight and stretchy, as per regulation, but something thorny got caught on my pant leg and the man grabbed the back of my vest before I could untangle myself and run.

He swung me around to face him, and I used the momentum behind that maneuver to help put more force behind my swing when I punched him as hard as I could in his face. I was aiming for his nose, but I caught his mouth instead. Pain exploded in my knuckles as they connected with his teeth. *Terrible aim, Bailey.*

My arms were still free, his sword too long to be of much use in such close quarters, so I slammed my left fist into his face. I was right-handed, but I could still wallop the hell out of someone with my left, too. Besides, adrenaline lent me strength. That time my aim was better, and he screamed as his nose spurted blood everywhere. I lifted my feet and used them to push against him and launched myself backward away from him.

His grip couldn't hold against the force of my legs. It

wasn't my best landing, my body crashing down hard on my hip. It was enough to get me out of his range and I ran as fast as I could, not waiting around to try to finish him off, which I might have been able to do. He looked pretty stunned beneath all the blood. But I was still following Nash's orders to run.

I felt better about taking off like that, knowing I had maimed one attacker enough to keep him from being able to fight anyone else. One of my teammates would easily finish him off if they found him. If they came after me.

A wave of heat trickled its way down my chest and pooled in my stomach, which clenched with the stress of the fight and the sudden thought that my team would only find him if they bothered to come find me. My breath panted out in gulps as I ran, dodging the trees, trying to think clearly enough to remind myself that I had the compass, I was the navigator, and they would come for me. That was why I learned to use the compass in the first place.

It was ridiculous to think about that while running for my life. The kind of thing we were supposed to go to the Corps therapist to work out. But I knew better. We all did. The second we admitted to having some kind of hang-up over something, they pulled us from duty and sent us away. The Corps training was great - for the Corps. It didn't get us a job anywhere else. And with a psych discharge, nobody would hire us anyway. Why would they? There were so many people and so few jobs that the Corps was typically the only chance any of us had.

My boots sank into the soft, sandy soil that lined a small creek I didn't notice in my hurry. I groaned. Wet boots sucked. They could be another cause of danger, especially if I wasn't able to dry them out. What a mess. Gritting my teeth, I kept up the pace, ignoring the growing discomfort, hoping my skin wouldn't slough off and give me blisters. Or worse, an infection. There was no telling if Ginger's meds would be enough to fix me up.

After a few clicks, my stamina gave out on me. I ran, jogged, and walked in intervals, but there was only so much ground I could cover before it became too much. I bent over and gripped my knees, dragging in several deep breaths before slowly walking around in a circle while my pulse slowed.

It gave me a chance to look around. There was enough light filtering through the trees that I could see a surprising distance ahead of me. The forest wasn't very dense, and many of the trees were long and skinny with the paper-thin white bark that identified them as birch trees. They didn't have fat leaves like an oak tree, which make it difficult to see. The ground was wavy, steep hills and low valleys in the terrain, but I figured I was in a safe enough spot to stop. I'd twist an ankle if I had kept running.

I pulled my canteen off my belt and drank a few sips. I didn't have any of the pills that we used to clarify drinking water and I didn't want to risk drinking from the very cold, very tempting stream trickling sweetly down a gentle slope that lay before me, and end up getting sick. But I decided that I might as well follow it for a while. Sticking near a water source was a good way to keep from getting lost. Not like I knew where I was to begin with. It would be a good rally point and my teammates would look for me near water, too.

My breathing finally evened out as I loped up the hill by the stream. My thigh muscles pulled uncomfortably, and I stomped off a cramp in my calf. Man, it had been way too long since I had been out in a Mention. Nash had made us all take a few weeks off. They all had somewhere to go and didn't mind, but unlike my team, that did not apply to me. I tried to keep up with my normal exercises, but the camps the Corps ran weren't safe. I ended up staying in my dorm the whole time.

The land dipped, and the trees cleared. The smell of smoke warned of a nearby fire, which almost always meant people. My pace slowed, and I searched for something dense to hide behind until I could figure out what to do next. The ground dropped sharply, rocks jutting out to form a wall against the backdrop of yet another steep hill. A potential hiding place! I walked around the stones and hopped down over the blind ledge.

Right into the middle of somebody's camp.

My eyes darted around, trying to take in as much as possible. Two men, who looked like they were in their thirties, and one teen were staring at me. I didn't have any kind of weapon out and my lack of height mush have been non-threatening enough to keep them where they were as we stared at each other in shock. I took the frozen moment to assess my situation.

Well, at least the locals looked like us. I didn't have much of a chance to study the man with the sword as I was fighting for my life. *Damn that stupid thorn bush.* It was a relief that I didn't have the added threat of looking too different, though. Different would get me killed.

It was unfortunate that the two women peering around the laundry they were hanging on a rope strung between a tent and a tree were wearing skirts. If women were wearing dresses in a forest while hauling around buckets of water and scrubbing laundry, then they must not be wearing pants because it wasn't allowed. Nobody hiked or camped or worked in skirts if they could help it. I may have broken a taboo or two without realizing it because I was wearing pants. Another strike against me, besides being a complete stranger who happened upon them in the middle of a forest without a reasonable explanation.

The tent they were using to help prop up their laundry line was made of woven reeds lashed together, ropes twisted from a thready material held it in place with stakes. It was large and likely had several rooms partitioned off inside. I bit my lip, concerned that there wasn't any way to know if there were more people lurking inside.

A quick movement caught my eye. I flicked my gaze to assess the threat level and caught sight of an elderly man sitting across the small open area from where I stood, hunched over as he leaned forward towards the ground, using a stick to make marks in the damp clay at his feet near a small fire. As my gaze continued to rest on him, his sleeve rifled in the wind, drawing my attention again. His stance and look in unconcern marked him as a noncombatant. My attention shifted back to searching the campsite for more details.

All that only took a split second to take in. We had been taught to evaluate a situation lighting fast. Since they didn't respond to my presence with drawn swords, I had hoped they would be more curious than hostile. But there was no telling unless I knew I had accounted for everyone. I couldn't wait any longer. I had to make a move and try to set the tone of our interaction as peaceful before somebody got antsy and started a war.

I lifted my hands up, showing they were empty, and I didn't mean any harm. Then I tried to take a step back the way I came, slow and easy in hopes I could just take off, but bumped into something I was positive wasn't there when I arrived. Damn. I slowly turned around and saw another man, one who had a short sword that was pointing at my neck. He said something that sounded really familiar, but I couldn't quite grasp the meaning. That happened in the Mentions a lot. It usually helped figure out how to communicate, but there wasn't time for that.

"Sorry," I said in a slow, gentle voice. "I don't understand what you're saying. But hey, look at how slow I'm moving. And listen to how calm I sound. That means I don't mean any harm." I looked him directly in the face but avoided eye contact so I wouldn't seem aggressive. I was small enough that even in the Mentions, where the people could sometimes be especially short, I still looked smaller than they were, and therefore weak and unassuming and submissive. I hoped.

Depending on the situation, Nash would send me out to make first contact. It helped establish communication quicker because nobody thought somebody small like me would be sent out in front unless our team meant no harm. Enemies protected their weak - unless they were trying really hard to get along. With me out front, we looked like we were extending trust, taking that risk, in hopes they wouldn't kill the little one. Or recognize the gesture as one of goodwill.

It was all an illusion, though. During those times, I wore a great set of lightweight armored vests, and I was a lot stronger than I looked. Of course, we usually had our strategist hiding somewhere that the locals couldn't see, waiting to pounce in case I needed to be extracted. But none of that happened without taking the time to observe them before any of us walked into a new situation. Too bad that wasn't the case now.

Footfalls moved closer, likely from the two men I had first observed, but I didn't turn around again to check. With quick movements, rough hands appeared in my peripheral vision and took my knives and canteen off my belt.

Did that mean anything? It was hard to tell. It was standard to disarm a stranger. We did that to people coming to see us and we didn't always have hostile intent. Maybe these guys still didn't, despite the sword at my neck. It could have been a precaution until they disarmed me. I kept my hands up and allowed them to remove my weapons without making a sound since the odds were against me.

If they didn't loosen up, I would wait for the right time to escape. There was a chance I could take out two of them, but not more than that. I had to bide my time.

One of the men behind me grabbed my wrists and yanked them up behind my back, high enough to cause my elbows to jut awkwardly and pain to shoot up my arms.

I winced at the rough treatment, which was totally unnecessary considering how docile and cooperative I was behaving. That didn't bode well.

The man holding the sword at my neck made some kind of a command, and the hands loosened up a bit while he tied them together.

I figured he was their Head Honcho and that he just told off the rough guy. I was non-aggressive and small, and it was obvious that there was no need to mess me around. Already I had two of the men at odds, which could work in my favor.

Honcho sheathed his short sword once my hands were tied. He said something else, this time to me. It didn't sound harsh, so I hoped they would now remain mostly civil until my team found me. All hope that this wasn't going to keep getting worse had vanished the second they bound my wrists.

They turned me around and led me into the center of their camp, close to the old man, who was still sitting on the ground. The women were nowhere to be seen. They were likely inside of the small tent off to the side of the clearing. The two other men and teen gathered together into a group, staring at me, while the Head Honcho pushed on my shoulder until I sat. It was my experience that it was best to cooperate unless I was in immediate danger. Sometimes these things could be settled peacefully.

Technically, we were supposed to establish diplomatic relations with the locals, especially if there were minerals or metals we wanted to mine. So even in a situation like this, we needed to do our best to get along. Make them feel like we weren't a threat. That they could trust us. Then we could negotiate and they could be used as cheap labor. Not that it mattered if they wanted to cooperate or not because if we had to, we would kill enough of them and they eventually complied. But then it was usually free labor.

Some dimensions were totally cleared of their original population. One world had a really rare metal that wasn't even found on asteroids relatively near Earth, so it made it worth it to the Corps to settle that planet no matter what the means. There weren't that many people on that earth-copy. Something in their history kept the plague going, and they never recovered. It didn't take much for us to wipe them out.

There were hundreds of thousands of slum kids growing up on that world now, being groomed to work the mines by their parents. Their loving parents, who signed away their own rights, and the rights of the three following generations of their descendants, in order to earn their place on a world that wasn't Earth. Indentured servitude was still better than where they came from.

Honcho barked an order, and the old man jerked upright. He had a look on his face that made it obvious he was thinking deep thoughts and indicated the type of genius that probably wouldn't be able to tie his own shoes. If the people here even had shoelaces. Or shoes. He stood and made a few swipes at his pants to dust them off before shifting his robe and then walked over to where I was sitting. Old Man said a few words. He actually looked surprised, then sad, and then raging mad. I guess he didn't like Honcho - or what he had to say.

Old Man studied me, a shrewd, assessing look in his eyes. They roamed over me from the top of my head to my toes. He took his time looking me over, dark eyes narrowing when they reached the area where my knife was hidden under my pant leg.

He didn't hesitate there or give any indication that he found the slight bulge suspicious in any way, but there was something about the shift in his demeanor that made me think he knew about the knife. Which was crazy. He ran his hand through his white hair, and I could hear the teen laugh when some of the clay on his hands remained behind. Old Man turned away and said one more thing, and Honcho pulled me to my feet, moving me so that I was standing directly in front of the old man.

He looked... apologetic. That couldn't be good.

The old man reached his dirty hands out and I couldn't help it, I tried to keep away from him. Honcho had a hard grip on my shoulders and I couldn't move very far despite my struggles. Then my entire backside brushed up against Honcho's body, my bound hands brushing a part of his anatomy I didn't want to touch, so I jerked forward to avoid any more contact. The last thing I needed right then was Honcho deciding I was interesting - interesting in ways I didn't want to be.

That put me within reach of Old Man. As he lifted his messy hands, a beam of early morning light reflected off his palm. He stood still, speaking in a low, even cadence that reminded me of a chant, hands hovering in the air. He moved his hands together and made a sharp clap, then cupped them palms up. That was when I noticed the metal embedded in his flesh. Dots and swirls and strange shapes that connected into a framework or some kind of netting that was a part of him.

My eyes widened when the metal shifted, tiny tendrils rippling along his palms and snaking their way to the top where they stretched as thin as threads along the length of his fingers, growing spikes from his fingertips.

Oh, hell no. But I couldn't move no matter how hard I struggled, fighting to get away as his hands descended upon my head.

"Stop!" I cried.

Old Man hesitated, looking at Head Honcho. A voice growled a harsh command and the old man's hands slid gently into the hair above my temples, cupping each side. Old Man continued to chant, then changed it into a constant hum, and then I felt something going on in my skull. Everywhere he touched me, erupted with heat and pressure. His vocalizations made my teeth vibrate in response, rattling up and down my skull.

Then the old man murmured several more words and forced me to look him in the eyes. I couldn't help myself even though something in the look he gave me hurt, like lava was being poured down from his gaze. Then a searing pain exploded in my head. I was silent for a split second, gasping for breath, shocked at the overwhelming, all-consuming, torturous pain.

I started screaming. I couldn't concentrate on anything except the pain, but I knew in a vague way that my legs must have given out because I could feel somebody crushing my arms in a bruising grip to keep me upright, a different and lesser pain, but still noticeable through the haze of agony.

The pressure in my brain grew worse, the heat unbearable, and from very far away, I could still hear the chanting and humming and all the bones in my skull vibrated in response. Then pain and pressure were the only things that existed for me.

Thankfully, I finally passed out.

CHAPTER THREE
New Ability

I WAS LYING ON the ground, my cheek touching the bare dirt when I woke. I didn't have my sleeping bag and that meant any number of bugs, snakes, or small animals could crawl up my pant legs or into my shoes or down my shirt. It wasn't until I tried to jerk upright out of danger that I realized my hands were tied behind my back.

Only then did I remember my situation and froze, wondering if I should give away my conscious state by struggling against the ropes. A short distance away, a chuckle filled the silence. Too late. My movements were noticeable. I recognized the laughing voice as belonging to the teen, smug little bastard.

"You're awake. Good," the old man said. He was sitting in the dirt right in front of me. As he reached out, my body responded instinctively, trying to keep away from him. Those were the hands that caused me so much pain. I didn't want him anywhere near me.

Even though his movements were slow and shaky, I wasn't in the best position and the ropes didn't allow me to move more than an inch. Old Man finished his task, and my hands sprang free.

I didn't know why he did that, but I used my newfound freedom to push myself up into a sitting position and looked around. From the angle of the light leaking through the leaves, I couldn't have been out very long. Or I guess it could have been the next day, but my hands weren't numb, so I knew not much time had passed. Something about that made me feel better - more reassured that something bad didn't happen while I was knocked out.

"You speak English?" I asked. It would have been nice if they had said something a bit earlier. Like before the agonizing pain and nose dive into the dirt. I searched the campsite. The look on Head Honcho's face as he skulked across the clearing alongside the other two men kept me from rising.

"No, I'm speaking my own language. Just as you're speaking yours." He leaned back, shifting his weight away from me. I breathed easier without him in such close proximity. "I'm Blackstone."

My name was no secret, either. "I'm Bailey," I said, sudden reluctance lending my voice a slight stammer. I hated when that happened. "What did you do to me?"

"I used my power to open the natural blocks in your mind. You'll be able to understand us now. As I could already understand you."

My body stiffened in response. "Can they all understand me?"

"No," Blackstone replied. "None of the others can. They would not trust me enough to request I change their minds the way I did to you. I wouldn't grant them that gift, anyway. As it stands, they believe this is only a power I possess, and that I required a mind connection to allow me the power to understand you. Instead, I made changes to you and you can now understand us."

Wait. "Are you saying you changed my brain somehow? Is that even possible?"

"Indeed it is, but I have not harmed you. Please heed my warning - keep your knowledge of their words hidden. When they speak to you, give me the time to seem as if I translate their words for you." He reached out, and I forced myself to remain still when he held out a hand to touch my arm. Thinking he had altered my mind scared me, but there was nothing I could do but listen to his explanation. "I regret the pain I caused you, but there was no other way. I'm glad you made it through the process. Many die during the ritual, trying for the Gift."

"Oh, wow, thanks. Quite the honor you've given me." I couldn't help it - I was furious and terrified and so far, sarcasm was a universal language and the easiest way to vent my emotions.

Oddly enough, the old man looked like he wanted to laugh. Like maybe he even liked me.

What a strange thing to feel. Stranger yet, it was an odd thing for me to even notice. But it was easy to pick up on his unconscious movements. I could read them like a book.

"You speak truly, though I can tell you do not know it." He lost his smile as he continued his explanation. "Rader, the leader, has taken his family from the main settlement. There is a death penalty issued against him and his family. He killed his patron to escape, and he wants me to make sure you aren't a spy. This backward planet allows women precious little freedom or autonomy, but they do allow them to pass along information. But he is most concerned that you aren't from this place and about who sent you."

I jerked back in surprise. Did he mean what I thought he did? But no, I could just have easily been wearing pants out of necessity and not because I was alien to them. He must have meant not from this region. And not being able to speak the language was a pretty obvious giveaway. Maybe my brain was still healing from that lava he had poured into it with his eyes.

"How would he know I'm not from here?" I asked, testing the old man. Blackstone.

"It's because your eyes are more deeply set, like the Outsiders. Like me."

"Ha, they are all a little bug-eyed, aren't they?" My mind raced, filled with questions. "So they think I'm not from this area? That's fair. How about you?"

"We came through a gate between worlds to this planet," he explained. His eyes were intent, as if he were trying to tell me more than his words. But my ability to read him had evaporated with my shock. "Like you, I do not belong in this world."

I gaped at him. "Wait. You're really not from here? From this planet?" That was a new one. We had never been anywhere that had other people who traveled in from another dimension before. That we knew about, anyway.

Maybe there had been some encounters by the teams that never came back. I eyed the old man suspiciously, but he didn't look the least bit threatening.

Was he one of the invaders we fought? But no, he may have an implant in his hands, but the Techs had far more drastic alterations and their base humanoid frame was different than his, formed on a world with too much pollution and not enough sun. The way the children in the slums were sometimes born, before they were taken from their parents and sterilized so they couldn't pass on the defects. Most of them never made it back because of some "medical accident," though. None of us were used to seeing that.

"Yes. I am also an Other, an outsider. My people have learned the secret of traveling between worlds. A group of us came here to explore, as I suspect you have. Our team planned on a short scouting trip, but there is a wrongness about this world that we could not counteract. We could not escape this planet and return home."

Well, hell. That didn't sound good. "How do you open the gates?" Maybe they had a different method than ours. Just because they were trapped here didn't mean we were.

The old man, Blackstone, glanced at Rader and then back to me. "There is not yet time to explain. I could tell when I touched you that you're not the same as my people, but you're similar enough that I could open your mind. I took a chance, hoping it wouldn't kill you. Many of my people die during the process, too, but you came through very well. You are from another planet, aren't you?"

We were supposed to gather information, not give it

away. But there was something about that old man that made me feel like I could trust him. I wasn't about to allow myself that luxury, but I told him a little anyway since it was more of a statement of fact than a question.

To deny it would be embarrassing for me and an insult to him. Besides, he had given me the advantage of understanding their languages without asking me to pay a price. If I kept him talking, cooperated with him as long as he didn't ask too much, then maybe he never would. Not if my team retrieved me first.

"Yes, I am. I came through a gate, too."

There was a flash of triumph in his eyes, but he hid his face from Rader, who finished his skulking and headed towards us. "We will speak of this later. I have been searching for a way out of this world for many years. Maybe we can help each other."

Before Rader reached us, I blurted, "What about navigation? Would that help you find your way? If not with instruments, then with the stars?" It was the only way I could think to ask without it being too obvious that was what we needed, too.

Blackstone leaned close, speaking low. "The skies here do not clear often. It took many months to chart even a small part of the sky. We use the position of the stars in our chants to open the gateway between worlds. I have memorized their patterns, but they have not worked for us yet."

Damn. If I couldn't see the stars, we weren't going anywhere soon. But what if this guy could draw me some star charts? I could use them to check his information and see if it would open a portal. He would have to be accurate, but if that was how they traveled between worlds too, then he would have to be. And years of work! There was no way he would let that go to waste. Nobody would.

My compass could use his charts to model the way back to Earth for me so I could do a preview. It would confirm the patterns and I wouldn't have to jump blind. Not every navigator spent the time to validate the path home, but that was stupid and reckless. Two things I avoided. It was hard to do, but I would do it ten times over if I had to.

I didn't want to be stuck here like Blackstone and his people had been, apparently for decades. And whatever kind of tech the Outsiders used, but it must be voice activated because he kept referring to his chants. I was still freaking out about the Outsiders existing at all, but I couldn't focus on that now. My first priority was to plot our way home. Figuring out what it meant for him to be from another earth-copy and could use the portals would come next. Maybe even before I figured out how to feel about him altering my brain.

"What are you two talking about?" Rader demanded as he reached us. He stood a short distance away, his eyes boring into me, drifting down my body. I realized my shirt had twisted around and I was showing some skin. I tugged it into place as quickly as I could, but he kept looking at me in a way that I found disturbing.

"I have asked this one who she is, and as you suspected, she is not from here. She is one of the Outsiders who was born on this planet and speaks only the words of the region where she has lived her entire life. She does not know the old ways and came seeking to learn from the original Outsider," Blackstone said, referring to himself.

It sounded absurd when he said it, but I kept my mouth shut. I didn't know what he was up to with that story, but it was better than the truth about how I was a member of an advance team sent to take over the planet and basically enslave its people - if they were lucky. Besides, it cemented the idea in Rader's head that I somehow belonged beside Blackstone, a situation that could prove beneficial.

"Ask her to tell me her name and why she is following my family." Rader looked pretty pissed off. I guess Blackstone's explanation about how I couldn't possibly understand anything wasn't working out. Figured. After all, the old man could be going senile.

Blackstone looked at me with raised eyebrows while he repeated Rader's question. Probably hoping I wouldn't speak too soon and give away the game.

"You can tell him my name is Bailey," I said, granting him permission to use my true name. It would be easier to answer to than something made up. "I wasn't following him - I got lost. I had no idea you were here or else I would never have walked right on in like that."

"She was mistaken in her direction, Rader." Blackstone translated for me in the loosest sense of the word. "She is not following you and does not work as a scout."

Rader grunted. I wasn't sure if he believed Blackstone, but that was the story and I was sticking to it as long as they held me prisoner.

"Tell her to clean herself. The dirt disgusts me. I will have my wives bring water and appropriate clothing. You

Outsiders are too promiscuous for us. My brothers keep looking at her."

The hair on the back of my neck stood up in response.

He was blaming me? They were the ones who were acting like dogs, watching my every move as if I were putting on a show expressly for them. And what was that snide comment about me being dirty after they had thrown me on the ground? Jerks.

Rader turned on his heel and strode across the clearing, smashing his shoulder into one of the men, forcing him to look away from where I stood. Once he disappeared into the trees, both his brothers went back to watching me. The look in their eyes increased my pulse, setting off my instinct for self-preservation.

As I turned my attention back to Blackstone, I caught him staring. But with concern, not menace. "You're doing a good job," he assured me. "Just hold on. I'll get you out of this mess."

I raised my eyebrow in surprise. As much as I appreciated the pep talk, there was something in his tone that made me feel strange. Different than ever before.

Oh. He was acting like he cared about me.

Which was weird, because he didn't know me. Then again, maybe that was why he cared. Once people got to know me, their looks were always cold. The ones I thought I could trust turned on me. That was why I spent so much time trying to make myself indispensable. Otherwise, I couldn't rely on them to take care of me when I needed them.

Soon Rader sent the teen to usher me into the

tent, cutting off any further opportunity to speak with Blackstone. Fortunately, the belligerent young man didn't follow me inside. The last thing I wanted was to have to defend myself from molestation in a tent. As it was, I had to dodge his groping hands. How repulsive.

Just as Rader said, there were buckets of water waiting. I touched a finger to the liquid, sighing with relief at how warm it was. There was also a strip of fabric that was the right size for a towel and a smaller one to use as a washcloth. A small square of stones was nearby, a small drainage channel dug into the hard-packed earth. There was no tub, so they would expect me to wash directly from the buckets.

My eyes darted around, taking in the rest of my surroundings. The colors were muted but pleasant, a lot of sage greens and browns covering the tent walls and pillows, which were heaped in different arrangements. Some with furs and blankets, others near a low set of tray tables that probably held food during meals. At the moment, they were cleared of any clutter.

A small fire was contained in a cast iron, cauldron-shaped vessel that had a small pipe attached to one side leading up and out a hole in the roof. Really fancy and kind of nice, which surprised me. There were also sleeping platforms and expertly made pots and vessels that held tasty-smelling food.

I admitted to myself that I had made some assumptions about them that were incorrect. Brutal and less technology didn't mean the inhabitants of the planet were stupid or lived like animals. If I weren't being held prisoner, I would have felt bad about being judgmental.

There were some interior walls made of the same reeds they used to form the tent, but I was certain there wasn't anyone behind them. Unfortunately, Rader's two brothers had stationed themselves on either side of the tent as I entered, keeping guard outside. Sneaking out the back wasn't an option.

There was no telling when I would be interrupted, so I hurried to wash off the dirt with what turned out to be some pretty nice smelling soap. Floral, but also clean and spicy. There were bits of petals and soft green leaf pieces embedded in the bar. It foamed well and rinsed clean. I bet there would be a market for it, even if the Corps wouldn't care. They made more money from exploiting precious metals and jewels.

Hesitating, I looked around to make certain I was alone. Nobody. In a rush that made my hands feel clumsy and awkward, I removed my shirt and pants, leaving my undergarments on and leg bandage intact, and washed the grime and sweat off my body.

I picked up a brightly colored bundle. It was a light, filmy fabric, not anything like what I saw the other women wearing. I held it up to my body and groaned. It was a dress all right, but it was slinky and silky and totally inappropriate to the environment.

Something inside me balked. I may be under guard and hostage to these strangers, but how cooperative did I need to be? But remembering their violence and weapons, I knew I had to play along. But not entirely. I yanked my dirty pants back on and then slipped the dress over my head.

Our uniforms were skintight, designed for flexibility and maneuverability, so it was hard to tell I had them on under the flowing fabric. Good. I felt safer wearing them. The dress was too large for me, so the neckline plunged daringly, which was confusing considering how Rader acted like he was so concerned about promiscuity.

But was he? How many men had I met back on Earth who said one thing but expected something else? Not just with me. There were any number of men and women victimized by those who claimed to have better morals or beliefs. Not to mention anyone that didn't fit into their idea of the "right" place on the gender spectrum. Too many were harmed, especially in the slums where even the idea of law enforcement was laughable.

Rader may be bug-eyed and contradictory, but he was in control. And power corrupts. Add that into a society that controlled women? Who went after an old man like Blackstone, pushing him to the ground? They had taken advantage of, forced into some kind of servitude, overpowered those weaker than themselves. Or viewed them as other and different, and therefore to be mocked and scorned.

It reminded me of home.

I was starting to get a really bad feeling.

The chain holding my compass was in plain view because of the large expanse of flesh showing in the dress bodice, but it was intricate and looked decorative. Almost as if it were a part of the outfit. More importantly, the chain was long, and the compass remained hidden somewhere near my belly button. I stamped my feet back into my boots. The hem of the dress hid them, since I was by all indication shorter than whoever wore it last.

I braided my hair tightly and coiled it into a bun at the base of my neck to keep it out of my way. I needed to be prepared in case I found a chance to sneak away, but I also knew that I might have to fight. Long flowing hair wasn't conducive to kicking butt.

Moments later, the two women entered the tent. I would have appreciated a little warning, but whatever. The taller one had brown eyes that bulged out under a fringe of dark brown hair. She clucked her tongue in disapproval as they tidied up the tent, tossing the fabric I used as a towel into a small pile of clothing in a woven basket that I hadn't noticed sitting in a corner of the tent.

"Look at her," she said. "Those Outsiders are such trash. Leaving the drying cloth on the stones instead of the basket. Slovenly pig. Exposing her neck and chest is disgusting, and she shows no shame at all!" Annoyance burned through my veins like wildfire. My knuckles turned white as I gripped my hands together, trying to hide that I could understand them now. They knew the dress wasn't my idea. So rude.

The shorter woman, who was still several inches taller than I was, had similar features. Her teeth stuck out almost as far as her eyes did.

"I'm just glad Rader decided not to give her the honor of marrying her," she said. "She would bring down our value with those low-class habits. I guess I can see why he thinks she'd make a good concubine, though. And the more women he has before we get to the settlement, the higher our position will be. It's too bad we already traded our daughters away, they could have made our numbers more impressive."

What the hell? I needed to get out of there, and fast.

I would have given anything to speak their language, because if I could, I'd make sure they knew exactly how low-class I could get while I knocked them flat. Screw it - my actions would need no explanation. And I could probably knock them out and then try to go after the rear guard and make my escape. But as I prepared to pounce, Rader and the brother who had been standing guard by the front of the tent walked in, Blackstone trailing behind them.

Apparently nobody felt it necessary to give warning before entering a space they knew was being used to bathe myself! I was so glad I cleaned up as quickly as I did.

"You two have done enough, go prepare dinner," Rader ordered, and the two women ducked their heads and got all submissive and started groveling and honestly, it made me want to puke. Usually I let people handle relationships how they wanted. To each their own. But they were such fakers that it churned my stomach.

Rader took his time looking me over. His eyes narrowed before he nodded curtly. He turned to Blackstone and said, "Tell Bailey that I expect her to behave in a manner that will honor me and my wives. I want you to spend time with her and get as much information from her as you can. I want to make sure nobody is following her and causes us any trouble. She has a look about her. I'd come for her myself if she had run from me."

I bit my tongue. I guess I should have taken that as a compliment, but kept my raving gratitude to myself. A snort of disgust almost made it past my lips, but I managed to keep my mouth shut and my face blank. I wanted to talk to Blackstone, anyway. He had the position of the stars I needed. That meant playing along.

Blackstone bowed to Rader, who left with his brother, leaving me and the old man alone. Unfortunately, I could hear the sounds of my guard returning to his position right outside the tent.

"Come and sit with me, please," Blackstone said. "They will leave us alone for a while. Are you ready to exchange information?" I turned my attention to him and was shocked to see that he didn't look well. He seemed smaller and older than when I first met him. My heart melted, the desire to protect him - and his knowledge of the skies over this earth-copy - overwhelmed me. Besides, I was a sucker for a nice older man, especially when they looked at me like that. As if I were worthy.

The Corps therapist told me I tried to replace my father whenever I interacted with an older man. I didn't think it took a degree in psychobabble to know that about somebody like me, so I wasn't overly impressed with his observation skills. He obviously couldn't read anything else right since he thought I was also open to him hitting on me. It was a good thing violence towards others wasn't a firing offense while working for the Corps.

Shaking off my bemusement, I finally remembered Blackstone was waiting for me to answer.

"Sure, I would love to." Not that I planned on a true exchange of information. I wanted to hear what he had to say but wasn't about to let him know anything about me. And by the looks of him, we needed to get talking before he keeled over. "Let's make our way to that giant pile of fur and hang out." I walked a few slow steps with him and then helped him sit.

"You truly are a gracious child." Blackstone made himself comfortable. I bit my lip with concern over the tremors in his hands and arms. "Rader took me prisoner when he left his master's house. He thought it would open doors for him in the new settlement because I am such a valuable hostage. And I do not boast when I say that it will, it is merely the truth. But I am an old man now and not up to exerting myself this much."

Warmth spread through my body, causing my scalp to prickle pleasantly. Something bubbled up inside of me, spreading the warmth further. Blackstone's deep black eyes, so different from anything I had seen before, compelled me to tell him something. He had offered me information, and now it was my turn. But what could I say that would make him happy?

Wait. Did I want to make him happy? Strange enough, the answer was a resounding yes. How unlike me. How unlike any conversation I ever had. What a nice change. I should probably say something before the open, kind look on his face changed to one of disappointment.

"I don't have any power," I blurted. "All of our tech is in our devices." I was about to tell him all about my compass and Ginger's reader, but what I said was enough because

Blackstone patted my hand and spoke again.

"Our abilities are centered in our minds, but enhanced with implants. The metal connectors on my hands are the only visible manifestation of this. The people of this planet think it's decorative. They have tattoos and piercings. I believe they would use metals to decorate their bodies if they knew how."

"How did they manage to capture you? How many of you are there?" He was so powerful. I could feel it coming off him in waves, even if he looked even more shrunken than when we sat down.

"I am the last of the Outsiders who traveled here from our home planet. And I had the most power. But there is something that you do not know about us, but Rader's people realized soon after our arrival. We are pacifist by nature, and they took advantage of us. We taught ourselves self-defense, but it isn't enough to keep us from harm. They find it easier to control our children, who never had the enhancements that we did on our home planet."

"How sad," I murmured. I couldn't figure out why Blackstone was telling me so much. He had no clue who I was, or worse, who I worked for. The Corps would take that information and do whatever it could to exploit him and his planet, and if they thought there was a threat, the Corps would kill them all.

It was more expedient to commit genocide than fight the kind of war we had to fight when the first wave of invaders came through a portal to Earth. We called them the Techs, because of all the tech we ended up getting out of the deal when they lost. They were warmongers and conquerors, but they didn't expect there would be so many of us. We overwhelmed them with sheer numbers.

Millions didn't make it through that campaign, but we won. And still we had issues with overpopulation. In fact, the war barely made a dent in the slums.

I still remembered the parade when they came back. My father marched in front.

Instead of the normal fear and revulsion that came with thoughts of the general, warmth spread through me again. Blackstone. It had to be him. Something he did to me made me want to tell him everything. To trust him with everything. It was the strangest feeling, especially since I knew in my mind that I couldn't. Yet, I wanted to. Needed to. Despite the rules and the conditioning we received in training.

But he was also sharing so much information with me. Didn't he know he couldn't trust me? "Why are you telling me all of this? You don't know anything about me at all. I could be a danger to you."

And I was. I was a real danger to normal, healthy people everywhere. But I was also an extension of the Corps and they wouldn't care how I felt about anything, wouldn't allow me to control what they did with my reports. Which meant giving me information was downright ruinous.

"I have very little time left. Rader wants me to collect as much information from you as I can. I do have the ability to pluck thoughts straight from a person's head," he said. I jerked away from him. "Before you start running, let me assure you I will not be doing that to you. I saw everything I needed when I was giving you the Understanding. I'm not concerned about the men you work for and I don't care who your father is, though he seems to be a figure of great evil. You are a good person, Bailey. You and I can help each other, if you'll let me."

I had no idea where Blackstone was coming from, but I did know when I was being buttered up. Compliments made me uneasy, and I wondered what he was trying to get me to do. "Ah. Well, I'm not sure where you really got all this information from, but I admit it makes me suspicious."

"I know it does. And it was from you, Bailey, just as I said. However, I don't have the time to earn your trust right now." Blackstone slowly placed his hand on my arm. I was not used to people touching me, so it gave me goosebumps. I felt heat and pressure, and I wasn't sure why, but suddenly I was totally open to what he was saying. "Tell me about your world, and the stars that shine above it."

I shifted so that a ridge in the mountain of furs would quit jamming into me and then I settled back, laying on my back with my knees in the air, feet on the furs, hands crossed over my stomach. The skirt flowed around me and I plucked at it while I spoke.

"There are too many people there. I used to look at the pics in libraries and history vids, and Earth was so beautiful. It doesn't look as nice anymore, but now that we can jump into other worlds, we are starting to unload the extra people and maybe it will get better. Then again, humans aren't very nice, so maybe not. Most people like me end up working for the Corps. The mission is to exploit and conquer. Advance teams like ours get a tiny percent of the loot. Even a minuscule percent of an entire world can be a whole lot of money. I want to do that so I can retire and find a nice place to hole up so people will finally leave me alone." I kept nattering away, telling Blackstone about my sister and father, about how my mom died when I was little and even cried openly when I told him about finding all those babies. And somewhere inside of me, there was a tiny voice screaming at me to shut up.

I wasn't the only one talking, though. Blackstone took a turn sometimes, too. Usually, it was about their abilities and tech. "The Outsiders are a peaceful but curious people. We learned long ago how to remove the blocks in our brains so we could utilize them to their full potential. There is no separation between the electrical impulses that spark in our brains and the power that is all around us. We use the metal as a conduit."

It looked like the strange metal that was used to make my compass. I shivered at the thought of having it infused with my body.

Other times he would share about how the power he spoke about worked. "Our world looks much like this one, but it is full of power. Every world has a magnetic field, and we tap into that often for everyday tasks. Some of us are talented enough to use the power in other things, like the sun, or the internal pressure between tectonic plates. This looked like magic to many of our people, and the ones without the ability viewed us with awe and respect."

He spoke directly about where he was from. And all the while, I filed it away into the back of my mind to dictate into a report. "It is very prestigious to have a family member to be a part of the Magus class, but many people died despite all their training. Our leaders became concerned. The mind is very powerful, but not everyone can handle the energy that surges through it. It often causes their blood vessels to burst."

And more about what it was like to arrive on this earth-copy. "Our leaders were about to rule that there would be no more Magus class when we discovered the first gateway. There have been many fruitful encounters since. The other worlds had less power in them, and so our minds were better able to handle the interaction between man and environment. We arrived here many years ago, when I was still a young man. There is something about this place that trapped us, so that our normal interaction with power didn't work. The magnetic field here is strong, and we can use it to perform many tasks, but we can't use it to open a gateway."

And then always, there would be a plea, spoken with urgency. "I hope you can help us, Bailey. Our children are dying here. There is something missing, maybe it's the lack of sun. But they are small and weak and cannot use the power at all. We can't seem to unblock their minds, even with the ways that predate the tech integrations. Once I am gone, they won't have anyone who could take them back home."

My head felt light, and it was swimming, wavering and hard to focus. I struggled to clear my thoughts. I kept picturing those poor, defenseless little babies my father killed while Blackstone spoke about the children of the Outsiders, trapped on this planet. Soon, they were the same to me, and I had to save them.

I also kept wondering what was wrong with me. I never acted that way, but I instantaneously trusted Blackstone with more than I had ever told anyone else in my life, and I felt like he had been my friend for a thousand years. A close friend. Maybe even a special friend. When I tried to tell myself that wasn't normal, my suspicions instead drifted away and my trust and love for his people grew.

"I can help you," I promised. "I can help them. But I need to know the star patterns. Can you draw them for me? Do you have some paper here, a pencil?" I sat up and wiped my face dry, the tears I wept for Blackstone and his people's doomed children still dampening my cheeks. I knew I could do something for them. It would help my team, and the Corps never needed to know. It wasn't like they made us give them reports about every tiny little thing, and they wouldn't care what I did on the side in order to get the information I needed.

Blackstone smiled at me with gratitude and assurance. My head was starting to clear, and I still wanted to help, but now I was feeling more like myself, more cautious. I was having a hard time remembering everything we had just talked about, but I could feel it in my bones that I could trust him. But I still kept certain things to myself, holding back, something that was normal for me, a second nature and not a conscious thought.

Blackstone was patting the robes he was wearing over his clothing, looking for something to write with. I knew the robes were a symbol of his status, even though I wasn't sure why I was so certain about that. He couldn't find anything, though.

"When I leave, I will find some charcoal and skins to write on. I have nothing to use in there. I can draw you the sky. It is rarely clear, but when it is? Ah, child, it's so amazing. I can see the milky stream of stardust connecting the other suns in the universe. It's like the power that runs through my people, linking everything. We're all made of the same substance that sparkles in the night sky, forming stars and planets. Everything is connected." Blackstone rose slowly.

I stood and grasped his hand, helping to heft his weight as he got to his feet. He wasn't that heavy, but he wasn't very steady. He actually looked thinner than he did when he entered the tent.

Taking a step back, I studied him, looking at the startling differences. My forehead wrinkled in my usual frown of concentration, and then almost immediately I heard my sister's voice, an unhappy echo from a distant past, telling me that I needed to keep my skin smooth and wrinkle free or else I'd never be pretty like her. It was one of the few things she said to me when I was little, before she abandoned me to the system. I guess it wasn't bad advice or anything. It was just pointless and stupid for me to try to be anywhere as smooth and beautiful as Shareen.

"Rader will come in soon," Blackstone said. "He wants to make you his concubine. You are a fighter, and you may need your skills at that time. I am sorry, my child, but there isn't anything I can do to help you."

And I knew he couldn't. His people were pacifists. Their very nature, everything that made them who they were, the deep empathic connections in their powerful minds made it impossible for them to do more than try to stop an impending altercation with their words or maybe even raise their hand to block their face. But that was it. They were incapable of attacking or even protecting themselves beyond some gentle attempts. I had no idea where all the information flooding my mind came from, but I knew I was right.

Once Blackstone was done and had left at the request of Rader, I heard sounds of frantic activity. After only a few moments, Rader entered the tent with one of his brothers and the two women. An icy feeling settled in my stomach.

Any woman would recognize the look on Rader's face. And if we spent any time in the slums, we knew when to run, too.

Despite the women in the room, it told me that I had just run out of options.

CHAPTER FOUR
Rescue

BEFORE ANY OF THEM could make a move, I jumped over the mound of furs in the middle of the tent and made a break for it. I ran straight for the back wall of the tent, ready to plow through, hoping the element of surprise would help me get past the man standing guard outside. It was a desperate attempt without a lot of thought behind it, but I didn't want to stay and find out what they planned next. I already had a good idea that it wasn't going to be anything I liked.

The damned hem of the dress almost tripped me, wrapping around my boot, causing me to hop a few times, yanking at the skirt until it loosened. As it was, it slowed me just enough that Rader snatched the extra fabric and yanked me backward.

He was strong. I practically flew towards him, not touching the ground at all. The women backed away and ran from the tent. Cowards. I tried not to feel betrayed, but

I did. They knew how awful men like Rader could be. Yet they left me there, anyway.

Rader spun me around and the other man grabbed my wrists behind my back, stopping my attempt to escape. A tall woven basket fell on its side, spilling the clothes and towel the women had collected.

It hurt too much to move, my joints protesting how hard they were being stretched. I stopped struggling and instead glared at Rader while his brother forced me to stand before him, helpless and trapped.

Something about the look in Rader's eyes caused me to jerk against his brother's iron grip once more. Pain lanced through my arms and shoulders as my captor struggled to contain me. But I just couldn't break free. Without a word, Rader slapped me hard. My head swam, disorienting me as I swayed on my feet, knees shaking.

"She's feisty, isn't she?" Rader chuckled. A shiver wracked my body and my skin broke into goosebumps. "It'll be fun to train her. I might even be willing to share her for a while. That usually breaks them faster."

His brother let out a bark of sickening, ugly laughter. I couldn't help it. Despite the pain it caused, I yanked against the hands holding me in place, desperate to break free. Then my instinct for survival kicked in and ideas raced through my head, my brain running through the different fighting techniques I learned from the Corps. None of them were very helpful when outnumbered in the small confines of a tent.

I was willing to give it a try, though. Rader leaned closer, and I took the opportunity to slam my forehead into his face while simultaneously twisting my body, trying to get my hands free. It hurt me, the pain almost blinding.

Thankfully, it also hurt him, if the roar I heard come out of his mouth was any sign. Unfortunately, there was only a split second of triumph. The man holding me in place tightened his hold and Rader hit me with his fist this time.

Things got confusing after that. I was still awake, but I couldn't think. My body slumped when my knees gave out, and I couldn't stop it from happening. When I hit the floor by the furs, it took me a while to clear my swirling head enough to realize my arms were free. I raised a hand slowly to my face, touching my cheek, and a small pained sound slipped out of my lips. It hurt so much, I couldn't tell which part of me didn't.

My mind swam and wavered and I tried to shake it off, knowing that I had to think, and think fast. It was difficult to grasp everything going on around me, but my thoughts finally cleared. I was alone with Rader. Very alone.

His shirt was off and he was using some of the water in one of the buckets to clean the blood off of his face. It looked like I had gotten him on the nose. With any luck, it was broken.

Rader must have realized I was coming to, because as he finished drying off, he turned towards me. "You're lucky I need to raise my status, you little bitch, or I'd strangle you where you lay."

A strangled moan escaped my lips. I bit my tongue, shutting myself up. He looked like the type to enjoy another person's pain. I had seen enough of them in my life.

I drew in a shaky breath, wondering if I should say something or remain silent. His bucket bath was complete. Maybe if I said something, he would treat me nicer. It was worth a try. "I'm sorry," I lied. "I didn't mean to upset you."

His smug laugh sent chills down my spine. "You'll learn what I want from you soon enough. I can tell you've been allowed too much freedom. Makes a woman spoiled and wild. But you're mine now, and I know how to deal with women like you. I'm a really good teacher."

Rader lunged at me, rolling me over onto my back. My thoughts scattered again, and I felt nauseous, forcing me to swallow hard. Then my mind cleared when the adrenaline surged through my veins. I panicked. I needed to get out from underneath him. Unfortunately, his body was already pinning me down, his weight trapping me.

I couldn't even get in a good hit because the ground kept me from pulling my arm back far enough to gather any strength behind my fist. He grabbed my wrists together in one hand and actually laughed when he managed to slide the skirt up to my waist before I could roll out from under his shifting body.

My pants stopped him from going any farther. I had never been so glad to be wearing them. He grunted when I twisted my body, trying to reach for the knife hidden under the bandage on my calf.

"You're making this harder on yourself, bitch!" He pressed his free hand against my throat. "You're not supposed to have on anything that denies me access. You'll learn to obey me or suffer. Starting right now."

Rader curled his fingers around the waistband of my

pants. I filled my lungs, ready to scream my head off in hopes somebody would help, but choked it back when I saw a movement behind him. Before I could process what was happening, Rader's body went slack, falling on me, smashing me into the ground with his dead-weight. All the air whooshed out with a stifled squeak.

My lungs jerked helplessly, trying to refill with air. But he was too heavy. I tried to shove him off. It didn't work any better than trying to fight him off did. A wild thought about suffocation flooded my mind.

Then the weight was gone, Rader's ugly, pop-eyed face disappearing from above me as his body flew into the air, landing with a thud a short distance away.

"You saved me," I gasped.

There stood Mason Bain, strategist and fighter, larger than life. His eyes caught the flickering light of the brazier filled with coals, burning brightly inside the interior of the tent.

Green. Amazing, glittering, stunning green. Wow. I could stare into eyes like that all day long.

He raised an eyebrow, then lifted his chin in an abrupt motion. Why was he nodding at me? Then reality snapped back. Right. He had saved me, and he was acknowledging my obvious statement.

Mason focused on me, his eyes running over my body, searching for injuries. The Corps taught us to make a visual check before making physical contact. My breathing slowed as I continued to lie on the floor for a moment longer, assessing my potential injuries.

How did I feel? No sharp or overwhelming pain

indicated that I was seriously injured. The rest of my system was in overdrive. My heart was pounding in my ears, pulse racing with adrenaline. My chest was heaving, and the bodice of that infernal dress was clinging to my chest, dark and damp. And sticky. I was covered in blood. Damn. Mason must have slaughtered Rader. Not that I minded.

He finished his perusal. In a flash, Mason reached down and pulled me up, setting me on my wobbly feet. Without a word, he yanked the dress over my head, then scooped up the wet rag draped over the side of the water bucket - miraculously still full and upright - dunked it and then swiped the dripping fabric from my neck to my belly button.

It was freezing. I tried to pull away, but Mason had wrapped his hand around my arm, steadying me. It also blocked me from squirming away from his other strong hand as it washed off Rader's blood.

Thankfully, it was over quickly, and he tossed a blanket at me. "Dry off. We need to get out of here." Then he reached down to pick up something off of the floor. He tossed my shirt and vest at me in one fluid motion. I automatically caught them, still bemused by my sudden change in circumstances and the punch to my face.

I pulled myself together and got dressed, my hands fumbling with the loops. Giving up, I left my vest unbuttoned. Meanwhile, Mason prowled around, checking for hidden enemies in the blind spots. There wasn't anyone there, not anymore.

"I'm guessing the rest of the team is outside," I said,

compelled to fill the silence. There was no way Mason was alone. He wouldn't have spent so much time taking care of me inside a structure that blocked all vision of what was going on around us if our teammates weren't outside playing lookout, handling the situation.

My brain settled, and I started to think normally again. What exactly was going on outside the tent, anyway? There were Rader's brothers to think about, and that one teenage punk. Plus those wives and Blackstone. Oh. Was the old man okay?

"Anything of value in here?" Mason asked, his voice gruff. He scanned the area for likely hiding places, looking in the dark corners, too.

I shook off my concern, the odd connection I felt with Blackstone rattling me. Better to avoid that until we were out of danger.

"No weapons anywhere," I responded. We weren't petty thieves - the only thing we valued while in the Mentions were weapons. Even food was potentially suspect if it belonged to the locals. Well, intel was important too, but I knew that wasn't what he meant even if this was our first trip together. The real riches were stolen by the Corps after we turned in our reports.

"You good to go?"

"Yeah, I've got all my stuff. How can I thank you?" I appreciated his help, even if he had seen my naked chest. I refused to think about that - there would be time to be embarrassed later.

Mason snorted. "Let's go," he said, ignoring my gratitude.

My hero. Well, I guess I couldn't blame him. If he asked me too many questions about my emotional state, I'd probably cry. How awful. It was a pretty typical response after an attack. He may seem uncaring, but that was the training. Although I guess it was likely that he really didn't care. It wasn't as if we had formed some kind of instant bond when we met.

Mason still had his sword out. Once he was through clearing the area, he wiped the blade on Rader's trousers to clean it off. He couldn't use anything else since the jerk was shirtless. I stared down at the body and tried to feel something. After all, a man had just lost his life. But there was nothing. Maybe it was because he died while assaulting me. But there could be more. I could be like my father.

My body jerked with a violent shiver. Goosebumps broke out across my arms, prickling at the back of my neck and head. No way. I was messed up, but I wasn't a psychopath.

Heaving a deep breath, I pushed aside the remainder of my distraction. Mason walked out through the front flap of the tent. I followed closely, not sure what I was going to find in the little clearing outside.

They were all there, my entire team still intact. Whoever the enemy had been that started this whole thing, causing me to run into an even worse situation, were gone. They had obviously beaten them.

Nash was at one edge of the camp site, speaking intently with Ginger. Tyler and Logan were a short distance away, sorting through weapons on the ground. Mason spoke with them quietly and then slipped off into the trees.

Both of Rader's brothers were dead, their corpses lying side by side, close to the entrance of the tent. The women and teenager were grouped together on the opposite side of the clearing, as far from the dead bodies as possible without disappearing into the woods.

My forehead wrinkled with worry as I scanned the area. Blackstone wasn't there. I needed to find him. With some effort, I ignored the emotional tie I seemed to have developed and focused on the practical. We had to find the man that was our ticket out of this Mention.

Will was standing near the women, trying to communicate. He was the linguistics expert and had an implant, but I didn't know how he managed to do it so well. Most linguists took longer. Was it some kind of additional training? Did he have extra tech for that kind of thing? Maybe he had implants not available to the other trainees?

He was so fast, it was difficult to believe that it was natural ability or standard tech. Good luck to him, though, because the women weren't cooperative. In fact, all they were interested in was crying and wailing like banshees.

Oh, wait. I was distracted again. Rader must have hit me harder than I realized.

My legs felt weak as I made my way to one of the stones lining the fire pit and sat. Nash sent Ginger to look me over. She wasn't always nice to me, but I couldn't fault her professionalism when she plied her trade.

"You're bruised pretty badly, but luckily your cheekbone isn't broken. That can be tricky to handle in the field and your face needs all the help it can get." Oh, yeah, I had to be fine if she already slipped back into her old habits. Oddly enough, it didn't really bother me. Maybe we could figure out some kind of level of friendship.

Even though I was paying attention to what she was saying, I still kept looking around for Blackstone. "Thanks. Has anyone seen the old man?"

Ginger snorted. "You're welcome," she said sourly. With a huff, she hightailed it back to where Nash stood. I couldn't tell what he was thinking, but he met my eyes and gazed at me for quite a while before he returned to scanning the clearing. It was hard to get a read on him, but out of everyone, he was the one who cared about me the most. He must have been worried about me, more than just for my ability to use my compass.

Logan and Tyler jumped up from where they had been crouching over the pile of weapons. They were loading into various carry sacks to haul them with us. Tyler joined me, sitting on a rock next to me, and patted my arm. He was the closest thing I had to a friend on the team and watched my back a little more than the others. Friendship made his obligation to keep the navigator safe rest easier.

Logan remained standing. "One man ran off when we showed up. We sent Bain out after him."

"Damn it," I groaned. "He needs to know that man is a valuable asset. I had time to talk to him and he might have the information we need to get off this mud-ball." Maybe they wouldn't realize I had done a lot more than talk with him.

The old man had been inside my head and I had blabbed too much when we were together. No need to tell my team that - Blackstone had told me more than I told him. Info that would help us beat his people if they ever tried to come after us. Not that it was a huge possibility, considering they were pacifists.

But I was actually worried about his safety. I had no idea if Bain was one of those shoot first, ask questions later types. And as odd as he was, Blackstone had the goods. We needed him.

The taller woman wouldn't stop wailing. It was getting seriously annoying, and the world's largest headache was blossoming in my skull. What was her problem, anyway? It wasn't like we had taken her hostage and forced to dress in some nasty gown so we could turn her into a concubine.

I walked over to where she was standing with the other prisoners. The teenager sneered at me as I drew closer. He looked a lot like Rader, probably a real chip off the old block, too. He stiffened and yanked against the ties that held his wrists behind him when I reached out and slapped the woman. His ties held, and she shut up. Ah, silence.

Will caught the younger woman, Buck Tooth, when she lunged at me, screaming even louder. "You stupid slut! Keep you hands to yourself. You've ruined everything! I'm going to kill you!"

"Looks like she's pissed at you, Bailey. What'd you do?" Will asked. Nobody else could understand what the locals were saying, but her spite was easy enough to read. So was the fact I was the one she was so mad at.

"Ha. Ha." I replied. "Like it's my fault her husband tried to rape me. This place blows."

Will let out a chuckle and manhandled Buck Tooth

into sitting back down. She continued to give me the stink eye, but I'd take my chances with her any day. I was itching for a fight to get rid of the lingering feeling of helplessness. But at least she wasn't screeching anymore.

Rustling sounds came from the trees. My team stood at alert, but relaxed when they saw it was Mason coming through the foliage, pulling something behind him. Hell. I ran over to him, and sure enough, Blackstone was slumped over, being dragged along by the back of his robes.

Mason dragged Blackstone across the clearing near the campfire, then dropped him on the ground. Worry made my mouth dry as I dropped to my knees by the old man and gently rolled him over. There was blood all over his abdomen. Oh, no. Gut wounds were the worst. A shock of fury filled me at the sight.

"What happened? This guy was a noncombatant when I got here. Did his mighty strength overwhelm you?" Who stabs an unarmed little old man? I checked for a pulse, but was having a hard time finding one. "Ginger! Can you come look him over for me?" I yelled across the way.

"He turned on me when I caught up with him," Mason explained. "I believe these are yours." My head jerked up to see what Mason was doing. He threw my knives and belt pouch down next to me.

He looked pissed. I didn't care. I bet Blackstone grabbed my things for me. He couldn't have known who it was that chased him down and was probably trying to keep anyone from discovering I was from off-planet.

Blackstone said that Rader leaving was illegal, and they all thought I might be a scout. The old man would have no idea who was friend or foe, and I was certain a six foot five slab of muscle with a sword coming at him didn't look all that friendly.

The old man groaned faintly as Ginger checked him over. "It doesn't look good. I think we'll have to pile him up with the others." She sounded cold, but I knew sometimes when she lost a patient, she cried. She didn't know I knew that, and I wasn't going to tell her, either. But this patient was a stranger she thought was an enemy. No tears for the old man tonight.

Hell. This whole trip was one disaster after another. I needed that info. I needed him.

"He has intel I need," I said.

Ginger's lips pressed together. "Then you better get it. Now. There isn't much time left." She stalked off and went directly to Nash's side. Well, fine. She could tell him to keep everyone out of the way while I tried to get the information that would save us from an eternity stuck on this earth-copy.

"Can you hear me?" I asked Blackstone, clasping his hand. Mason snorted in disgust, and Ginger was happy to lure him to her side. I was glad, though, because explaining why I could understand a total stranger would have taken up too much time and I still didn't know how it worked. Or if I wanted to share my new skills. "Are you awake?"

Blackstone's eyelids fluttered as he struggled to open his eyes. Oh yeah, he was definitely in pain. The least Ginger could have done was give him something. I dragged my belt pouch towards me and pulled out my emergency rations. There was a pill in there that would help. I smashed the capsule between my fingers and placed the powder into Blackstone's mouth. In a few seconds, his face relaxed, and he could focus on my face.

"Bailey," he rasped. "I'm afraid I couldn't get away. After all this time, I finally found a way home, and it's too late."

Dread burned its way through my veins. "No, it's not. You're going to be okay. Just hold on."

"That is a lie, my girl, and you know it as well as I do." He coughed, and a trickle of blood beaded at the corner of his mouth.

"Please. I need your help. Your people need your help," I begged.

Blackstone's lips tightened. "Listen to me. This place, it's like a trap. The forces messed with my abilities, and I couldn't open the gates. They will mess with you, too. But I can help you. Together we are the key to getting home."

Did he feel that connection, too? It wasn't just a way to get me to talk? But why else would a stranger care so much about what happened to me? Maybe he hadn't been as in control in the tent as I thought.

"Then hang on! You can make it through this. Then we can figure it out together."

His hand gripped mine with the desperate strength of the dying. "I am the last of the elders. The children of my people need help leaving. Please, promise me you will help my people get home. There are so few left, so weak and vulnerable."

I didn't have time to argue, or find a way to avoid making a promise I might not be able to keep. "Okay, I promise. I will get them home." The hand that gripped mine grew hot, a sharp pain stinging my palm. I had forgotten about that metal tech.

"Yes, you will. Now, lean closer. I'm going to perform the Transfer. You will receive the information, but I don't have enough time to show you how to use it. Trust yourself, close your eyes and try to feel your way through the new connections in your mind. "

"I'll do whatever you say." What else could I do? The guy was dying right there in front of me. And if he wanted to transfer something to me, I'd take it. Especially if it was the star charts.

There was something else happening inside me. I was focused on Blackstone, desperate for the information I suspected I couldn't get any other way. But for some reason, I felt like I was losing somebody very close to me. Somebody I loved. It didn't make any sense. But I couldn't seem to stop myself from making stupid promises.

"Come to me now," he said.

I leaned closer, helping him lift his hands. He was trying to place them on my head like before. Well, hell. That was probably going to hurt. But it worked last time - I understood what everyone was saying. So I took a chance. I lifted his hands to my head, settling them on the same place as before.

Blackstone said a few words I didn't recognize, despite of my ability to understand everything else he said.

"Ah, you really are a good child," he murmured. "Better than you know." Then the heat and pressure filled my head. I tried as hard as I could to stay quiet because I didn't want my team to get the wrong idea and interrupt what was happening.

The sound of Ginger's soft laughter stood out. It was hard to see, impossible to focus, but that sound told me my team was still going about business as usual. As long as they didn't interrupt, I didn't really care what they were talking about.

A quiet groan escaped my tight lips when the pain amped up, unable to keep silent under the onslaught of Blackstone's power. Then, like before, I got slammed by agony. I kept from making any noise by biting my tongue. I could taste the blood, the only thing I noticed besides the pain.

It went on forever. Much longer than before. Waves of nausea rolled over my body. Then I got hit with another wave of agony, so much worse than any pain I've ever felt, and that was when I started screaming.

CHAPTER FIVE
Compass

"HOW MUCH LONGER DO you think she'll be out, Patel?"

Nash's voice was clear and strong despite being hushed. I was awake, but I couldn't make my eyes open or my mouth work to tell him so. It was like I was trapped in my own body. My brain told me to freak out, but I couldn't do that either.

"I have no idea," Ginger replied. Oh, wow, she actually sounded concerned about me. Either she liked me more than she let on, or I was really bad off. "It's been three days. She's able to take in a limited amount of water and broth, so she should be okay once she's up and about. But if she doesn't wake soon, it'll be time to worry."

Oh, right. She didn't care about me. She was worried about not being able to use the compass. Not that I blamed her. I wouldn't want to be stuck on this dirt ball forever, either. "I can tell you one thing, though. She isn't in a coma. Bailey may have been for the first day or two, but she's in a regular sleep now. She was crying again last night."

What?

"Good," Nash said. "At least things are returning to normal."

What?

Then other sounds encroached on my eavesdropping. Somebody else walked up, their footfalls muffled and slow. "We need to head out soon," came Mason's voice. Relief flooded through me to hear him so near. He had saved me, and the gratitude flooding my veins made me want to call to him. Unfortunately, my voice still wasn't working. "The farther we get from the bonfire, the better."

Memories flooded my mind breaking through the pain from Blackstone's efforts to fill my brain with information. They must have burned Rader and his brothers, which was standard practice. That way the enemy couldn't connect their disappearance to the new people who showed up the same time the dead bodies did. I wondered what happened to the others? The tall woman and Buck Tooth. The bratty teenager.

A cool hand slipped around my wrist, then a gentle pressure. "Her heart is beating faster. She might be ready to wake up. Bailey? Can you hear me?" Ginger was probably the one patting my cheek, quick and sharp. Maybe a little too sharp. But whatever, she's the medic. Nobody was going to stop her, including me. Unless I could shake off the lethargy that held me prisoner.

After one good smack that stung like crazy, I finally found the strength to lift my eyelids. I groaned, the light blinding me at first. After the ache from the brightness dulled to a bearable level, the blurs and blobs were revealed as people.

Ginger hovered over me, staring into my face. Her hands were gentle when she lifted my head and held a canteen to my lips. I sipped some water. My head still hurt. It seemed like it was too full, like maybe it was going to burst open and I would feel better once it did. Or maybe die. I wasn't even sure which I wanted, considering how bad the pain was. At least my voice worked enough to moan as I tried to sit up.

Nash was crouched down beside me, across from Ginger's position. He helped prop me up. "How you feeling, kid?" Good old Nash. Another person who made me feel safe despite my weakened state.

"Like hell," I ground out. My vocal cords felt too dry. I took another sip of the water Ginger offered to wash down the pain pill she handed me. Then another need made itself known. My bladder, climbing to first place on my priority list. "Give me a sec to pull myself together. I'll just be over there behind those bushes."

I had to roll onto my knees before I could climb to my feet, but I made it. Ginger must have moved my limbs, kept them from stiffening too badly because I could stand, if a bit shaky. I refused to look at anyone while I hobbled away as quickly as I could. Walking like a drunk pirate wasn't nearly as embarrassing as wetting myself in front of everyone.

"You need help?" Nash called. Ginger should have been the one, but now that I was functioning again, she had her lips pinched together with reluctance.

"No, I've got this," I declared with more confidence than I really felt. Ginger may be a professional, but the second she could get away with it, she left me to my own devices. My earlier optimism about her feelings towards me crumbled in the face of reality.

I managed to do my business and not fall over, though it was touch and go for a few minutes. I felt almost human after I splashed some water on my face from the nearby stream. Nobody told me if it was safe, so I kept my mouth tightly shut while I did it.

My legs were feeling steadier, and I walked a little more normally on my way back. I was still stiff, my thighs and back especially. What surprised me was my stomach muscles were killing me. But the pain pill was kicking in and it was a manageable pain. Fortunately, my head was feeling almost normal again.

Being unconscious for three days was pretty bad. Some teams would leave their injured partners to fend for themselves. Or worse, euthanize them. But that never happened to the navigators. My career choice had once again saved my butt.

Nobody would ever leave me behind. But it didn't guarantee they would be very gentle about it. Or willing. That came from bonding, and I couldn't seem to break through the barrier I felt between myself and the rest of the world. Not that I was comfortable letting anyone in. It was my fault I was so cut off.

Nash narrowed his eyes as he watched me return from taking care of business. Ginger was also assessing me, but I could tell from the look on her face it was only out of duty. She didn't look concerned the way the boss man did. Although I had to admit to myself that was somewhat comforting. She would have been the first by my side if there was something still wrong with me.

I scooped up the canteen. "Alright, Nash, tell me what I missed," I said.

Nash looked me over, eyeballing my stance. I tried to straighten up. "After that old man did whatever the hell it was to you, the two women went crazy. They kept screaming, but none of us could tell what they wanted. Eventually the younger kid said something, and it shut them up. We piled all the dead bodies and lit them on fire. We didn't know what to do with the live ones so we let them go."

It was within our rights to kill them all to cover our tracks, but Nash hated to hurt women and children. It was something I admired about him, even if it placed us in danger. Not everyone felt the same way I did, but he was a strong enough leader to force the rest of the team to go along.

"Makes sense," I murmured my agreement. It didn't hurt to show him my support.

"It put us in a bind," Ginger added. She didn't sound as angry as I expected. More resigned, and even supportive. That was new. She usually pushed for the most expedient method and guaranteed way of hiding our presence. "That's why we're hoofing it as quick as we can. It's not easy dragging you around."

Right. "Well, thanks for that," I replied with a straight face. I wanted to smack her, but that would make our interactions even harder.

"We're going opposite of the settlement we came to see," Nash informed me, his words causing my guilt to rise in response. I was the one who had crashed into the camp and ruined the original plan. "The women headed a different direction, so I doubt they were returning there to tattle on us, but we didn't want to take the chance. As far as I can tell, we're going the right direction for the secondary contact point. We tried to use your compass to pinpoint the exact location, but it won't fix a direction."

Damn it. Blackstone was right about this planet. It messed with him, and now it was messing with my compass. It was a good thing the inner workings didn't rely on a magnetic field or else we'd be totally screwed.

"Okay, give me a second to check it out. Then I ought to be up to a bit of walking so we can get back on the road." I was talking tough, but I had no idea how long I could last. I'd been out for three days, so I figured I was going to want to die before the day was over. Not that I would admit that.

They must have returned my compass after using it, because it was still around my neck. Come to think of it, I was wearing a fairly clean set of clothes. Ginger must have bathed and changed me at least once while I was incapacitated. Probably helped with the less pleasant bodily functions, too. Damn, now I owed her another one. That woman was going to own me one of these days.

I looked around for a decent place to sit. Mason had returned from scouting the trees. He, Tyler, and Logan were walking around the perimeter of our campsite. We were in a sheltered area with water nearby. The land sloped down on all sides, placing us on high ground. Nash stayed by me, but Ginger wandered away to talk to Will by the campfire, both of them packing the cooking implements.

There was a flat spot a little way from the bushes. After chucking a few stones, I sat cross-legged on the ground. It made it easier for me to keep my hands steady if I rested my elbows on my knees. I pulled the compass out from under my vest and looked it over.

It was a nice dusty brass color. I wasn't actually sure what kind of metal it was made of, but it was one of the first things we dug up from the first world Earth-prime traveled to. The scientists had spent a ton of time trying to find it, but they could never figure out how to predict what would be waiting for us on the other side of the portal. But there was something specific about that metal that enhanced our location technology and practically drew us in.

Until they figured out its value and put it to use, we were lucky anyone made it back from the earth-copies. Nobody had a good compass back then. Way more people died, too. Now that we had the tech to handle the gateways, it was better. I guess. If the continued loss of teams at a slower rate was really an improvement.

My hands were small but broad, but the compass fit exactly into the palm of my hand, like it was made to fit there. It looked exactly like any normal compass, with a button to pop open the face of it so I could view the little red arrow and the usual face with the four direction indicators printed in black on a white background. There were also a few other little buttons, one that released inner dial to go spinning so we could find north, and another to lock it back into place.

That was where all sense of normality ended. I pressed my finger hard enough against the center of the glass so that I smudged it with my finger. There was a slight flash, barely detectable, made by a scanner that took a reading on my print and the DNA left behind from the sweat and oils from my finger. Then I widened my eyes and turned towards it while I focused on a tiny hole in the center so it could take an eye-print. I needed to delve into all the features, and that was the only way.

After my identity was validated, the metal sort of expanded, looped around, flowing like cold lava around the back of my right hand. The metallic ooze was really thick, and I could never understand where all that extra volume was coming from. In just a few seconds, the glass that had covered the dial floated into place, the direction markings disappeared into nothingness.

When it was over, I was holding a large rectangular device, the length of my forearm and about half as wide as it was long. There was one hell of a lot more buttons on the front, and the red arrow was now pointing to the glass inset towards the top. It actually looked a lot like an old-fashioned calculator to me, but my instructor almost broke his walking stick across my back for daring to make that comparison.

He said it was because I wasn't taking things seriously enough, but I knew it was really just an excuse to beat the hell out of a recruit. I think they wanted us to obey blindly, but obedience never worked out so well once a navigator was on a journey and there wasn't a teacher or boss to tell them what to do. It was a stupid, needless lesson to learn.

I concentrated on the glass view-screen and keyed in the code to run a calibration. Damned if it didn't start clicking at me in overtime. After a moment, a whirring sound indicated something was spinning inside. Then it threw an error code.

Damn it all. I was going to have to do everything manually. That meant a year of clicks, tracking the position of the earth-copy using a complicated set of calculations that thankfully the compass did for me, but also using the movement of the planet, rotation, position in space in relation to the sun and all sorts of other cosmic things that I managed to grasp, but just barely.

The mechanism had a lot to do with timing, but I was a natural. I had to learn the math to pass the exams like any other navigator, but I didn't need to use it. My talent for the numbers helped me feel where the proper calculation had to go in the string of formulas and equations. Like knowing when to hit the right note in a symphony that depended on the one instrument only I knew how to play.

Manual input also meant I couldn't look into the viewer and see brief glimpses of Earth through the portal. We would have to travel completely blind. It also meant we were more likely to survive if we skipped.

My body shuddered at that. Skipping meant we jumped to another earth-copy instead of going home first. The initial sequence to open a portal to Earth was the most complicated one ever created. It was actually a lot easier to find another planet to go to instead of home. The problem was, teams that skipped were in danger of getting lost - forever. Nash would never allow it. No good leader would.

The navigators who skipped had to add in extra calculations to get back to Earth and most couldn't do it. Maybe the teams survived and were out there somewhere in the Mentions, but it wasn't likely they'd ever be found. There were too many earth-copies for an accidental rescue to take place, and the Corps didn't have the technology to find them directly.

At one point, a team of scientists and mathematicians set up security to keep people from an earth-copy from opening a gateway and invading Earth. Some of them were still alive, but none of them would ever talk about it. Too dangerous for anyone to know.

But it complicated everything. I had to apply the type of math that was so convoluted that half the time, I thought I was making it all up as I went along. Maybe the Techs made it all up, too, and they were the ones we stole the technology from so we had to copy them.

I had to know where I was before I could complete the first sequence that opened the security hatch. Then I had to calculate how to generate the portal and make it home at the proper time. Most navigators couldn't do it if they had to add another layer to account for the skipped Mention. And when they did, they ended up at the wrong place on the timeline.

Things used to blow up a lot when people came home at the wrong time. Time flowed one way on Earth and there was no getting around that. Coming in too early was an impossibility that destroyed the jumpers and the entire surrounding area. I always knew when I was, and I always knew where to put that information. I could handle it, but none of that did me any good when I had to work manually. Not that Nash would let me try.

With a defeated sigh, I tapped in the end sequence. The device turned back into a compass, smaller and more manageable. I hooked it back onto the chain around my neck and tucked it away.

Nash had remained nearby, watching me from only a few steps away while I did my evaluation. My stomach filled with dread.

"Sorry boss," I said. "But it looks like everything is going to be hard about this one. I need to get an accurate read on the stars and then go after a year of clicks." Damn, I hated delivering bad news. But there were four other successful journeys to fall back on, so I hoped he wouldn't think I was incompetent. One of my teammates still might stab me in the back over it, though. After we get back, of course.

"No way, Bailey. I know it's been overcast the entire time we've been here. Let's complete the mission and then worry about stargazing when the weather clears. We can make your compass work once we get out of this area. There's probably some kind of interference. You know compass tech doesn't just stop working." I loved how straight-up focused Nash was, even if it put me in a bad place. But it usually got him results. Put the burden of the problem on the right person, and they find a better way.

Did anything ever ruffle him? Man, I hoped not. But if something finally did, I didn't want to be there to see it.

Nash let out a low whistle, and the team came back into camp. Mason walked over to where Nash and I were standing and asked, "How are you doing?" It really did take me a full beat to realize he was talking to me. I wasn't trying to be rude on purpose by waiting a bit to answer.

"Oh, uh, I'm fine I guess. I know I've been off my feet for a few days, but I'm sure I'll manage."

Mason grunted. "Whatever, Hawke. When you slow, I'm hauling you along just like I have the last three days. Let me know when you can't hack it anymore." Nash must have seen me wince when Mason called me Hawke, because when he chimed in, he emphasized my first name pretty heavily.

"Don't be a hero, Bailey. Mason tossed you over his shoulder and hiked just fine. He can do it again as long as needed. I can't have you slowing us down. Your ego isn't as important as our safety. We need to get far away as fast as we can."

Well, no wonder my stomach muscles hurt so bad. I bet Mason carried me over his shoulders like a sack of potatoes when he got tired of carrying me like a deer carcass. He probably did it for fun. Maybe he even jogged a bit to show Ginger how manly he was, and that was why I felt like a cement truck had spent the last several days ramming repeatedly into my abdomen.

"Ah, well," I said. "Thanks, big guy. Appreciate you and all that." And there was me, being completely unable to sound grateful, even though I was. I was also flustered, thinking about how damned strong he must be, and what it might have felt like to be wrapped around those shoulders while awake. Which I would probably find out soon enough, if my weak knees were any sign.

Mason snorted. He eyeballed me again, really hard. "You don't keep up, I'm picking you up. You don't have to thank me, because I'm doing my job. I want to get home, too." He easily put me in my place. He helped me because he was forced to rely on me, not because he liked me. Check.

To hide my embarrassment, I pulled on my pack. It felt a lot lighter than usual. I bet I would find that they redistributed the supplies I was supposed to be carrying, and all I had left were my clothes and personal items. Talk about not pulling my weight.

At least they weren't making a big deal out of it. For now. With a word from Nash, we all lined up. Then we were on our way.

CHAPTER SIX
Hot Springs

IT WAS THE LONGEST day of my life. Nash had always set a quick pace, but we were in the kind of hurry that kept us alive, so we moved faster than usual. I managed to get through the worst click I'd ever walked when Mason made a sound of disgust. He slowed his pace until I caught up with him and we were walking side by side.

"Look, Hawke, I know you're not going to like this, but we need to get a move on. Logan spotted some campfires in the direction of the funeral pyre, and they've been moving steadily in this direction every night. Hop on and quit slowing us down."

There were so many things I wished I could say, but the only thing I did was nod curtly. He was right. I was holding up the team and that could get us killed.

Mason skipped a step and in one fluid motion, he adjusted the long strap around his shoulders so his pack was resting lower on his body. Then he bent over just far enough that I could make it onto his back when I jumped. Mason grunted when I landed, and the heat in my cheeks told me I was blushing like a freak. It probably clashed with my hair.

What a ridiculous thought. In danger, and all I was thinking about was how I looked. I was crazy.

He slid his hands behind my knees to help me adjust my position. I was plastered against him tightly, my weight resting on his pack so it would be more evenly distributed across his shoulders and torso. Then I was set for the longest piggyback ride I was ever going to get. Fun times.

Nobody said anything. The pace was pretty grueling and their focus was on keeping up. Surely they had to know how humiliating it was. They were still being nice to me, though. Maybe I could handle their teasing later - much, much later. But not right then.

My head was only pounding a little, but my stomach and legs were getting worse. I was doing the two of us a disservice by holding myself so stiffly. With a sigh of resignation, I relaxed into the movement of Mason's body.

I wasn't a very large person, so my legs were stretched wide to wrap around his waist, my body pressed close. The pack was a huge help - holding my knees up against his hips without it supporting my weight would have been just as tiring as running.

Mason looped his arms around my thighs, tucking his hands under my knees. It helped even more. The entire experience was bearable, but exhausting. Whatever Blackstone had done to my head had drained me of my stamina, and the downtime after had finished it off.

As much as I hated to admit it, I was flat-out too tired to make it on my own. I rested the cheek Rader hadn't hit against Mason's back, giving in. Holding myself stiff wasn't giving me back my dignity.

My body settled into the rhythm of his stride. I had been trying to keep my hands clasped around his chest, but he was so broad that it was straining the muscles in my arms. I was strong, but I wasn't used to that kind of position.

I slid my hands apart, lightly tucking my fingers under the long straps holding his weapons in place. They were widely spaced on his chest and therefore easier for me to reach. It was comfortable enough that I probably would have fallen asleep if I wasn't so damned aware of him.

It had been a long time since I had a man that close, and the motion of his muscles pressing against my flesh was reminding me of that. Mason had long, even strides, and my body shifted slightly with every step. I bit my lip, trying to ignore exactly how that made me feel.

After another few clicks, it was finally midday. We stopped in a rocky area, still surrounded by trees. I had gotten a lay of the land through the compass before we jumped. This planet was heavily forested and didn't thin out until closer to the coast. So different from the concrete and asphalt on Earth.

There was an enormous gaping hole in the ground roughly fifty feet from where we were standing, with a small stream nearby. There didn't seem to be any shortage of water on this earth-copy, which was helpful. Will, Logan, Tyler, and Ginger all went over to investigate, and it must have been clean because they filled their canteens.

Huge piles of rocks made out of cinder were scattered everywhere, and there were several different lines of steam rising from the ground nearby, even more in the distance. This was an active volcanic area, and we were going to have to be careful, despite our desire to move quickly.

Nash remained standing, on the lookout as always. "Mason, take Bailey with you and see if you can find a hot spring," he ordered. "A pond or stream deep enough for Bailey to soak the weakness out of her body. Ginger said that would help and we can't keep asking you to haul her around. So far the water's all been clean, but use one of the kits to test first."

The strategist and the tracker typically teamed up, but I felt bad that after hours of hauling me around, Mason still had to cater to my injuries. He didn't bat an eye at the extra duty, though, and he was surprisingly gentle when he reached his arm around and shifted me to the side of his body.

I pulled my leg up to dismount. A moan popped out before I could stop it. Damn, I was so sore. My leg wouldn't move any farther, but it was high enough to allow Mason a solid grip. He pulled me around to his chest and then eased me down on the ground.

He was so tall, a little more than a foot taller than I was. I felt tiny standing in front of him. It was a good thing he had kept his hands on my upper arms, or else I'd have fallen.

It was agony to straighten my legs. I moaned in distress and kept my eyes firmly away from his face. I couldn't stand to see pity, or disgust, or really any emotion at all. What I needed was a moment to collect myself, and Mason was giving it to me.

He was being so much nicer to me than I deserved. After a few minutes, I leaned back to stand on my own. "You okay?" he asked.

"Yeah, totally awesome." I didn't groan at how idiotic I sounded, but it was close.

Mason snorted. "Come on, Hawke. Let's hunt down a place to fix you."

If only that were possible. "There should be hot springs all over the place in this terrain," I replied. He nodded, eyes scanning the forest around us.

"The thickest steam cloud doesn't look too far. That's the likeliest place. Let's go before you stiffen up."

"I hear and obey," I said. Me and my mouth.

But he only snorted, one corner of his lips lifting. Wow. He thought I was funny, not annoying. That was a nice change.

We headed off towards the largest cloud of steam. I focused on keeping upright so I wouldn't have to think about the fact we'd be alone together. And how much I liked that idea.

"Mason," I said, hesitation making my voice quieter than usual.

He cut me off. "You don't need to thank me. It's my job."

What an ego, thinking I was going to thank him. Then again, that was exactly what I was about to do. But still. He should have let me give him credit when it was due.

I did it anyway. "You're right. It's your job, but you really helped me out and I want to tell you I'm grateful. I know you guys are stuck hauling me around right now if you want to get home, but you made it easier on me. I won't forget that."

How embarrassing. I watched where I was placing my feet so I wouldn't have to look him in the eye. I wasn't all that steady anyway, and that made a great excuse. We finally came across the source of the steam and sure enough, there was a large pool tucked up against a steep cliff. A waterfall dumped cold water into the pool. It was really quite pretty, but the fresh water would cool the hot spring enough for me to swim.

We used the water test kit, and it was pure. There was nothing stopping me from the treatment Ginger had suggested and Nash ordered. Which was a huge relief. I didn't have to worry about the optics of my being carried around while I was unconscious. But now that I was awake, it had to end as quick as possible. I could lose my spot on the team if they thought I was milking it.

This earth-copy was a lot nicer than Earth Prime. There wasn't clean water anywhere at home. Actually, there wasn't polluted water, either. The aquifers were bought up and controlled by a few billionaire families, purchased hundreds of years before.

Mason turned to me and damned if he didn't have a smile on his face. He seemed so different from when I first met him. "The temperature feels great right about here," he said. "If you stick to this side, you can have some privacy and I'll keep lookout up top the cliff where my line of sight is clear."

"Wow. That's downright decent of you, Mason. If you keep this up, I'll be forced to keep you." And he laughed. It wasn't even all that funny, but he did. Huh.

The height of the surrounding rock allowed us to see for miles. Nobody was coming. The pool had made a deep depression in the ground, and if anyone showed up, we could hide before they noticed us. Relative safety in the danger zone. A relaxing thought.

Mason turned his back and headed off to stand guard. I waited until he disappeared from sight, then slipped out of my clothes and walked into the hot spring. Ah, the perfect temperature.

Ginger may have changed my clothing, but she hadn't washed anything. Not that I blamed her. I piled together the ones I had been wearing and the ones in my pack. As I suspected, it was almost empty inside, the supplies removed and handed off to the rest of the team.

I left my clothes on the bank near the edge of the water, along with my compass. Discomfort filled me - I actually felt more naked without it than I did without clothes. Popping a painkiller to help relax my sore body, I lowered myself into the pool to soak. Heat baked into my bones and soothed my muscles.

After a few delightful minutes, I dragged my clothes over and scrubbed them. I used the Corps issued soap that cleaned them up really well and dissipated in the water quickly.

I wrung them out as best I could and laid them on the rocks completely flat. The sturdy fabric would dry quickly so I could dress when I was done. To my relief, it was a quick enough process that I had enough time to wash my hair.

Unwinding my braided bun, I scrubbed my hair and body as quickly as I could and I dove under the water to rinse off. If I hurried, I could give Mason a chance to clean up, too. It was the least I could do.

He whistled lightly every so often, letting me know where he was. And I would whistle back to let him know I was still okay. We sounded like a couple of birds, and I really hoped they had those kinds on this earth-copy in case anyone overheard us.

I landed us in a sparsely populated area, and we were now three and a half days away from the small camp I had stumbled across. I didn't think there was anyone around for miles, and there had been no sign that we were being followed outside of the campfires that never seemed to get close enough to overtake us. If those people were really coming after us, they wouldn't have set their evening fires where we could see them.

After a few more stretches, I allowed myself one more soak before offering to trade places with Mason. We had maybe another hour before we were expected back, so we had plenty of time. I was standing where the water came to my knees, facing the waterfall, the shore and cliff to my right. I placed my feet shoulder length apart and stretched my arms up straight above my head.

My entire body hurt, and I groaned loudly enough that I could hear it echo off the cliff. I slowly stretched side to side, bending and twisting my body carefully the way Ginger told me to. I leaned back as far as I could and moaned loudly, my stomach muscles still protesting the abuse they had received over the last few days.

When I glanced down, I noticed a fish near my feet. Ha, protein might be nice, if it was edible. It probably fell from the cold waterfall and was just sitting there, confused by the heat and wiggling against the ripples. I leaned forward, stretching my hands to slide them under the fish when I heard Mason growl, "Damn." Right behind me.

My brain still hurt, but it didn't take me long to realize that my moaning and groaning caught Mason's attention, and he'd come to check on me. When he came around the other side of the outcrop of rocks, he had a full view of me standing there naked.

A gasp burst out of my chest as I dove forward into the water. Screw wishing a hole would open up and swallow me - maybe I could drown myself right then instead.

"I'm sorry, I didn't mean to sneak up on you like that. I thought something was wrong," Mason called from the edge of the pool.

Please let me die right here and now.

I tried to answer, but nothing coherent came out of my mouth. Mason laughed, his voice clear and loud above the sound of the little waterfall. The sound drilled into the deepest, most vulnerable parts of me. Humiliating, hot tears fill my eyes.

It was bad enough to work beside somebody as beautiful as Ginger Patel, but to be laughed at when he saw me naked was more than I could take. I choked back the sobs that threatened to overwhelm me and moved out closer to the center of the pool, trying to disappear into deeper water.

"No, wait. I was just surprised that anything could render you speechless. You always have a comeback for me."

I refused to turn around. My plan had been to let him clean up, maybe feed him a fish, do something nice to thank him for being so nice. Instead of being grateful or touched, he was laughing at me. There was nothing I could do to make people treat me the way I wanted to. Frustration burned in my eyes, threatening to loose the tears I struggled to hold back.

The only reason my teammates kept me alive was because I was the navigator. I didn't sleep with any of them the way Ginger did, so they had no close feelings towards me. I knew I should have, that it was a part of the job, but I just couldn't do it.

The Corps provided the implant, and I tested free of diseases like the rest of them. There was no reason to hold myself back, and it kept everyone at a distance. Nobody had hang-ups about sex the way I did. By our second trip, I overheard what they were saying. They thought I believed I was too good for them. As if.

Teammates were expected to help each other out in the Mentions. I had always felt guilty that I didn't do my part, but nobody pushed. Nash would never let them. The few times I let myself join in back at the Corps camp, I felt so inadequate, or too serious, to enjoy it. But this was a new low for me. Nobody had ever laughed at me before.

I cleared my throat a few times. But it wouldn't stop. Humiliation crashed over me. The one man I actually wanted, and he thought I was a joke. I let the tears fall, crying silently, facing away and hoping Mason wouldn't see.

My father had taught me the value of silent tears, my childhood tormented by a man who hated fragile things, including his own daughter. I only shook a little bit and thought maybe the ripples of the water would hide what was happening.

But I knew it hadn't worked when Mason swore under his breath. I wasn't sure what he was saying, but he was on a rant.

Then splashing noises came from the shore as he entered the water and made his way to my side. Mason surprised me, really and truly shocked me when he slipped his arms around me. He turned me to face him, pulling me closer when, in my confusion, I didn't resist. He hugged me to him.

"Look, I know you're injured and tired and miserable. It's all right. I understand. There's nothing wrong with crying, especially since you've been through hell." Who on earth could be so infuriating and frustrating and rude and then be that sweet? He had been so kind since he saved me from Rader. And gentle. It was something I would never have expected, but it drew me to him.

He had removed all of his clothing except his boxers, and his skin felt good. Then he slowly pressed me closer, and I let him. There was comfort in his arms, despite the awkwardness of him seeing me when neither of us had expected it.

"I guess it shouldn't matter what you saw. I don't know

why I'm so embarrassed. Except I'm sure you think I could never compare to somebody like Ginger, and everybody else thinks so too." I nearly bit off my tongue when I realized I said that last part out loud.

Mason's arms tightened around me. "Is that what you really think? Holy crap, Hawke, I've never seen anyone as gorgeous as you." I would have argued with him, but I was close enough to know how his body had responded to mine, and that kind of reaction was impossible to fake. I couldn't help it - I actually smiled.

He groaned and took it as the invitation it was. He slid his hand across my jaw and down my neck, causing me to shiver. At that moment, all I wanted was to be with him, but my muscles were still so sore. I let out a small sound and, like before, it was as if Mason could read my mind.

With two fingers, he lifted my chin until my eyes met his. "If you want this, I can make sure it doesn't hurt." I ran my tongue across my lower lip, thinking about it. The second I nodded, Mason crushed me to him, kissing me.

And man, did he have skills. All I could think about was him and how he made me feel. Then he deepened the kiss as he walked me backward towards the shore. The water was barely to my ankles when he pulled back and kissed my jaw, then my neck.

Every motion, each movement, was designed to make me feel good. None of my other partners had taken the time to do more than copulate. But Mason made it all about me.

My lifelong barriers evaporated when I realized I was finally wanted for who I was and not just because I held the compass. A thrill surged through me at that thought, heightening my enjoyment, which in turn elevated his. For once, it was everything I had ever wished for. And Mason was the key.

We were both panting. I was on my hands and knees, breathing hard onto the surface of the water, when Mason said, "Damn, Hawke, that was hot as hell."

I couldn't help it - I stiffened and jerked away. "Don't call me that," I begged. We were so close, had been through one of the best experiences of my life, and he brought my father's name into it?

Mason groaned, running his hand through his hair. "Okay, Bailey. I'm sorry. I won't do that again."

With some effort, I lifted myself until I was kneeling upright. Before I could stand, Mason dragged me backward against him, slipping his arms around me, pulling me against his chest. A shiver rippled through me as he nibbled on my ear, his warm breath washing over me.

The shock I felt at the sound of my father's name dissolved under Mason's lingering passion. I wanted to tell him how he made me feel, but I had no idea what to say. I wasn't sure how to react. All I knew was that it was wonderful and women my age should know how to handle normal interactions. Maybe now I'd learn.

Children in the slums didn't trust easily. Too many people tried to use our vulnerabilities against us. But Mason broke through and made me feel normal for once.

The idea came to me that if any of my other encounters had been even half as good, I would have given Ginger a run for her money. All the guys on the team would be my friends.

But the second that thought came to mind, I realized it wasn't true. Sex with Mason had been great, but I couldn't stand the thought of anyone else touching me. Damn. I would probably have to go in for another psych evaluation. It wasn't good to focus too hard on a man who wasn't my contracted partner. Not when I had a team full of men who should have had a fair share of my time.

"Come on Bailey, you can help me do laundry so we get back in time," he said, teasing me into a different topic. But I appreciated it. I didn't want to talk about what had happened between us or my dad. Both subjects were too full of emotions I wasn't ready to share.

"Oh, sure," I played along. "Show a girl a good time, and then make her do laundry. I knew you were a throwback, Bain."

Mason laughed. We cleaned ourselves off, then he helped me walk over to where he had left his pack and the pile of his clothes. We pulled them out and washed them quickly, laying them out to dry in the murky sunlight.

The heat from the magma far below the rocks dried them quickly. There wasn't enough sun because of that infernal cloud cover. Then I returned to the pool and soaked a while longer in the heated water. When our clothes were dry, I got dressed alongside Mason. It wasn't embarrassing when I was prepared. Especially after what we had shared.

The stretches and heated water had done the trick. I could even walk almost normally on the hike back.

"Bailey," Nash called when he saw us. "That did you

some good. You look downright human." I grinned and bowed slightly. I wish Nash could have been my dad. He always seemed happy to see me. "I hope you're ready to eat. We caught something that looks a hell of a lot like a rabbit, only bigger. It tested fine so Will made the best lunch I've had in a long time. As soon as you two are done, we need to head out."

A huge smile crept onto my face. The rabbit sounded good, just the thing to make my afternoon even better. But I made the effort to settle my features into a more serious look, trying not to be too obvious about what I had been doing and exactly how great it was.

The guys had always respected Nash's mandate to leave me alone. And knowing them, I didn't think they would have pushed me to do it anyway, once they knew about my reluctance. But I didn't want it to cause any problems, or even worse, have any of them approach me now.

Teams did a lot for each other out in the Mentions. The closeness was meant to be cemented by our interactions. I've always known holding myself back was to our detriment, another reason I made myself as valuable as possible with my skills. We had a fragile balance, and I didn't want my willingness to be with Mason to alter the understanding I formed with anyone else.

My skin prickled with awareness - I felt eyes boring into me. I looked up and sure enough, Ginger was staring me down. She looked seriously pissed off. I raised my eyebrows at her, not sure what her problem could be.

It wasn't enough to distract me from the rabbit we were eating, though. Will was an amazing cook, and when I finished, I licked my fingers clean to avoid missing any of it.

Since I was no longer focused on my food, I didn't know where to look. Ginger was still giving me the stink eye, and I didn't know how I was supposed to act around Mason. He was eating seconds, so I looked down at my boots, thinking about what would come next.

"Mason, you don't need to haul me around this afternoon. I feel better after that long soak. I can probably keep up." Maybe I was okay. Or maybe I would collapse after a click or two and ruin all the good the hot water had done me. It was a tossup.

I was known for my sheer pigheadedness and I could make that work for me. I didn't want Mason to think I was some kind of wimp or that I wasn't willing to pull my own weight. Or worse, that I expected special favors.

"I'm good. You really aren't that heavy." Mason glanced around before lowering his voice. "Besides, I love the feel of your legs embracing me. You smell great, too. By the time I set you down for our break, I was so tuned on I almost took you behind those bushes over there."

It was a good thing that I had finished eating because I sucked my breath in sharply, flustered by his casual confession. Then it was my turn to glance around to make sure there wasn't anybody within earshot.

"Really?" I had always come out lacking when compared to my sister. And being on a team with Ginger didn't help my self image, either. He obviously wanted me, but it was hard to process.

"Don't look so surprised, Bailey, you're the sexiest

woman I've seen in a long time. And when you finally relaxed into me, I got a sense of your rhythm and kept myself busy thinking about how that would feel with you under me, your legs spread out, gripping onto me with all your strength."

Heat rose from the center of my body, spreading into my cheeks. But I didn't feel embarrassed, I felt turned on. I wasn't sure what I should do or say. Again. That was going to turn into a habit if I didn't watch out.

I tore my eyes away from him licking his fingers clean only to catch Ginger's eyes on me again. She was fuming. As she stalked off behind the bushes, I decided to go see what was going on.

It took me a few minutes to spot her where she was standing near some trees. I walked over to her side. "What's up, Ginger? What'd I do now?"

"Oh, shut the hell up, Bailey. You've left all the work to me for the last four trips and now that I finally find a guy I really like, you jump all over him."

"What are you talking about? I work my butt off, too."

I thought Ginger might slug me. She had clenched her hands into fists and her arms were shaking with tension. Nash didn't allow any fighting, and that was probably the only thing that kept her from jumping all over me.

"You know exactly what I'm talking about! You've been a freak woman eunuch, and I've had to take care of everyone by myself since Abilene died. And you might be the best navigator out there, but I'd settle for second best if that meant I could get a break once in a while."

"Yeah? Well, the second best is Jamison and he wouldn't

be helping you with that, anyway." I was so stupid, goading her like that. There was no reason why I should be so snarky, because she was right. It really wasn't fair. "Look, you know none of them want me. You're magnificent. I look like a dishrag standing next to you."

"Don't flatter me. You know damned well Will and Logan can't stop looking at you, no matter how much I've done for them. And if you quit looking at Nash like he was your daddy, he'd take you, too. So screw you, Bailey. Screw you for taking the one damn man I actually want."

I stood there like an idiot with my mouth hanging open. My head was pounding again, and I couldn't think. But for some reason, I actually believed her. Before, I told myself the men didn't really want me, so it was okay I didn't help relieve the tension.

But I was lying to myself, giving myself an excuse to remain separated from the rest of the team. Maybe I was the throwback, not Mason. "I'm sorry Ginger. I don't know what's wrong with me, but I just can't make myself do it. I don't know why."

"It doesn't matter why, Bailey. When we get out of here, I'm turning you into the Corps for dereliction of duty. You better hope we strike it rich because you're not going on another journey. I'll make sure of it. You'll go back to the slums and then we'll see how easy it is for you to keep them off you. And enjoy Mason while you can, because I sure as hell don't want him now that he's touched the warped little freak-show, Babykiller's Spawn."

I might have tried to talk sense to her if she hadn't said that. I had no idea she knew who my father was, and I froze. It had been a while since I'd been called that with so much hatred.

Hearing that name sent me right back to the day I found my father's secret room. My mouth refused to open, to deny the things Ginger had said, even if they were true. But I was frozen in place, stiff and horrified, the memories of dead babies blinding me to the forest around me. And the screaming faces of the media looked like they were right there again, surrounding me, all shouting for my attention because they couldn't get to my father.

"That's right, you scum," Ginger said, her face coming into focus. She looked triumphant. "I know exactly who you are. It isn't any wonder you can't function like a normal woman. And don't worry about the guys, I'm going to keep them busy and away from you just like you want. Because they're my teammates and I'll protect them from a psycho like you." Ginger walked off, back towards camp.

I stayed where I was, unable to think. The old panic was back, trapping me. Voices, images, memories all crashing into my mind, bringing me back to the worst time of my life. Locking me into the eternity of terror I lived through and could never shake.

Then I heard a whistle. I must have been holding everybody up. I unfroze, duty moving my feet back towards my team. All eyes were on me when I got there.

Tyler winked and nodded his head towards Mason and waggled his eyebrows. Sweet Tyler, a nice friend who I never had to worry about pressuring me. Seeing his handsome face helped anchor me back into reality.

Logan and Will were both gazing at me with the same

look Mason gave me while we were down by the waterfall. How did I never notice that before? What was wrong with me? Maybe Ginger was right. I was even more warped than I realized.

I couldn't look at Nash, though. Ginger was lying about him. He didn't want me like that. Every part of me rejected the idea.

Mason was looking at me quizzically. I had been teasing and laughing with him just a few moments before and I came back into the clearing looking like a zombie. I shook it off as best I could and jogged over. Pretending to be normal was something I was good at. "Hey, let me walk a while, okay? The exercise will probably be good for me."

He nodded, but kept his eyes on my face until Nash gestured for us to go. Then he had no choice but to turn his back.

I always knew that my past would catch up with me. The moment I'd been dreading since I joined the Corps finally happened. Right when I thought things were going to change for the better.

Hardly anyone remembered I had found the babies, my sister's fame fogging the memories of so many, drawing their focus to her. Sometimes there was even a reference to her in the news vids, as if the world had collectively decided she would make a better heroine.

Not that I was one. It didn't take any bravery to tell somebody about those babies. I just wanted to terror to stop.

They would have gone after her if her husband's men hadn't protected her. But to give her credit, if she deserved any after abandoning me to the system, she left it alone. Shareen let the media think she was the only daughter, allowing me a shot at hiding my own existence. Not an easy thing to do when my ID chip told everyone my real name.

But what was I supposed to do now? With a shake of my head, I reminded myself I had a plan. I would do my best, pull my weight, and be as valuable as possible. They might all eventually turn on me, especially if Ginger had her way, but I was going to make damned sure they remembered they needed me to navigate. It was the only power I had.

CHAPTER SEVEN
Encounter

WE TRAVELED FOR TWO more days before we saw signs of a village up ahead. There were no more private spots on the road, and Mason learned pretty quickly that I didn't feel free to be with him while we were surrounded by our teammates. It never seemed to bother them when they spent time with Ginger, but I simply couldn't.

He didn't pressure me, and I was grateful that he didn't decide to turn to Ginger for attention. Despite her declarations that she wouldn't touch Mason now that he had been with me, I bet if he glanced her way for a second longer than necessary, she'd start up on her flirting again.

That was how it had always been, ever since I met her. Ginger was territorial and all over every new guy. Even when I wanted to explore more than the occasional brief camp coupling, she got in the way. I wasn't sure if she really had any feelings for Mason or if she was just playing games, as always.

But she was serious about my dereliction of duty. I wasn't sure why I didn't realize how much she would resent me not helping with the guys once Abilene was gone. Or maybe she always had. But I was a fool not to think it would be a problem.

I had always walked a fine line, forcing people to accept me for my skills rather than relying on personal connections. The Corps expected both. It was too dangerous to get close - Mason was the first to figure out who my dad was without betraying me somehow. Ginger reacted exactly like I expected. But knowing it would happen didn't mean I knew what to do about it.

And I couldn't think about it, couldn't make plans about how to counteract her schemes. My headache had finally faded away, but thinking made my brain feel too full. Like there wasn't enough room for anything else. Not after what Blackstone had done.

Then there were the spells of dizziness. It hadn't taken me long to discover that they were often accompanied by random thoughts that sounded nothing like me. It took a while to piece it together, but Blackstone told me that he could pluck thoughts out of my head if he wanted.

If he could do that, then maybe I could, too. I wasn't doing it on purpose, but I did wonder if I was hearing something somebody else was thinking. Which was strange and scary and I was glad I couldn't process anything too deeply because that was simply too much to handle.

I felt a wave of anger crash over me again. Even though there was something growing between Mason and me, I was mad at him. If he hadn't been so quick to attack,

Blackstone would be here to tell me what was going on inside my head. Not to mention he would be able to help us get home.

It made me sad he was so close to finally going home when he died. That the poor old man would never see his heart's desire. Instead, he died on this jacked up mud ball.

Was it really Mason's fault? Blackstone did have my weapons in his hands. How would Mason know he was a pacifist?

I kicked a stone, sending it skittering into the trees. It was past time for us to continue our mission, which meant meeting people. Will noticed the path and Nash decided we'd take it. That would be a better thing to think about instead than Mason.

My heart sank as I admitted to myself that I had too many strong emotions for a man I barely met. It made it difficult to see things clearly. It also distracted me in a way I'd never had to deal with before. I gave myself a shake, trying to divert my thoughts into a more productive direction. Like how to use the information Blackstone put in my head.

I cleared my mind and focused on the rhythm of my boots hitting dirt. My skull felt weird, like it was trying to expand as I opened my thoughts. Unfortunately, no star patterns came to mind. But it got me thinking about the old man again.

Looking back, it was obvious Blackstone played some kind of trick on me in the tent so I would tell him everything he wanted to know. It had erased years of protective instincts and made me trust him. The tech installed in his body gave him abilities that were beyond anything I had experienced. Not that I was all that familiar with Psych Ops outside the usual fit-for-duty evaluations.

Whatever it was he did also made me feel like he had been a part of my life for a long time, and it actually hurt me that he was gone. My heart ached over his loss. I was trying not to hold that against Mason, especially since it wasn't real. But it was hard.

Part of me suspected I was avoiding further intimacy because of that, as much as the lack of privacy. If I wanted to be with Mason again - and I definitely did - I had to reconcile my rioting emotions. But how did I do that when I was so obsessed with Blackstone's loss? Was I going crazy?

My body shuddered violently, goosebumps covering my skin. Was I? But no, if I was scared I was insane, that meant I wasn't. Didn't it?

Nash whistled, indicating we were close to a village. Yes! Finally, something outside myself to focus on.

We targeted a different settlement, but they attacked us that first night. Now we realized they likely thought we were with Rader and didn't necessarily mean strangers any harm. But that made the territory too hostile, forcing us to abandon our original plan.

Mason stopped near Nash. I soon caught up. The rest of the team sped up so they could join us sooner and hear what the boss had to say.

Smoke rose in the distance, a haze on the near horizon indicating a large settlement. "We're close enough," Nash announced. Standard Corps protocol dictated teams scout before entry into a potentially hostile situation. It was also basic common sense. "Bain, take Nakamura with you."

Will's language implant made him the obvious choice to partner with the strategist when scoping out a new location. The more conversations our linguist overheard, the better. Also useful if they came across travelers.

Too bad I couldn't think of a reason to tag along. Since Blackstone fiddled with my head, I could understand the locals and help my teammates. But unless I wanted to let everyone in on my secret, I was going to have to let them handle things as usual.

We waited in the trees a little way off the pathway we had been following. It was large enough to allow a cart and horse to pass easily. If this earth-copy used carts. Or had horses. But most did and there were some ruts in the dirt, as if wheels had left tracks during the last storm.

"What's up with you and Mason?" Tyler asked, almost whispering. Ginger and Logan silently passed the canteen to each other as they leaned against a tree far enough away they wouldn't hear quiet conversation. Nash was close to the path, waiting for Mason and Will to return.

"Nothing, unless we get some privacy." I wasn't going to tell him what else was going on. I couldn't figure out my own emotions, much less talk about them.

Tyler snorted. "Why would that stop you? Ginger was going at it with Logan all night."

"Well, I'm not Ginger," I snapped, the strain of keeping my voice down causing my voice to shake. What if he asked why? I mean, surely he thought it was weird I didn't help keep up morale, too.

"Easy there," Tyler coaxed. "Listen, I was just trying to

pass the time. I didn't mean anything by that."

My shoulders slumped. I reached out my hand, resting it on his arm. "I'm sorry. I don't know why I'm so snappy." Except that I did. Not that I could confide in him. Telling him would only make sense if I told him who my dad was. And Ginger was already threatening me over it.

As if she heard my thoughts, Ginger's eyes snapped to mine. Then she glanced down at where I was still squeezing Tyler's arm. A sneer crept onto her face. As clear as day, I heard her voice in my head. "Freak."

I casually moved my hand back to my side. No need to remind her I wasn't doing my part. Or that the only other man I had let close to me would never be interested.

"Probably because you haven't gotten any in days. I know I need an attitude adjustment, myself."

I chuckled. Tyler had all sorts of euphemisms. Every Mention had willing partners for him, but some earth-copies were more open than others. He once told me that he didn't want to out anyone living in a Mention so backward they harmed those who didn't conform to their narrow beliefs. It was one of those things we sometimes encountered in the Mentions that was hard to believe. Then again, there were terrible humans in a lot of the earth-copies.

"Maybe we can do something about that when we meet the locals."

"One can only hope." Tyler shifted his stance, narrowing his eyes at the shadows along the edge of a small stream. There was nothing there, though. The leaves were rustling in a slight breeze, not because we were about to be raided.

A low whistle sounded through the trees. Nash took off, the rest of us staying where we were in case it wasn't Mason or Will. Then a louder whistle in Nash's distinct pattern, calling us to his side.

"We passed a few locals. None seemed threatened or even that curious. I don't think they have hangups about strangers," Mason said as we all gathered around. "The settlement's close, soldier types here and there but not on high alert."

Perfect conditions for us. Relaxed locals who thought they were safe were easier to deal with. Not that we didn't always have to be on guard. People were people, no matter what side of the gateway.

"You heard the man. Time to go." Nash didn't go over the plan again. We were all versed, including the backup plans. The Corps insisted we all train in the same methods so swapping out teammates would be seamless.

The path widened into a legitimate roadway, with wheel grooves stacked two or three vehicles wide. There wasn't anyone currently traveling, but there was evidence it was occasionally a high-traffic area. Nash set a quick pace, requiring me to exert more effort than I had to since the incident with Blackstone. But I was pleased to note I handled it without the usual strain.

Soon we came across a wood bridge over a river, then around a bend. The settlement lay before us, a collection of huts and larger buildings that had the unmistakable signs of a village.

The various structures were laid out in a grid. It would be easy enough to learn our way around in a short time.

They were made of reed-like material woven together into the walls of buildings, several groupings deep, and ended with a great wall off to one side made of sharpened poles and stone.

Behind the wall was a large wooden building, much like the ancient castles we'd studied. While there was no telling what we would encounter while out on a mission, our own history was by far the most helpful subject to study in our Corps classes. Some earth-copies missed the same leap in technology or invention that Earth Prime did.

Fortifications and other amenities made it a more significant settlement. Our original plan was to arrive at a more vulnerable place to begin our negotiations. My stumble into Rader's camp had put an end to that.

Nash pointed at Will and Tyler. "Nakamura, I want you and Moreno to come with me and Bailey, standard formation." It was normal to split into two groups. It gave us the advantage of distance observation of the other half of the team. "Bain, you take Patel and Jackson."

Ginger and Logan were hard to read, but it was obvious Ginger hated to rely on Mason. And Logan was following her lead. It was a tense threesome, but they would do their duty. Nash's leadership had seen to that. If anyone failed to follow orders to the best of their abilities, he'd boot them.

We approached the village, going slow and with caution. We wanted them to see us, but not think we were a threat. All weapons were secured to our backs so we didn't seem aggressive, but also let no question about defending ourselves if we needed to.

Then there was nothing left to do but enter the village.

No going back.

Several people were roaming around, doing the manual labor chores we see when in the no tech Mentions. Digging drainage ditches, herding animals around looking for some scrub grass to eat, collecting eggs from under scrawny chickens, chopping wood, and, in the distance, working in fields of vegetables.

An unnatural silence had fallen, ushered in by our arrival. The locals held back, but they kept working as if to prove they weren't afraid. Or maybe hoping if they acted non-threatening, so would we.

We had reached the center of the village when a group of men approached us, appearing from behind the spiked-pole wall. They closed the gate behind them. I bet the villagers were thrilled to be locked on the same side we were.

I moved up to stand next to Nash. Since they were a male dominated society, I hung back slightly behind him. Giving a subtle appearance of submission would soothe them subconsciously. It even helped that my presence at the head of the line would display our so-called vulnerability. Me, the weak link.

Will and Tyler walked behind us, while Mason, Logan, and Ginger dropped into a spot quite a ways back, positioned as if they might even be a separate group. It looked like it would be easier to take us on when we walked in like that, and that was what we wanted them to think. Really it gave them a tactical advantage to observe from a distance and potentially attack from behind.

Every one of the men had on a matching patterned cloth draped over his shoulder. It looked a lot like the old vids I'd seen of the Scottish wearing their plaids. Considering how many were grouped together, it was safe to assume the patterns marked them as a squadron or clan or whatever they called it in this Mention.

They had weapons galore, so it wasn't a huge leap to assume these guys were soldiers or warriors. One man stood in front of the group, in a position of prominence, likely their leader. He was tall, well over six foot six, and had muscles bulging all over the place.

His features were so strong that the large, almost bug eyes typical of the locals were set more deeply into his face, which made him one hell of a lot more attractive. And holy hell, he was looking at Tyler like he wanted to eat him up. It was so hot I could practically feel it singe my skin.

"Who are you? Why are you here?" The leader demanded.

Blackstone's gift kicked in, enabling me to understand his words. It sounded just like English, the language I had spoken since childhood. When I concentrated, the words were different, and I got a sense of the way the native language really sounded.

I held my hands at waist height, palms up, and let my chin drop, deliberately avoiding their curious glances. It was annoying. And trying to act all humble and submissive at the same time I was speaking for my group wasn't the easiest task.

"Nash," I murmured. "Put your hand on my shoulder so they know I belong to you." He did as I requested.

It didn't matter if my teammates thought that was strange. I was the one in charge of initial contact, earning that extra duty by our second trip. Another good reminder to Ginger and the guys that they needed me more than I needed them. Hopefully, it would keep them from joining her case against me when we got back to camp.

Keeping my eyes at the level of the leader's chin, I made my voice sound soft and shaky. "I know you can't understand me, but we mean no harm. See? Our weapons are not out." I pointed to Will and Tyler's swords, strapped to their backs.

Even when people didn't understand our words, they could hear our tone and see our actions. It encouraged them to verbalize as well. Will needed to hear them to get his implant enough input to help him learn their language.

The man in front glanced at our weapons, but he had already assessed the situation. No leader would wait for us to point out the obvious threats.

I moved one step forward and bowed my head a little further, reaching out my hand. "It would help if you could speak to us. We need to hear your language for this to work."

The leader responded by giving his men orders in a firm and even tone. It wasn't overly aggressive, which was a good sign. "Spread out. See if they will let us form a half circle around them. If they make no move to withdraw their weapons, then we can invite their leader and his woman to sit with us. The rest can stay where they're at."

None of us moved while the soldiers positioned themselves around us. They looked us over, coming close to each of the men, but we didn't touch our weapons. The men remained calm, but some of them bristled and threatened more than the others. They were the type that would fight dirty, but then again, so would we. Nash never held that against a potential ally.

After a few moments, the leader approached us, holding his hand out towards me. I wasn't sure what he intended. After spending time with the delightful Rader and his wives, I knew women weren't exactly treated like royalty.

I didn't even know if Nash giving my hand to the leader would also indicate a transfer of property, and he'd want to spend some time with me. The kind of time I wasn't interested in.

Then again, the way he looked at Tyler made me feel safer. And Rader had been really possessive and interested in me up immediately. This man wasn't eyeballing me the same way, so the likelihood that I'd be harmed was small.

Nash probably thought the same thing because he pushed me forward and released my hand. The leader grasped it and tugged me closer. Without warning, he wrapped his arms around me and kissed me.

It was deep and fierce and sudden. It was also so fast I didn't have a chance to pull away. He then grasped my shoulders, holding me still as he studied my shocked face. He chuckled. What a jerk.

"Little woman, I embrace you and accept your family into our village. You will be treated well while I negotiate with your master. I have placed my claim upon you and no other man will harm you." I took it back. Not a jerk. That kiss was ritualistic and gave me a modicum of safety.

A small group of bug-eyed women walked up. They had blankets and food, as if they wanted us to go on a picnic. The leader gestured towards a line of trees, casting their shade on a flat grassy area. It looked downright pleasant, so I shrugged and followed them.

The rest of my team followed at a short distance, and the soldiers moved closer. This was the part when things became tricky. They were now close enough to cause damage before we could react. My team's tension prickled against my back, but we had been in several situations like that before and always made it out without injury. We'd be okay - if our luck held.

CHAPTER EIGHT
Feast

THE SOLDIERS TALKED AMOUNGST themselves while we ate. We couldn't have asked for a better situation. All of that input would speed Will's ability to understand them. I wasn't exactly sure how the implant worked, but it clicked in fast. It stimulated certain parts of his brain, and I suspected what Blackstone had done was similar.

After maybe twenty minutes of chitchat from the locals, the rest of us silent as much as possible to allow Will to soak in only one language at a time, Will looked at the soldier next to him and pointed to the bread. "What do you call this?" he asked.

The soldier didn't know what Will was asking, but he said, "Do you want more bread?" And then picked up a piece, handing it to Will.

"Got it," Will announced, triumph ringing in his voice. Then the way his words sounded changed. "I greet you," he said, and I recognized the strange syllables of the local language. "I do not know many words, but I can help your leader to speak with ours."

The soldiers exchanged glances, wary and surprised. That was always the first reaction we got when Will started speaking local languages - they wondered why we had hidden that from them. It was tough on the rapport we were trying to establish, but we couldn't explain that Will had just learned most of it in twenty minutes.

The leader narrowed his eyes, looking us over again. "I was not aware any of you could speak our language. Why didn't you introduce your team instead of sending that woman to be your mouthpiece?"

I tried not to look up and respond to him like I understood. Nobody, not even Mason, knew that Blackstone had changed me to understand what people were saying around me. Or that I could hear some of the things they weren't saying.

Will answered haltingly. "My leader wanted to show you that we meant no harm. I did not want to insult you with my poor speech."

That seemed to make sense to the leader. The other soldiers relaxed as well. This place was so full of machismo, I could practically feel it. Almost as if it left an oily residue on my skin. I wrinkled my nose, but looked down at my hands quickly to hide my expression.

Out of the corner of my eye, I caught a few of the men staring at me. I didn't want to inadvertently insult anyone with my obvious annoyance. Or start a war because they thought I didn't like their cooking. Things like that happened a lot. Then I let out a soft laugh at the absurdity of it all and hoped nobody heard me.

"Honored leader, my name is Will. I speak for this man, Nash."

The leader nodded to Nash, acknowledging an equal. "I am called Javilin. I am the head of the soldiers garrisoned here. What is it that your group wants from us?" Javilin was nice and direct.

Straightforward communication was a gift - and a problem. It was nice to know where we stood, but direct speech and honesty went hand in hand. That was too bad. We needed to figure out who was corrupt to move forward with our plans for these people.

"We have come to speak to your leader about trade goods. We come from far away. Can we meet him soon?" Will knew how to move things right along, and he could tell that Javilin would respond better to straight talk, too. Or what seemed like straight talk. Most of what we said in the Mentions were lies.

Javilin spent his time assessing us again. I tried to read his expression and guess what he thought about what he saw.

We weren't dressed like they were, especially Ginger and I. Pants weren't normal for women. And we spoke in an unfamiliar language. That made me wonder if they all spoke the same language. Most earth-copies had a variety of languages the same way Earth Prime did, but every once in a while there was a planet where everyone could communicate with a common language.

Earth Prime's president had suggested that we should do the same, but once we got into traveling the dimensions, the more people who knew different languages, the better. Often locals spoke a similar, or even almost identical, language to one of Earth Prime's. When they didn't, the language implants kicked in and communication became even more refined.

But the openness to our presence and willingness to hear us out remained in force. Javilin poured himself another glass of wine from the fired-clay vessel in navy blue. I had marked that one as safe to drink after Ginger had surreptitiously tested it for safety. It was harder to ensure the proteins they offered were safe to eat, but she had taken the bread and ensured it was safe as we walked in.

Will and Logan were both eating the meat. Brave men. But Will was also the cook and Logan the botanist. They took more risks when it came to food. Logan had already tested a ton of vegetation during the days of our long hike, and one or two of the offerings were definitely edible.

As the navigator, I was forced to eat only the foods that had been tested. The others could take the chance that these locals could eat or drink only the same things we could. And they probably didn't have any special immunities. But there was still a chance. In the last Mention, the water had too much arsenic for us. We had to filter it all, but the locals were either born with an immunity or built one up over time.

The drawback to me choosing a valuable profession was sitting out some fabulous looking meals. I couldn't risk my safety any more than my team could. They might owe me for their ticket off this planet, but I owed them to keep myself alive long enough to get them home. It was the deal we made.

When nobody got sick, Mason and Nash grabbed up some of the meat, too. Tyler stuck with the same foods I was eating. Maybe out of solidarity. Or maybe because he didn't like to take any more risks than necessary to get on and off planet. Not everyone had a lot of good luck, and he once told me he was saving his up for when it mattered.

Javilin had to decide if he was going to introduce us to his leader or not. I hoped he hurried because I was getting pretty sick of this place. The sooner we moved on to the next stage of our process, the sooner we could get out of here.

"I will take you and your leader to see Tellar, the ruler of this region," Javilin announced. My shoulders relaxed. One obstacle gone. "You must also bring your women for their own protection."

Tension returned to my shoulders. It never boded well when the locals flat out told our team that women were in danger. "We would be honored to meet Tellar," Will responded. He didn't acknowledge the warning, but then turned to us and spoke in our language. "Nash, they'll take us but he said to bring the women so they won't get hurt."

"I'd rather they come than stay behind, anyway," Nash replied. He took a swig of the beer-like beverage in his clay goblet. I loved how much care he showed for the people on his team. It was one of the things I admired most about him.

Will turned back to Javilin. "My leader has agreed to take the women, if you feel that is necessary."

Javilin nodded towards me and Ginger. "They do not

look like our women. Their faces are pleasing to my men. Please warn them to make sure they do not wander off on their own. My gesture of protection over the little one will only go so far to protect her."

Yeah, that was me. The little one. Javilin could bet his dirty leather boots that I wouldn't be wandering off anywhere on my own. I wasn't stupid. Neither was Ginger.

Will nodded gravely. "Our team usually stays together," he said.

It didn't work, though. "Tellar will not allow any more than the two of you in his presence. Your guards will remain outside."

"Understood." It would have been better if we could've brought all the guys along, but at least the four of us would be together. It really wasn't too bad of an arrangement, although we would be locked up in that castle fortress with no way out if something bad went down.

We'd do it, anyway. The Corps considered our teams dispensable. Disposable. Cannon fodder, if needed. Either this place was worth plundering, or the gateway would be closed forever. There was no in between. Our job was to figure out which.

Getting home was optional as far as the Corps was concerned. There were too many of us to matter as individuals. That was the worst and best thing about Earth Prime. Too many people and all the disastrous things that went with it. But it was also the only conceivable way that somebody like me could get lost in a crowd. It was nearly impossible not to.

The Corps had also trained us to fight - to survive. If we

couldn't, a Mention wasn't worth the effort to send another team. They moved on and sealed the coordinates. There were infinite earth-copies. No need to waste too many resources, regardless of the continually growing population.

The only exception was if my compass went off. It was set, the same as all compasses, to alert the navigator if there was more of the same type of metal that they used to create it. It was too rare, and too precious to worry about a hard colonization. We would return home to unimaginable riches as a reward for finding it, no scouting needed. Getting the message back was the priority.

Then the Corps would throw every soldier they had at the Mention and keep sending them until they were victorious. Like ants building a bridge of dead bodies across a body of water. They'd keep piling us up until they won.

"As soon as we are done eating, I will lead you to him," Javilin explained. "The guards would not let you pass without my permission. Then I will return to my soldiers to stay with the others in your party as you seek Tellar's favor. We will show them around to keep them occupied."

Javilin gave Tyler another searing look, and I could hear Tyler gulp all the way from where I was sitting. Man. I'd bet my own dirty boots that Javilin would be personally escorting Tyler to explore some of the more titillating sights. Whew.

The women who had invited us along on the picnic came back and cleaned the food scraps away. Ginger and I had been the only women at the meal. Considering the Mention we were in, having women there had to be a big shock or great honor or maybe both.

Will gestured to us and repeated what Javilin said. Logan didn't look happy, and he moved closer to Ginger, hovering over her as if she were made of spun glass. That was new. I studied them, and while Ginger's narrowed eyes and nasty look didn't surprise me, Logan's possessive actions did. He noticed me looking at him and returned my curious gaze with a hostile one.

Ginger's face shifted from nasty to triumphant, her arm sliding around Logan as she skewered me with her eyes. She was responsible for the change in his attitude and wanted me to know it. Damn. How much had she told him? Apparently, that was another thing I needed to worry about.

I tried to force aside my growing uneasiness. There was too much going on to spend my time thinking about her tricks or what to do about them. But I couldn't help it. She wasn't letting it go, and I couldn't afford to just let it happen without a fight.

The problem was, I had no idea what to do. I never had. People had so many different reactions to who I was that I could never figure out how to counteract their assumptions. Not to mention their revulsion. Or worse - their sudden flattery and desire to use me to get at my father. As if I would ever go near him again.

But why would Logan turn on me so quickly? We had worked alongside each other out in the Mentions. Surely a sexual relationship wasn't the only way to ensure his loyalty. What else was I supposed to do?

I'd probably waste the rest of my life trying to solve that mystery. Better to build up my own connections, or remind them about how much they needed me. Then I would stay safe.

Wouldn't I?

As we were dusting off our pants and trying to wash up a tiny stream nearby, Mason walked over to where I was kneeling by the water. We didn't talk much on the last part of our hike to the settlement, and I was worried that I had caused a wedge with my hangups. "How are you doing?" he asked.

Nice opening line. "Fine," I said, not helping him at all. It wasn't on purpose - I was still feeling awkward. But in the middle of all my worry and confusion, I thought the irritation that flickered across his face was funny. Hm, yes, I really was a little crazy.

Grabbing a small towel from my pack, I dried off my arms, face, and neck. Then I stood, still not saying anything. Mason was waiting for me to show him what I wanted, to flirt or reject or whatever. But my tongue felt as if it had been glued to the roof of my mouth.

My eyes studied his face. The look in his eyes relieved the tension in my shoulders. He wasn't mad or irritated. Not really. He was offering me the lead. Giving me what I wanted. Waiting for permission.

Heat shot through me, pooling in my stomach. I had thought he was hot before, but it was nothing compared to how it made me feel to be wanted like that. Respected like that.

The tip of my tongue flickered across my lips before my teeth sank into my bottom lip. It was a nervous response, but Mason's eyes followed my movements. His gaze heated, causing my breath to hitch in my chest.

Desperate to seem normal, I returned to my preparations to meet the big boss of the village. With a quick side glance at his smoldering look, I unwrapped my hair from its usual bun and shook it out. A waft of mild floral scent rose around me, the underside still damp from that morning's river bath. I pulled out a brush and used it to work out the knots and smooth the fly-aways.

Mason made a soft noise. Then he tangled his hands in my hair and tugged a little. He had taken my glances as an invitation - and I was glad.

I hoped nobody else noticed how much I obviously liked it, though. Goosebumps covered my arms, and I didn't stop Mason when he leaned in close to me, his body pressed into mine, his warm breath tickling the back of my neck. Not one part of me wanted him to quit touching me.

My toes curled when he whispered into my ear. "Take care of yourself in there with the locals, Bailey. You're a sexy little thing, and I've been watching how these men have been looking at you. I don't blame them, but that doesn't mean I want them to touch what's mine." And damned if I didn't really like the sound of that, too.

A low groan sounded in my throat before I managed to straighten, pulling away from his body. I wanted nothing more than to stay there, wrapped in his arms. But Nash wasn't going to wait all day. He'd flip if I made them late because I was busy flirting.

"I hate to say this, but I need you to let go, Mason. I've got to get my hair back under wraps before these soldiers get the same idea as you and I start an inter-dimensional incident." Mason chuckled and let go. He knew the drill. Personal time came after the mission. And there was no telling what the men in this Mention would do if their sense of entitlement came up against Javilin's protection.

I ran my brush through my hair again and pulled it back into a bun as Mason moved away to inventory his weapons. A movement caught my eye, and I turned, catching both Tyler and Logan staring at me. Tyler was smiling and encouraging, Logan angry. I would have to deal with that eventually, but I wasn't sure where to begin.

Whatever. I needed to concentrate on the upcoming meeting and leave the personal interactions for later. Although Logan didn't seem as hostile as he had when Ginger was hovering nearby. Maybe he would give me a chance to explain my side of things, after all.

Nash didn't lecture me when I reached his side. That meant I wasn't holding them up. Good thing, too, because I'd come out smelling like a rose compared to Ginger, who was still primping by the water's edge. She was making quite a show of it.

Will was watching her, too. I glanced around. Logan and Tyler had joined Mason. Of the three, Logan was the only one interested in the peepshow. He couldn't tear his eyes away from surveying Ginger's wares. She was always trying to be the center of attention, but this was something at a whole other level.

The way she moved, slithering and wiggling, jiggling as she tugged her clothes into place, pressing her breasts together as she styled her hair. It was so overt and obvious.

I could barely stand it. Nausea threatened to crawl up my throat and I had to swallow hard.

I glanced at the boss. Nash was grinding his teeth, obviously ticked off. The last thing we needed was for a bunch of soldiers to cause a ruckus over Ginger's cute little display. Still, she didn't walk over, didn't get ready for the mission. Instead, she "accidentally" dropped her brush and bent over, legs spread and backside aimed at us when she picked it up.

My eyes squinted as I braced myself for Nash's bellow. He was calm in a fight, deadly and in control. But when we needed the slack jerked out of us, he was as loud as any trainer in the Corps.

But he didn't say anything. Shocked, I snapped my attention to his face. His jaw was still clenched, but it wasn't anger that made him so tense.

No. There was no way he would fall for those trash moves. He would never. Nash was a good man, strong, respectable, fatherly. Smart. Too smart for her.

His whistle broke through my fears. Oh. He was calling her to attention, using the report sequence. That was it. He didn't want the locals to know he didn't have complete control over her. It wasn't her display that held him enthralled. It was his legendary focus on the safety of his team.

Ginger finally completed her ministrations and loped casually up the hill to where we were standing. I sneered, allowing my disgust to show on my face. Will might be panting after her, his desire painfully obvious. But not Nash. He saw right through her, same as me.

"Ready, boss," she said to him, smiling as if she had just won some kind of award. "Sorry I took so long. The water felt so good. I've been so hot lately I needed something to cool me off."

Unable to keep watching her or her effect on Will and Logan, I tilted my head to soak in Nash's reaction to her foolishness.

Damned if he didn't smile back.

CHAPTER NINE
Performance

JAVILIN LED US THROUGH the gate into the garrison. Soldiers milled around, running errands or practicing with wooden swords and bows and arrows. There were more women walking around on this side of the wall. It was probably safer for them.

The wooden building was the seat of power, prominent and well-made. It stood at three full levels, with square towers in each corner of the rectangular main building, each sticking up another two stories. Long, thin slits wide enough to shoot arrows from lined each outer wall, allowing for defense of each floor. They had stained it a deep chestnut, but most of it was almost black.

I touched a wall as we entered through a giant wooden door bound with bands of iron. My fingers came away with soot on them. I had seen something like that in some of the Mentions that build with wood. They charred the outsides to waterproof the walls and drive away bugs.

The doorway opened immediately into an enormous room with ceilings reaching the second floor, lined with structural beams painted white to match the ceiling. Five enormous chandeliers covered with candles lit the room.

There were several fireplaces lining the perimeter of the room, with a slim staircase leading up, spiraling close to the wall so anyone who was right-handed would have a hell of a time using their sword. Which clearly was the point. That was how we used to do it on Earth Prime.

They led the four of us to a smaller room that opened right off the side of the entry. Egg-shaped chairs made of woven reeds were dangling from chains hanging from the ceiling, with long wooden tables pushed against the wall filled with a variety of multicolored containers and pitchers made of glazed, fired clay.

"I shall inform Tellar that you have arrived. Please help yourself to a sample of our best wines and delicacies."

Will perked up while he translated. None of us were hungry, but Ginger poured herself a cupful and brought one to Will, flirting heavily. Time to make her move to convince Will to hate me, too.

With a snort, I wondered how she thought she could turn Tyler against me since he wouldn't be interested in her skanky lady-parts. Maybe I could keep at least one friend.

"Take it easy on the wine, you two. You don't know how strong that is." Nash was back to sounding gruff and monitoring his team. I relaxed, not even realizing my body had been so tense. Nash not telling off Ginger earlier had freaked me out.

There were tapestries hanging on the walls, brightly

colored and embroidered with a good amount of skill. They were edged in the same fabric pattern I saw the soldiers wearing, indicating they were family banners. Each pictured lions raging and battle scenes, obviously a power display.

Somebody had embroidered grapevines along the edges - this family likely had some orchards. There were also images of cattle, sheep, and fruits included. It wasn't too hard to figure out where the wealth of these locals came from.

Javilin and a young boy returned to the waiting room. "Tellar will see you in the great hall."

Will relayed the message. I could tell his understanding was getting better because his translations were more accurate. We headed back into the cavernous room, and sure enough, they had set up a platform on one side, supporting a chair with Tellar sitting in it. I assumed that was him, anyway.

He had the typical bulging eyes I was positive I would never get used to, and was actually quite slender. He wore fussy and superfine clothing made of garish red silk, his brown eyes lined with black markings and black hair styled carefully to show off the shaved sides peeping below the longer locks braided all along the sides.

That was a good sign for us. Vanity usually went hand in hand with greed. That trait always helped us lead the locals right on into corruption. If there was anything our Corp training could help us with, it was how to use the corrupt locals to get our way.

"You may approach," Tellar announced, waiving us

closer.

I kept my face directed at my feet, struggling to keep the grin from spreading across my face. What a peacock.

Will picked up on the cues, well-trained in his job, too. Nash never would have let him on the team if he weren't. Once he began his opening spiel, Will became distinctly flowery with his phrases. "Great ruler, my leader offers his greetings and best wishes for your health. We come to you with open arms, desiring only to encourage a mutually beneficial relationship."

Yeah, he definitely read that right. Tellar got all puffed up and allowed Will to move closer to the platform. I was almost disappointed when I heard Tellar say, "Come then, let us retire to my private study and speak business. I will have my men see to your ladies' comfort."

It would be nice to overhear their important initial discussions. But whatever, women weren't important here.

Javilin had left, so only the boy remained to usher us out of the room. Ginger looked annoyed, too, but that could be because she had to hang out with me a little longer and not that we were being left out. She was never one to care about negotiations or manipulative tactics.

They showed us to another chamber down the opposite side of the hall from the waiting room. My eyes had trouble taking it all in at once. The room was draped with cushions and silks lining the walls in bright jewel colors with sitting pillows and lounging couches. It looked like a combination of brothel and harem. Tacky - and gross.

There were five ladies already there, saving me from Ginger's foul mood. Nastiness needs no translation, so she had to force herself to be on her best behavior. Ha, how long would that last?

Two of the women were fair-skinned and had blond hair, and the other three had darker skin with an olive overtone and black hair. All were beautiful in their own way, even if they had those creepy eyes. Definitely a rich clan.

This society based its power structure on valuables and how many women they owned. Presumably they cared about looks, because none of the wives were plain or ugly. The shorter blond woman even had smaller than usual eyes. The way the others tiptoed around her, patting her arms and hair, it was obvious they were kissing some serious butt. She was probably wife number one if I was reading them right.

"I hope they aren't a part of the negotiations," the small blond said.

"Oh, no Jaycee. They couldn't possibly interest our husband. He only wants unused women, and these two travel with many men, who touch them freely in public."

Oh, hell no, she did not just call me and Ginger a couple of sluts.

What a nasty little piece of work. Not that I could do anything about it. Even if they knew I could understand them, I still wouldn't have said a word. We needed to keep these people cooperative and lulled into a sense of security.

"Hey, how much do you want to bet the little blond is queen bee?" I asked Ginger, hoping to draw her out. Sometimes a common enemy was a good start. It was worth a try, once.

Ginger's eyes glittered as she snapped at me. "You aren't funny, Hawke. Quit trying to kiss my butt. It won't work."

My jaw clenched with fury. Why didn't she try showing some loyalty to me for once? The least she could have done was talk to me about wanting help. Not that it would have changed anything, but I may have been about to divert her anger before it had gotten so bad.

The local women watched us out of the corner of their eyes. Ginger might have been regulating her voice, but her body language made it pretty obvious we weren't exactly best friends.

"It would be nice if you could at least pretend we're a united front while in enemy territory," I responded. When in doubt, fall back on rules and regulations. Not like that ever seemed to calm anyone down. It certainly didn't work with Ginger.

"Look, you little hypocrite, don't go quoting policy to me. Women always let down their hair when they're alone. I'm setting up the groundwork to have them soothe my hurt feelings and take my side. Then I can get in good with the first wife so she'll promote the deal with her obnoxious husband."

Damn - Ginger just out did me. She thought up that plan on the fly while she was talking to me. And it was a pretty good one. I could have turned to that page in the manual without effort. It was a standard ploy and why it came so easily to her.

But once she threw it out there, with her as the Injured Party in our not-so-fake drama, that basically obligated me to be the bad guy in this scenario. And the sad thing was, it was true. If I was being honest, I was the bad guy to leave her without help because I wasn't into sleeping with a different man every night.

Well, fine then. May as well embrace it. Turning my face so most of the locals could see my expression, I rolled my eyes at Ginger, every movement exaggerated. Then used the nastiest voice I could as I launched right into my new role.

"You want to play it up? Fine. You're more likely to have something in common with those stuck up bitches, anyway. And since you're so willing to spread your legs for anyone you meet, I'm sure their husband would take you up on anything you offer him, too. Have fun with that."

I cringed at the words that had bubbled up without a thought. They wouldn't help with the war Ginger had started between the two of us. The locals didn't understand anything I said - there was no reason for me to get personal. My tone and expression were all I needed to set the stage for those women.

But I was so tired of feeling like a freak for not sleeping around with my teammates. Nobody else cared about it the way I did. They didn't take interactions with other people as seriously. And that didn't mean I was wrong.

So maybe it was time to remind Ginger that not all people thought the way she did. And just because it was an accepted rule, that didn't make it right. Even if the Corps agreed with her to the point that they made a policy of it, backed by Psych Ops.

My little jab about her having so much in common with these bug-eyed locals was on purpose, though. It reminded her that even though I was a killer's daughter, my pedigree was still light years better than hers. I had to work for the Corps to survive and was never granted the advantages I was born to possess, but Ginger had never understood that.

I could pull out my supposedly superior bloodline and taunt her because she was the one who felt my ancestors defined me. They were so distant they really had nothing to do with me. There was only one family member close enough to have influence, and I had spent my entire life trying to make sure I wasn't anything like him.

Ginger and the others had been conditioned to reject those with higher status. The ones who weren't a part of the nameless, faceless masses who live and died in the slums. And in typical fashion, had developed a superiority complex about how hard they had it. If I took her sense of pride away, she would lose control. Basic psych principles.

She was waging a war against me. I couldn't think of anything I could do to counteract her actions. My only hope was to throw her off balance. Make her think she couldn't win because people like me had connections and got away with whatever they wanted. With luck, she wouldn't turn me in, even if she ruined the relationships I had with my team.

Did it matter that I didn't actually have those connections? My sister did, but she had disowned me when our father was arrested. Ginger may have figured out who I was related to, but that didn't mean she had a clue about my life. Nobody ever did.

"Don't act like I'm the freak, you abomination,"

Ginger hissed. "I followed the rules! Look how easy it is for them to take my side because of it. Maybe you have connections I don't, but I've been smart about my camp hookups, too. You might not be able to hide behind your fancy connections after all. I guess we'll see when we get back, won't we?"

Damn it. What did I have to do to get one over on her? I had to protect myself. Had to! But how? And there were the locals to consider, too. Ginger had the worst timing.

My eyes slid from hers, landing on our rapt audience. The local women weren't even pretending to ignore us anymore. Fine. If Ginger wanted to play the victim, then so be it. But I wouldn't back down. The battle line had been drawn, and I couldn't afford to look weak. She might give up her plans to turn me in to the Corps if I never let her see how scared I was.

I slipped smug superiority over my entire being, channeling my sister, my father, and all the people who turned their backs on me. Images of them flickered through my mind as I mimicked them. I knew how it looked when somebody looked down on me. It had hurt me my entire life. But that meant I could do it too.

"These women may be stupid enough to believe you could ever be better than me," I sneered, putting everything I could into my act. I had to keep her from turning me in. "But everyone on Earth Prime can tell I have more to offer than you and your used up, slum-trash body. Enjoy the fruits of your labor while you still can. Take advantage of the men you cultivated. But remember, filing a formal complaint and failing will get you kicked out of the Corps, not me."

A thrill of excitement shot up my spine as Ginger and every other woman in the room recoiled. They didn't even know what I said, but the locals knew what a monstrous bitch looked like, and that was me.

The crack of her hand on my cheek echoed against the silk-draped wall. I froze, my entire body growing perfectly still. I had spent years working on my fight response, but so much talk about my family and connections had put me right back into the mindset that had plagued me as a child. The muffled sound of an infant's cry sounded in my memory.

"I knew you thought you were better than us," she spat. "I'm going to tell them to bring Psych Ops into it. You're delusional if you think somebody as broken as you can win."

Broken. Her words laid me out, raw and exposed. But I couldn't let her know she was right. I had spent so many years building a life for myself. No way was she going to take it away from me before I got my payout and disappeared into one of the pastoral Mentions that had become a favorite destination of Corps retirees.

"You need to rein it in," I ground out, my throat straining to remain quiet. Ginger might have forgotten about our audience, but I hadn't. We had to look at odds, but not enough to derail the plan. Good thing the women in this Mention had no problem hurting each other. My experience in Rader's camp had taught me that. "And honestly? I don't *think* I'm better than you. I *know* I am, you insufferable bitch."

She didn't have any idea I was lying. Good. And I had to give her credit. Even though she obviously wanted me dead, she maintained her distance long enough to gain control of herself. But her eyes promised me retribution. "Just you wait until we get out of here," she threatened.

"Yeah, yeah," I scoffed. There was no way I would show her how terrified I was. She would pounce on any weakness I revealed. I knew her type better than any other. "Now do *your* duty. Go schmooze with those women and leave me the hell alone."

Ginger hesitated. I thought she would screw everything up, but her core professionalism won out again. I hated that I admired anything about her, but she pulled it off. She forced her eyes to fill with tears. She wasn't a natural for the role of Injured Party, but she really was working it.

The local women drew closer together and the first wife, Jaycee, whispered quietly to the others. Two of them broke away from her little sphere of influence and came over to Ginger. They approached her and patted her arm. Ginger let them coax her over to stand near them, and they provided her with some wine and food.

Disgusted yet pleased at my performance, I snorted and swiped a container of wine as I sauntered over to the opposite side of the room, kicking aside two large sitting pillows. I poured myself a glass and acted like pretty much anything, including staring at the wall, was more interesting than they were.

I was used to being on the outside. But it turned out this was a better role for me to play after all, even though Ginger was the natural born snob. But I had learned from the best. Besides, sitting alone would have been too hard for her. And the thought of letting those women fawn all over me when I could understand all their backhanded compliments was too much to handle.

By the time the boy came by to lead us back into the main hall with the men, the women had styled Ginger's hair and lent her some of their cosmetics. She looked pretty good, too. I chuckled to myself when I saw them smile goodbye to her. The idiots were so snotty they didn't even realize they invited a viper into their nest.

Jaycee seemed particularly happy to have another admirer kiss her butt, though. She'd be positively inclined towards anything associated with Ginger.

Since she was watching, Ginger walked over to Will and slid her arm through his to align herself with him. Now Jaycee would support Will.

I did my part and walked off to stand near Mason, Logan, and Tyler, finding a way to touch all three of them. With a few gestures and looks, I made it seem like I thought I was hot stuff being the soldier's girl. To every single one of the soldiers. Somebody the women viewed as no better than a total slut.

Oh, yeah. Jaycee would do anything to support Ginger and her man, and trash me in the process. Wives couldn't stand the women who serviced their men when they had their backs turned. And the guys did a great job. They let me play it up without question. They probably recognized the ploy from the manual, too. Tyler even ran his hand over my butt, which almost made me laugh. I wondered which of us was more weirded out by the contact.

Will was finally done groveling to Tellar. We walked in as he promised to provide us with protection as we performed our negotiations. That meant a large escort of guards, including Javilin. Lucky Tyler.

CHAPTER TEN
Assessment

NASH UPDATED US ON the progress of the mission later that night. We gathered around a campfire encircled by our tents not too far outside of the village in a small glade. Far enough away to hear or see an enemy coming.

"Now that Will is done licking the headman's boots, we have a pretty good foothold in the area. Tellar is exactly the type of local that works the best. We shouldn't have any trouble with him."

Will chimed in. "Greed is the name of the game and he loves power. He was practically salivating over our basic offers." That meant power and riches for Tellar and carefully measured benefits for the rest of his people to keep them motivated.

"He also likes how our women look. He said there is something about them he finds 'foreign yet fascinating.'" Nash snorted. We all knew he meant we didn't have eyes that looked like they were about to jump off our faces. "If more of our women come into this Mention, they'll be ours without effort. As long as the Corps arranges a reward for him."

I wrinkled my nose. Yeah, the women who traded themselves got paid a lot of money. Certainly more than I ever earned, and I held the most complicated and vital role on the team. But yikes, Tellar was no peach. They had to really want their paycheck.

Then again, I knew full well that those women would do anything to help their families out of the slums. The Corps was taking advantage of their desperation. But I knew the drill. The world was built on the backs of desperate people.

"There was one small blond that was obviously the favorite," Ginger added. "I got in good with her, so I'll cultivate that relationship over the next few stages. Men like Tellar think with their gonads so he'll find a way to feel righteous about selling his people off to the highest bidder with her support." Yeah, Ginger did so much. Apparently without my help. But whatever. It was her call as point person, and she could tell it however she wanted.

Tyler laughed. "I thought it was hilarious when Bailey came out on the prowl and stroking her menfolk. Nice ploy. By the way, nice butt, Bailey."

My face flooded with heat. All the guys were looking at me. Tyler meant well, but his teasing brought attention to the messed up dynamics of our team. But then Logan cracked a smile and winked at me. Tyler bringing me into the normal realm of sexual innuendo had actually helped. Maybe I could use that to get Logan on my side.

Mason's face showed nothing of what he was thinking.

Did any of this bother him? Or was he the same as all the other men I had met?

I had to tighten my lips to keep from denying that thought aloud. Every part of me rejected that idea. There was no way. He knew almost from the second he met me who I was, and it never occurred to him to either judge me or expose my secret for his gain. That alone proved how different he was.

"Alright, you idiots, quiet down," Nash said to interrupt their banter. He stared at Tyler as an amused silence fell over us. "Ginger, keep it up from your angle, you're doing great. Bailey, see if you can find any camp followers to get buddy-buddy with. Some of them might like to take on a hunky foreigner and spill some good intel on their troop capabilities. You can introduce them to our boys."

Ginger snorted. I bet she loved the idea of a high-class lady like me being humiliated by my assignment. She really had no idea who I was. Camp followers were one hell of a lot nicer and way more accepting of me than anyone else has ever been.

The ones that stationed themselves near the Corps camps never got too close to me, probably because they knew I didn't belong, but they were always nice. I had nothing but respect for them and the work they did. Especially in a place like this, keeping the troops happy and lessening the tension, which left unchecked led to infighting.

And they saw things other women didn't. Sometimes, I thought they might have truly seen me.

"No problem, boss man," I replied as jauntily as I could. "Maybe they can give me some pointers." Everybody laughed except Ginger. Even Will. But then he stopped abruptly, as if he remembered he was supposed to hate me. Yeah, apparently one joking comment wasn't going to fix that.

The look Mason gave me warmed me to my toes. And thankfully distracted me. But it also flustered me. I rearranged some of my gear so I had a reason to look away.

"You guys are all a bunch of jokers tonight. Just watch your butts, we've got locals staying in our camp with us. They can't understand what we say, but they've still got eyes. Keep your tech on lock-down and standard watch patrol tonight." Nash huffed his annoyance, ready to bust our heads together.

"I'll take first shift," Mason volunteered. He was the strategist and determined our watch schedule while in enemy territory. "Then Bailey, Moreno, and Jackson." Mason pointed to me, Tyler, and Logan when he mentioned our assignments. I was grateful I could get my watch done sooner rather than later. "Ginger, I want you and Nakamura on roaming detail before dusk."

I was disappointed he paired those two up, but how was he to know that the more time Ginger spent with Will, the more likely he'd never talk to me again? Damn.

Even worse, because Javilin gave me his protection in the beginning, she had to be partnered up with one of the guys every time she went out to keep her safe. It made sense, but that gave her more opportunities to pull her tricks.

Tyler had the worst shift, but I figured he wouldn't mind, considering it gave him time to get to know the locals a little better before getting some much-needed sleep before his shift. If he could calm down enough to sleep. It had been a while, and Javilin looked like he had stamina.

I whispered as much to Tyler as we were walking over to our sleep rolls. He laughed, keeping it quiet enough to avoid another Nash lecture.

We were sharing a tent with Mason, so we entered together. After a brief talk about Javilin's potential as a partner, I took off to wash up. I hated being dusty and dirty and while this planet was the pits, there was plenty of water.

Ginger had finished her tests, and the whole place was clean. We could eat, drink, and bathe without restriction. Another trait of this Mention that kept it from being the absolute worst place in the Multiverse. Barely.

I had overheard the men talking about their regular bathing spots and walked upstream to find a more private place that had one of the many hot springs feeding an offshoot of the river. It was more like a pond, the current filling a pocket along the bank, forming a pool perfect for bathing.

My groan of delight echoed back from the shore as I sank into the heated water. Finally, a moment to myself. It was small and remote enough to not be the first place the local soldiers would frequent, perfect for my needs. Unfortunately, my peace and solitude didn't last long.

I was standing with the water to my knees, washing my hair, when I heard voices. My hands froze, and I strained to determine whether they were coming closer. Uncertain about their direction, I shuffled to the deeper side of the pooled water that was tucked under a jutting overhang.

My pulse quickened. I didn't want anyone to see me, and I wasn't sure if it was the locals we were traveling with or strangers. Or what any of them would do with a naked woman who made it really clear that she was available to lots of men. My stupid ploy instigated by Ginger. Damned bitch put me in a worse position than I realized when she stole the Injured Party role.

"Come on, Ginger. I'm dying here," Will's voice rang out. My body jerked in surprise. I would have thought they would be in their tent, getting some sleep before their early morning shifts. "Help a man out."

Ginger chuckled, a purr in her voice. The rustling of the undergrowth and crunch of gravel indicated their position nearby and made it clear they were getting closer. Oh, man. There was no way I could afford to let them know I was there, stark naked and vulnerable. "Come on, there was a little place just by the stream that you'll love," she replied.

Ha. Will wasn't interested in nature. "I don't want to wait any longer. Hell, I'll take you right up against this tree. You're so damned hot." He groaned and I could hear some scuffling, and then a slurping noise. *Ugh, not what I wanted to hear.*

"Here we are," Ginger said. She was close, really close, but I couldn't see them. That meant they couldn't see me and I could sneak off when they got busy. I leaned my head back and rushed to rinse out the soap.

"Hell yeah!" Will was kind of loud. Then Ginger giggled. Gross. "Damn, Ginger, that feels so good. You take it better than any woman I know."

And that was more than enough for me. My bath over, privacy interrupted, and by the last two people I wanted to see. I was desperate to get out of there. Not to mention, I felt a little queasy.

Like anyone in the camps, I'd heard people having sex before. It was also quite a normal thing in the overcrowded housing I grew up in, although when I was little it never made sense. But it was impossible not to hear and eventually grow used to other people's interactions.

I was also used to blocking out the sounds when Ginger or Abilene were with the guys. But this was close, too close, and I was exposed in a way that put me at a disadvantage. Knowing she was trying to draw Will further into her web, trying to influence him by using sex as a weapon, bothered me more than their interactions had ever done before.

Peering out from beneath the ledge, I searched the surrounding foliage. There was no sign of the couple, no black silhouettes against the backdrop of a shadowy forest. I may be able to hear them clearly, but here was no visual on them.

Would they move closer? Decide to wash off when they were done? They were already so close, I couldn't remain where I was and avoid getting caught. Better to disappear while they were otherwise engaged.

Slipping out of the water, I slid my feet into my shoes. Fortunately, I always brought a light pair of sandals to wear when I bathed. I couldn't stand wet boots and gladly gave up space in my pack to carry them with me.

Wrapping my towel around me, I gathered my damp clothing and draped it across my naked arm. Not ideal, but I wasn't sticking around to get dressed. Ginger and Will's moans and shrieks filled the night, all the incentive I needed to move even faster as I hurried away, walking the long way around the stream to ensure I missed them.

When I drew closer to the campsite, I found a tree to hide behind and hurriedly slipped my clothes back on. I didn't want any of the locals to see me with nothing on but a threadbare towel. It simply wasn't safe.

I then wrapped up my wet hair in the towel and jogged as best I could while wearing sandals. Men's voices rose directly in front of my path to the camp, forcing me to veer away. My clothes may be on, but I was alone and didn't want to be outnumbered in a place where nobody could observe any potential attacks.

Damn it. I should have waited for Mason to get off duty or asked Tyler to delay his meet up with Javilin. Either could have watched my back while I cleaned off - and escorted me to and from the camp. I should have known better.

The haze from campfires concentrated in one place grew thicker and the terrain became more familiar. Soon a path appeared, and I searched for signs of activity. Fortunately, nobody was there. I nearly lost a sandal, but kept up the pace as I reached the passageway through the forest.

Soon, a pile of boulders appeared around a bend. It was the formation I had marked in my mind to ensure I wouldn't get lost. The tension spurring me on dissipated. I was close enough to camp to shout for help if a determined soldier cornered me. The officers were aware of our new arrangement and wouldn't allow me or Ginger to be molested.

Javilin had given me nominal protection when we first arrived, but Ginger's antics with the local women had effectively removed it. The agreement between our team and Tellar helped, but the locals didn't consider women to be autonomous human beings. Better to keep a knife handy and watch my back. I had left my blade in the tent, but that was a bit of foolishness I wouldn't repeat.

The clearing came into view. I rushed to my tent and ducked inside, avoiding eye contact with the men milling around, engaged in various activities. The interior was dark enough that I had to light the small oil lamp we had set right inside the opening.

It was empty. Mason was already on watch, and Tyler with Javilin. I wasn't sure what the local conventions were about anything other than heterosexual relationships, so it was possible they traveled quite a distance away to be discreet. Either way, he wouldn't return anytime soon.

I changed into clean, dry clothing and rubbed my hair vigorously, trying to get it as dry as possible before I twisted it back into a bun. It would be wet all night if I left it styled that way, soaking wet. But if I didn't, it would be a tangled, frizzy mess by morning.

After tacking up my damp clothes to dry overnight, I shifted my focus to more technical matters best performed while alone.

Plumping up my sleeping roll, I made a little nest for myself and took a seat. My compass was still hanging on its chain around my neck. It was completely waterproof and I would never leave it behind, even if Nash hadn't ordered us to keep our tech on lock down.

The sky was still overcast, as it had been since our arrival in this Mention. By all indications, it would remain that way for most of the year. Every year. No doubt the result of having so much water and volcanic activity. I had nothing to enter into the device, but there were options I wanted to explore.

I pressed my finger on the glass to change it from the smaller, standard-looking compass into the true navigation device. It soothed me - I loved that complicated tool. It symbolized safety and gave me a sense of accomplishment.

Although it wasn't necessary to convert it to the other form to click on our astral position, I wanted to. It was almost like visiting an old friend. I also wanted to try an experiment.

Over the last several days, the changes in my perception alerted me to the possibility that Blackstone had made more changes to my brain than I realized. It was clear to me that I could hear thoughts and emotions, and even understand the motives of the people around me.

Despite having never seen terrain like this, it was recognizable to me, as if I had lived here for a very, very long time. I kept getting flashes of actual memories of plants or objects I knew I had never seen before, yet at the same time, were as familiar to me as my compass.

As crazy as it made me feel to admit it, I suspected Blackstone gave me everything he could. His memories, his knowledge, his abilities. I had heard about some freaky scientific experiments where they tried to remap brains. I think Blackstone might have remapped mine. Even more, that he filled it with everything he was.

Whatever those memories and abilities were, I could occasionally feel them pressing against my skull like they wanted to get out. But after a while, the fluttering and pressure ceased. It all sank deeper into my mind instead.

I took a deep breath and then let it out slowly. I shifted into a more comfortable pose, one I learned in my many counseling sessions. After clearing all thoughts from my mind, I lay my compass in my lap, resting my hands on it. I concentrated on my breathing, in and out. Slowly. Deeply.

My body settled into itself, and the sounds of the camp disappeared completely from my consciousness. I hummed a lilting melody that I couldn't recall where I learned it. But I knew it was my own memory, and not Blackstone's.

No. That thought made me tense up. I cleared my mind again, breathing, humming. Let it come.

There. The stars. I reached into the empty blackness within, searching for the constellations. I focused on my own memory - Blackstone drawing in the clay at his feet. Then something more that was beyond what I had experienced on my own. Old hands smudging charcoal on paper, marking up boards and stones, always the same patterns.

And then there they were, as clear as could be against the back of my eyelids as if I had memorized them myself. I opened my eyes and gazed down at my compass. I let my fingers move as if they had a mind of their own, pushing the buttons, inputting the precise positions of the stars in the sky here.

Blackstone likely had an eidetic memory - no details

were missing. I continued on with the sequence, pushing my observations to the back of my thoughts so I wouldn't derail my progress. Once it was set, I raised it up to my eye to look.

Normally, when the star sequences entered properly, I could actually see bits and pieces of the planet we were standing on, but viewed from space, its astral location set and humming. That information helped when it came time to jump through the gateway - I could see the planet on the other side of the portal in glimpses I interpreted for my team.

Even though it was never as accurate as when I had the right stars while standing on the planet itself, I was good enough at it that we could make plans about the best place to land. It was one of the talents I had cultivated to make me the best navigator in service.

I groaned when I saw the blackness inside. "Damn it!" I exclaimed. Then I tensed up as I looked around. Empty. Nobody was there, nobody could hear me talking to myself. Good.

Those stars were correct, so why didn't they work? We would never get back to Earth Prime if I couldn't see it.

This Mention was so jacked up, it was going to force us to skip, and I wasn't sure if I could pull it off. I didn't know the homing equations for anywhere but home, and with the interference I was getting, we'd be skipping planets totally blind.

Except now that I had Blackstone's brains meshing with my own, somewhere in my new memories I probably had a detailed map of the stars in his home dimension. I could use them to skip into the world of the Outsiders, and then once there, recalibrate and head back to Earth Prime.

I didn't bother to look around again when I laughed to myself. I was too damned happy I just figured out how to get out of there to care who could have heard me. Besides, they needed me too much to dump me off with Psych Ops. Not that there were any of those creepy doctors around here.

A crunch of gravel and cinders warned I was about to have company. I flicked my eyes to the viewscreen where my compass showed me local time. It was probably Mason - his shift had just ended. I slid a knife into my hand in case it wasn't.

Sure enough, he was the one who appeared when the tent flaps parted. "Your turn, Bailey," he said instead of a greeting. "Watch the men to the south, they're drunk."

I nodded and collapsed my compass, tucking it back under my shirt. There wasn't time for more than official business as we changed shifts. Nash would be all over us.

Grabbing my vest and boots, I headed out, tugging them on as I went. A wistful part of me wished Mason had given me some sign of how he was feeling. Until we were both off duty, I didn't really expect that to happen. But still, a girl could hope.

With a shrug and a sigh, I started my rounds. I didn't go far since the locals were guarding the campsite, but I did keep an eye out for my teammates. It was better to know where they were as I watched out for their safety. Nash and Logan were the only ones I saw. That meant Ginger and

Will were still out there somewhere in the dark. I shivered, wondering what they were plotting.

CHAPTER ELEVEN
The Blackstone Effect

TYLER MET UP WITH me at our tent when my shift was over. It was easier for us to trade off our watch when we knew exactly where the other person would be. He'd go to Ginger and Logan when it was their time. Nobody would dare to come up missing when it was their turn to guard our backs.

"Hey sexy," Tyler greeted me. "You find any hunky soldiers you want to get to know a little better?"

"Hell no! Besides, for the juicy stuff, I need make friends with the ladies. They're the ones who know the good gossip here. You better be nice or else I'm going to point a few of them in your direction so you can coax them to shower you with their secrets."

As a threat, it lacked all force. Tyler knew I would never put him in that position. Not like he wouldn't take one for the team, because he actually would and has. Any of us would if it would set us up for life. But he didn't like it and

I wouldn't do that to him unless he gave his consent.

"Yeah yeah. I'd be happy to do my duty if I wasn't so damned tired." Tyler yawned.

"Why, Tyler Moreno, you're positively glowing. You better have enough energy to handle your watch." Despite my teasing tone, my concern was genuine. We all knew what Nash would do if somebody was too tired to do their duty.

"Nah, I'm good. I took a nap earlier. I couldn't stay awake as long as I wanted to, not after some of the things I learned tonight. It exhausted me. I can't believe I don't have the stamina. Javilin is educated, if you get my drift." Tyler winked at me and waggled his eyebrows. I laughed and slugged him on his arm as he walked off to start his rounds.

Before I entered the tent, I kicked off my boots and unfastened my vest, setting them aside for later, right inside the flap. Tyler was kind enough to leave the lamp burning so I could see. His connection with Javilin had already paid off - a watertight vessel filled with warm water to wash off had been added to the back corner of the tent.

It was attached to a series of tubes made of hollowed bamboo-type shoots. I had never seen anything like it, but it was easy enough to figure out. One tug on a little sliding square of wood and the water flowed. A plug made of ceramic and a rubbery substance covered a drain that flowed out through a tube leading out of the tent through a small opening we used for ventilation.

A quick wash removed the dust from walking through the camp, and I was working my fingers through my still-damp hair when Mason returned. A shiver of anticipation covered my body in goosebumps and I turned my head to the side to look at him over my shoulder. He actually grunted and then dropped the pile of clothing he had been holding onto his sleeping roll.

I smiled at him coyly, hoping to remind him about our time at the waterfall. It must have worked, because he walked right up to me and wrapped his arms around me from behind, sliding his hands over my stomach and breasts while he pulled me back against his body.

"Anything to report, Bailey?" Mason murmured in my ear. My breathing hitched in my chest and I shivered.

"Not really. The boys were being boys, and the girls haven't arrived yet so they are getting drunk to pass the time. They have their own watch set, though. Strictly professional on that side." I stopped talking when he took my earlobe between his teeth. It felt so good. When his hands cupped my breasts, I began to babble. "So I was wondering what was going on earlier. Everyone thought it was pretty funny when I came on to you guys, but do you think it worked? Did it look real? I don't normally do that and I felt stupid. Did I look stupid? Did it look real?" I was repeating myself when Mason finally said something.

"I was actually jealous, watching Moreno running his hand over your body, rubbing your butt when you walked by."

My heart fluttered. Corps members weren't supposed to be jealous, and I certainly wasn't supposed to encourage that behavior. But it felt good that he wanted me all to himself. "Women aren't his type, Bain. No need to be concerned." I pulled away and turned around to face him, putting some distance between us. I wasn't sure what I should say or do, and it was too hard to think when we were that close.

Mason wrapped his hands around the fabric of my shirt and tugged me up against his chest. He looked down into my eyes. "Baby, I don't care who he likes. He needs to keep his hands off. You're mine now, do you know that? For as long as you let me, I'm your man, and nobody else."

His words sank deep into the very center of my body. I let out a small groan, reveling in how he made me feel. He wanted to be with me as long as I wanted him to be? How about forever? But only a quiet gasp escaped my lips.

Mason lowered his head slowly, watching for my reaction to his declaration. I said nothing, barely able to think, much less decide what to say. Instead, I waited for him to get a little closer. Just before his lips met mine, he whispered, "And you want me, right, Bailey? You want me."

I couldn't think of the words to answer him, to respond to the need and question in his voice. His warm breath stroked my lips as he breathed out, and I couldn't stand it anymore. I reached up and wrapped my arms around his neck, then gripping his short hair, I pulled his head towards mine, bridging the distance, and kissed him with everything I had.

Mason and I woke when Tyler came into the tent at the end of his shift. He was careful to be quiet, but we were all more alert while out on a mission. Nothing crept by us.

"Anything to report, Moreno?" Mason asked, sitting up as he spoke.

"All good, Bain. Ginger and Will are out and about." Tyler let out an enormous yawn as he stripped down and slipped into his sleeping bag. Mason nodded his acknowledgment and lay back down.

I was glad we were sharing a tent with him. Tyler didn't expect anything from me once he realized Mason and I were sleeping together. Even with Ginger's games, I had gotten some looks from the other guys.

My night had been wonderful. The privacy of the tent, alone time with Mason. Everything felt amazing. But now that I was awake, should I move over to my sleeping roll? I shifted, but Mason tightened his arms around me. A smile crept across my face as I stayed put.

Nothing in my past had ever worked out into a full relationship. Not even a short contracted partnering. That meant I had never shared quarters with anyone. I liked how it felt to have him resting up against my back, his muscular arms wrapped around me and holding on. It was like I finally belonged somewhere.

Mason's breath evened out as he fell back asleep. I snuggled closer and closed my eyes, content to remain where I was. Only a few hours more passed until it was time to get up and get ready. Tyler's addition of a camping sink was a godsend.

"So Javilin just gave it to you?" I asked as I brushed my teeth. Mason had just left, checking in with the rest of our team to see if anything happened while we were sleeping.

"Yeah. He was surprised we didn't have one. But they haul them around in those carts along with their provisions and when I pointed out we only had what we could carry on our backs, he offered us the use of this one."

"Well, it's awesome. No wonder they picked a campsite near the flowing hot springs. It's as good as any indoor plumbing I've ever had." I used the glass of my compass to ensure my hair was in order before ducking out of the way to allow Tyler access to the sink for his morning routine.

"You hear about today's schedule?" he asked.

"Yeah." I sat and tugged on my boots before rolling my sleeping bag and tying it to my pack. Mason had taken care of his stuff and all that was left was for me and Tyler to get our personal things stashed away and break down the tent. "We're touring the region. It's weird they don't ride horses."

"Right? I guess they don't have many of them so they use them as cart animals, mostly. It's another sign of wealth but they didn't develop riding skills for some reason." It was standard to leave cultures alone, but once the Corps came in, they had no rules against changing things for our benefit. And more advanced techniques or limited access to different technology kept them complacent. Maybe somebody would teach them to ride.

"Well, I don't mind walking," I added, looking around to ensure everything was packed away. Once Tyler was done washing up, we'd be ready to go. "But it'd mean less time in this Mention if we could get where we're going faster."

I didn't want to admit we didn't have a way to leave yet. But it was true enough that it would be faster riding horses. There was no reason for the guilt I felt hiding my troubles from one of the only friends I had.

"We're going to be exploring for at least a week or two. I saw the maps - Tellar's territory extends over an extensive region. Will had them mark the places where they mine metals or other precious materials. We'll skip the rest."

All the better for us to cash in on. Nash and Will didn't take long to convince Tellar it was in his best interests to work with us. They had things to show the locals, like gold or jewels. We gave them away as a gift and to use as an opener in negotiations.

Nash was the best at it - he didn't look like the political type, but he was brilliant at posturing and establishing a rapport with others. That played out in our team, too. He wouldn't be the leader if he wasn't so good at it.

I didn't want to be the focus like that myself. Not that I wanted to be in charge. I wasn't sure I had the skills to do what was required of a team leader, anyway. Another reason I became the navigator besides avoiding the spotlight - I couldn't withstand the extra background scrutiny they went through, and I wasn't a people person.

It behooved the local leaders to cooperate. Not only did we have better technology and riches to share, but as first dimensional contact, men like Tellar would be richer than the rest of his people, not like that would to matter on this mud ball. What would he buy?

The more items they showed us that the Corps could use, the better off they were. They had some say in how things would be handled and were even put in charge of all the locals. It was more expedient than a war. Then anyone from Earth Prime who was experienced in colonizing the Mentions would handle the rest.

It wasn't something I wanted anything to do with. If it looked like politics would be involved, it reminded me of my dad or my sister, and that was always to be avoided. I stuck with my dangerous job because the payoff was better and the cushy jobs working on established planets weren't for people like me.

"Ready?" Tyler asked, fortunately interrupting my darkening thoughts.

"Yeah. Let's go."

After breaking down the tent, Tyler tied it to his pack and called one of the young errand boys over to come get the camp sink. Then we trotted over to where our team was speaking with Javilin.

He had six soldiers with him. I wasn't sure if that was the usual size of a unit, or if they were being careful not to out-number us. Either way, it made for a better working relationship when the locals were deliberate about how we perceived them. It showed they were thinking about a future when we would work together.

Our entire team would go on the tour, though, regardless of what they wanted. It was dangerous to split up and our policy was to never do so unless absolutely necessary. Fortunately, none of the locals even suggested that we separate.

I peered around Nash to check out the itinerary on a small table in front of him. They marked the first place we would explore on their map with a circle and several lines drawn coming out of the top like a crown. A memory not of my own flashed across my mind. The spot on the map showed a place on the far side of a densely packed forest with a wide dirt road cut through the center.

"It's field rations for breakfast," Nash announced.

"We're heading out immediately. It'll take about three hours to get to our first stop."

"Got it, boss," I said, adding my acknowledgment to the rest of the team's responses. Nash turned and slid his arm around my back, patting my shoulder with his approval.

"How's the compass work coming, Navigator?" he asked. He left his hand on my shoulder, leaning in to hear my response over the sound of our team and the locals chattering as they got ready to go.

"I have some intel on the star patterns," I replied. He knew I was having issues. But I'd figure it out. No need to make him wonder if he made the right choice by selecting me to join the team. "I'll need time to work it out, but my goal is to be ready to jump when you say it's time to go."

"That's my girl," he said, giving my arm a squeeze. I grinned up at him, thrilled by all the positive attention. I didn't think Ginger could get to him the way she did with the others, but she was too good at playing games for me to not worry about it at the back of my mind.

Our eyes met, and it occurred to me that we were standing a little closer than normal. Or was it? Maybe Mason's comments about me being his were making me more sensitive to Nash's usual proximity. What if his joking about Tyler turned into something more when it came to the boss?

Nah. Mason knew better. Besides, the man was like a father to me. And fathers hugged their kids. Maybe not mine, but I've seen it in other families plenty of times. Mason would know that.

Still, to make sure I wasn't breaking any unwritten

rules about new relationships, I gave Nash a quick squeeze back to let him know I appreciated his kindness, and then slipped out from under his arm to join the others.

Javilin had his men line up. The rest of us moved into our normal formation behind them and started our trek to the first map marker. Time passed quickly enough, my thoughts centered on star patterns rather than the hike. There wasn't much to see. It was dark under the canopy of trees, the overcast sky keeping the sun from lighting our path.

The locals passed back torches for us to use. Nobody talked much, and we kept up a grueling pace. It took a lot to break into my concentration, but even I noticed the good-natured competition that had sprung up. There was no way the guys were going to let a group of local rubes see us straining to match their pace.

Not that we were. We may have vehicles and moving walkways on Earth Prime, but the Corps required constant physical conditioning. Javilin's men were in for a shock if they thought we were soft because we had women on our team.

After three hours of quick walking, the trees ended abruptly. Nash stopped and let out a low whistle. "Well, would you look at that? That's pretty impressive for such a backward society."

I studied the wide open area in front of us. A massive hole that looked a lot like a crater of a volcano dominated the expanse, but instead of lava or boiling mud, it was a giant hole in tan, fine soil that had a path along the rim, spiraling down into the earth. A great, stark, yawning void.

My own memories told me what it was. An open pit diamond mine. As large as it was, it had nothing on the ones I'd seen on the vids of several of the other planets. Then again, there wasn't truly a way to compare. But even a small mine could produce enough diamonds to make us a respectable finder's fee.

The mine looked massive there in the middle of nowhere. The locals didn't have the machinery and equipment and technology that we had when we made our pit mines. They made this one using mostly human industry and a lot of greed. The area was probably pretty at one time, if the river in the distance was any indication.

"This is our first stop. We rarely show anyone our mines, but Tellar seems very interested in showing you everything we have to offer." Javilin didn't sound happy, but Will's translation was dead-on accurate.

Things were moving too quickly for Javilin. Soldiers, especially officers, hated to let anyone know anything about their assets, vulnerabilities, and resources. They certainly didn't like to hand over a really, really good reason to wage war on them. Like a large diamond mine.

Nash walked over to Javilin and gave him a friendly cuff on the shoulder. "You have no idea, my friend. You've already lost this battle."

Will didn't translate. He smiled at Javilin, his entire demeanor comforting and reassuring. He really was good at his job. "We're ready to take a look," he informed Javilin.

It was a strenuous walk down into the pit. The path spiraled down in circles along the outside edges of the crater, each level wide enough to carry some kind of conveyance to haul diamonds and excess soil. But it was steep enough that we could really feel it in our thighs about halfway down. At least, I sure could.

Javilin remained silent on the way down. He wasn't being unfriendly, but really, what could he say? Hi, here is a load of stark, stripped earth with no useful purpose anymore?

Not like that was a drawback. There were plenty of paradise planets for the upper class. And even some of the rich prospectors that were once team members like we were, looking for planets to loot, got lucky and lived in paradise once they became rich. Planets like that weren't really in demand, so the state of this one had no bearing on our decisions about exploitation.

Although, the Mentions were used mostly as vacation retreats. There was a sense that no Mention was as good as our world, regardless of the amenities or clean air.

Earth Prime was still the place of power in the Multiverse. The President was in control, the highest ranked human alive and whatever he wanted, he got. So when the world started its final descent into barrenness, he demanded we create more domes, more places for the rich to live in luxury despite the environmental disaster that stripped Earth Prime of natural life.

The result was a series of massive domed cities. Some were better than others. Like the Corps camps were covered in minimal protection to support life. But the cities of the rich rose like golden bubbles across the continents, reflecting rainbows and shining, glowing colored lights that could be seen for miles. It was actually quite beautiful, if unnatural.

Even though I was forced to leave at a young age, I would never forget the golden light of the sun filtering through the ultraviolet shields, arching over the President's city like the gods lived to shower us with beauty. A glow fell on the pale cream stone facades, statues, and sparkling fountains, making a modern day Roman paradise.

My father was the highest ranked military general, and we lived in quarters suited to a man of his rank among the ruling class. The President had moved his seat of power into what once was the Vatican. Many of the golden icons, treasures, and other works of art were brought out of their archives and storage facilities for all to view in a display of intimidating wealth.

When I was three or four, I had gotten lost. I still remembered the shiny gilded walls inside of a grand hall, almost like giant mirrors, reflecting my tears back at me until my nanny had found me and led me away.

The inner golden haze drifted off of my eyes. I had never felt a memory so deeply before, almost as if I was there again. The changes to my brain kept developing, deepening, and clarifying. I would have to start calling it the Blackstone Effect.

Whatever he had done to me, it was obvious that it was not only his memories that were filtering through my mind with startling accuracy. Apparently mine had come back in high definition, as well. That didn't bode well for my peace of mind unless I learned to control it.

We finally reached the bottom of the pit. Walking through the tunnel entrance helped me shake off my reveries and focus on what was going on in the present. Javilin led us from the entrance and down into the tunnels. There were torches spread out periodically, but Javilin didn't light them. He took one off of the wall for each of us and we carried our light as we toured the mine. There really wasn't anything special about it, though.

Like most mines I had seen, there were carved out tunnels in the ground, wide and smooth, braced with huge wooden posts. They had ensured it would be easy to transport the goods and waste materials as men dug and dug and dug into the depths.

It took a long time to get where we were going, which was an open face in the tunnels that was currently being worked. There were shining indications of an active work site, diamonds in the dust. Logan spent a lot of time poking around, and once he was through, he seemed satisfied. It was his job to ensure quality and that the locals hadn't salted the mine.

It looked good, but there wasn't enough to be our ticket out of the Corps. I shrugged it off. The mine was only one of many places Tellar wanted to show us. Plus the exploring we did on our own - locals rarely knew the true wealth of their worlds. We needed to search it out ourselves.

We then made the long and dirty trek back to the surface. It was stifling in the dark, and I was glad I wasn't claustrophobic because that trek into the bowels of the planet would have driven me insane. Once we reached the top, it still took a click or two before we reached a nice, cool stream and the shade of trees. Even Javilin and his soldiers unbent enough to splash cool water on their faces and necks before moving upstream to drink.

Will walked over to where I was standing by Nash and Mason. "They're going to take us north into the forest for a few days. There's a place marked on the map with interesting shapes, colored gold. That's our next touring place."

"Sounds like a blast," I said. "Nothing like a jaunty little hike through the creepy woods after soaking in the dirt for an afternoon." Mason sorted, and Nash ignored my quip like usual. Will continued to look at Nash as if I didn't exist. I didn't know what Ginger said or did, but it worked. Every bit of friendship I thought we might have had was gone. Will couldn't even handle the thought of my existence, apparently. Whatever.

Mason's eyes narrowed at Will. He had noticed how Will was acting, but I wasn't sure what he would do about it, if anything. At what point does a man take the side of the woman he is sleeping with over another man? Another team mate? If at all?

"All right, let's get moving. The day isn't getting any longer while we stand here yapping." Nash hustled us along and we fell into line with our escort.

CHAPTER TWELVE
The Outsiders

OUR GROUP HAD HIKED for another few days when we came across a band of people near the base of a cliff. Javilin's men went on high alert, their actions warning that it was an unexpected event.

It looked like they had been living there for quite a while. The camp had a settled-in look about it, using the environment to create separate areas for different activities. I left my knife in my belt - there was nothing about the place that made me feel concerned over our safety, but I hung back just in case.

We had entered the foothills the day before and the land was once again pockmarked with holes and cinder blocks and huge piles of pumice as tall as real mountains. The strangers were located by a naturally formed rock bridge over a cave set into the side of a large hole in the ground. It wasn't high ground, but it looked easily defensible.

If any of them bothered to protect themselves. After

I had the chance to study them, I realized they were the Outsiders. I could tell by their lack of creepy, bulging eyes. We had just come across a group of non-combatants. Not like my team would understand that. Not yet. But they should get a sense of the Outsiders and their inherent pacifism.

My curiosity went wild. These were the people Blackstone wanted me to help. And while my obligation was to the Corps, that didn't mean I wasn't going to at least entertain the idea. A large part of me felt compelled to do so.

A man wearing a robe in blue strode forward to meet us. A memory niggled at the back of my mind. It wasn't one of mine, but I let it play out despite how nervous it made me feel to allow something foreign to filter through.

Blackstone had transferred an incredible amount of information, and I was trying to accept it without freaking out. It would be foolish to ignore the wealth of intel he had given me. Ah, there it was. Blue was considered to be the most tranquil color and the Outsiders who wore it were thought to be the best at communicating.

"We mean you no harm," the one with dusty-blond hair announced. "What can we do for you? Do you need help? There are healers here who are at your service."

Nash looked at Will, who shook his head. The words had sounded different to me, a sign the language was different from the one Will had to learn to communicate with Javilin's men. There was nothing he could do to help our team understand.

One soldier stepped forward. "You speak in the

language of the Outsiders. We were unaware your people have settled here."

I felt compelled to translate, but I remained quiet to keep my secret safe. It wasn't my job, but I still felt guilty.

Dusty Blond exchanged a cautious look with two other men in blue before answering. "The local magistrate gave us permission and our leader moved us here. He hasn't returned to us yet. He went into the city to get Tellar's mark on the homestead board."

Javilin grunted. "Who is your leader?" he asked. It didn't surprise me that a man in his position would know the languages of the people around him. It made it easier for him to do his job.

"Blackstone."

My body jerked in response. I couldn't help it. It was the first time I had heard anyone say his name since he died. I also felt the desire to answer, as if they had called out my name instead of his. Memories threatened to overwhelm me by their sheer numbers, so I deflected them. A twinge of pain met my efforts.

"Nobody by that name has come to see Tellar," Javilin said. "You will come back with us and sort this out."

Dusty Blond looked nervous, but he agreed. I felt bad. Blackstone was dead. We were the ones who killed him, and these poor people were waiting for him to return with the plaque that proved their land claim.

Thanks to my team, that would never happen. And it was as plain as day that Javilin thought they were lying. Guilt filled me. What a mess.

My gaze slid to Mason, the man who had killed their

leader, even if it was to protect us. He returned my look with a searing one of his own. We obviously had different things on our minds, and after a look like that, my guilt faded as my knees went weak.

But I embraced the distraction. Blackstone's memories and my feelings about the people I had sworn to help were threatening to overwhelm me. There were worse things than clinging to the thoughts of shared passion Mason's gaze brought to mind.

Dusty Blond trotted back towards his people to give them the news. A ripple of disappointment worked its way through the Outsiders while Javilin turned to Will and Nash to explain what was going on.

"We need to bring these people along with us to see if they have been granted rights to live in this area. They are peaceful and shouldn't cause us trouble. But they must come with us regardless of our plans. Living on this land without permission or even staying here without a plaque posted for all to see is prohibited." He didn't say it, but it was clear that Tellar's authority would be weakened if they did nothing.

Usually, Javilin was more stoic. Maybe his association with Tyler was making him more verbose. Or it could be he was warming to us. If so, that was a good sign.

It was telling that he shared the inner workings of Tellar's territorial government. He probably trusted us now. Or at least thought of us as equals to the point where he wanted to ensure we knew the laws. That we were a group of people that were on his side and he wanted to keep up the status quo.

The locals did that a lot. It usually turned out the same way, though. But maybe Tyler could save at least this one.

Will translated for Nash, who then nodded curtly. I could tell by the tick in his cheek that he wasn't thrilled by the addition of a large group of hostiles. There was no way for me to reassure him without explaining a lot of things. Things I still couldn't really explain to myself. I pinched my lips together and kept quiet, letting it play out.

"Be on alert," Nash ordered. There was a subtle shift, and we were once again standing in order, paired up and ready for anything. Needless expenditure of adrenaline, but it meant Mason was walking by me, so that part was nice.

Hopefully, it would be a good enough distraction to ease my guilt. I hated hiding things from my team. It went against my training, which was so ingrained that it overcame my natural protective instincts. At least when it came to Corps business. They had spent a lot of time developing their techniques, and I wasn't immune to it.

The compulsion to throw myself at Nash and explain what happened to me once again crashed over me in waves. I wanted to tell him everything. What I knew and all about the things I could do. Even if I hadn't worked it out yet and would probably sound crazy.

Obviously that would be a grave mistake, so I kept my mouth shut. I didn't need another stint with the therapist. They weren't exactly the laying-on-the-couch types in the Corps. No. Hell, no. They were all about Tough Love. Without the love part.

It didn't take the Outsiders long to pack. They were such a biddable lot. No wonder they were constantly victimized. What made them so willing to drop everything and come along like lambs to the slaughter?

I was bombarded with a slew of agonizing memories going back decades. First-hand experiences of Blackstone, and memories of the tales from his people after they were harmed and came to him for help, battered around inside my skull. I nearly collapsed under the pain it caused as I fought to control the torrent of images and emotions. Finally, I came back to reality.

Note to self. Quit asking questions. The answers hurt.

It was maybe thirty minutes later when we hiked out again. We were close to that interesting gold symbol on the map, and my teammates were taking bets on what it could be. The obvious answer was a gold mine, so my contrary side bet against that possibility.

I put down one shiny rock I had found on the trail as collateral against the possibility that it was something we don't have in large quantities on Earth Prime. Our terms were a little vague, but we all agreed normal metals like platinum or caches of helium and most especially diamonds, didn't count in order for me to get a win.

Truthfully, I was fine with whatever it turned out to be, even gold. It didn't matter if I lost - I just wanted to participate. It was vital for them to see me, count me as one of their own in a real way. I finally realized that our bond was completely lacking, and it was dead easy for Ginger to manipulate everyone because of it. They hated me for no reason now, because I hadn't given them a reason to like me.

Focusing on the relationships I had already started

to build, I shifted my weight until my arm "accidentally" brushed against Mason's. He smirked and looked at me in the eye with something behind them that made me stumble.

Ginger made a strangled sound. Damn. She saw and had to know what I was doing. My actions were just like rubbing salt in her nasty, spiteful, gaping wound of an ego. But I had to keep going. Her way led to my destruction.

"Okay team," Nash said. "Looks like we're about there. Once we get to the campsite, I want your packs down and guard up immediately." We nodded acknowledgment and silently followed Javilin's lead.

Unable to ignore the new additions to our group, I glanced back to there the Outsiders straggled along behind us. One woman stumbled. Gentle, helping hands lifted her up, and the others brought her along with them, encouraging her. I wondered what it was like living with a group of people who cared.

Damn. I asked a question again, and with a blow like a hammer knocking into my head, I had a pretty good idea. Families, friends, leadership. Care and support. And parents, taking care of their children, molding their growth and feeding them as varied a diet as available to them in this Mention. There was a sense of other memories from Blackstone that went back farther, but I was able to cut them off.

When the detailed images were done playing out in my head, I was left with more than knowledge. I had an emotional connection and crazy enough, my other senses were engaged. Like I suddenly knew what boysenberry jam on toast tasted like. It was a favorite of Blackstone's. I had never had the pleasure myself. On Earth Prime, it was a crossbreed berry that disappeared long ago during the time of famine.

It was amazing. If I ever had the chance, I was going to put in a request with the Corps to be on the lookout for those things on their produce planets. Maybe I could taste them again for the first time, using my own tongue.

I tried to ignore the fact that it was all the sweeter because of the lovely dark-haired woman who had handed Blackstone the toast. She was his mother. I cut off my musings, struggling to keep from wondering what it would have been like if my mother had lived. I was positive I wouldn't have been able to withstand the flood of memories that would have brought me. Either Blackstone's entire childhood, or my own - or both. Something like that would likely kill me.

Or worse, make me cry. Distraction and inner focus I could explain away. But tears? No way.

Finally, Javilin called a halt. We had arrived.

My team spread out, looking for a flat place where we could all huddle together without cramping our fighting style, which often consisted of standing wide enough apart to keep from hitting each other.

"I'm going to check in with Javilin," Tyler said. The side of my mouth quirked up. He had already learned a lot of words in their language, not a surprise considering the amount of time he was spending with the sexy soldier. I was happy for him.

"I hope he can keep it in his pants long enough to remember where his loyalties lie," Ginger snapped. She was such a nasty piece of work. I couldn't understand why the men found her attractive at all. Sure, she had a killer body and was basically sex on a stick, who apparently took it better than anyone Will knew, but really. What a snot.

"If I think he's having trouble, I'll yank him back." Nash frowned, his eyes narrowed as he watched Javilin hand Tyler a canteen, and he happily quenched his thirst without even smelling it to see if it was poisoned.

Oh. That was it. Ginger's plan. She couldn't whore herself into turning Tyler against me, so she was going to turn everyone else against him instead. A wave of fury flowed like acid from my head to my toes just thinking about it.

"I'm going to go check out the new people," I said. Nash raised an eyebrow at me, recognizing that I didn't ask permission. Oops. I had been channeling Blackstone. He was the boss and had been for decades. "Uh, if that's okay with you, bossy-boss," I added as I batted my eyelashes at him and gave him a coy and vacant smile.

He snorted and shook his head in disgust at my playacting. But it was something he found familiar, and his stance softened. A smile flashed across his face before he got serious again - and gave into my wishes. "Quit your foolishness, girl. Take Mason with you and don't stray far. You know we can't trust them."

I actually knew we could, but whatever. I wasn't about to tell Nash that.

With Mason only a step behind, I walked to the other

side of camp where the Outsiders were still unpacking and setting up their campsite. Like several other tents I had seen in this Mention, they used animal skins tanned into leather for the base material. There was something they had rubbed in that was waxy and made it waterproof. Not that I could prove it, since so far it hadn't rained, even though the infernal cloud cover was our constant companion.

Another material the locals seemed to have in abundance was a type of reed they wove into walls and floor mats. I wasn't sure why they chose the material they used, but the richer, more established people used the reeds. It was possible that animal skins were more in abundance. That was typically why the lower classes and poor used certain techniques and materials.

The man with the dusty blond hair straightened up when we approached. Blackstone may have been their leader, but this man acted as such in his absence. Eventually, I needed to tell him that his temporary role had become permanent.

The man's worried look transformed into one of cautious welcome.

"Hello, strangers. I can see you do not belong to Tellar's barony. It confuses us that you look like we do, yet we know you are not one of us. Where did you come from? Have you come for us? Do you know our leader?" Dusty Blond spoke slowly and openly, looking both me and Mason in the face, yet not making eye contact. We had mimicked those peaceful and submissive traits when we were trying to make first contact, but I think they came naturally to the Outsiders.

I jerked my chin towards Mason, and he shuffled off a short distance away to give me privacy. It was natural for him to follow my lead in that circumstance. I was the person who handled first contact, and when I did, my teammates always followed my instructions as long as it didn't put anyone in immediate danger. Especially myself. But the Outsiders weren't armed, and he stepped back.

As soon as he was out of earshot, I began. "I know Blackstone. He helped me learn your language. Can you understand me?" Unfortunately, Dusty Blond looked at me without comprehension, except when I said Blackstone's name.

"You know our leader, Blackstone?" he confirmed.

I nodded my acknowledgment. How did I communicate with these people? There had to be a way. Knowing what everyone was saying was invaluable, but not being able to reciprocate was a significant enough drawback that I couldn't believe those who created the techniques Blackstone used on me hadn't addressed it.

Unfortunately, as Blackstone told me, none of the children born out in the Mentions could handle the mind transfer. It would have been so easy for us to talk if they had the same mind-alterations I did. It was strange that I could handle it when his own people couldn't. But the human mind was still a mystery to our scientists as well.

Dusty Blond cocked his head to the side, studying me carefully. Then I saw his eyes light up. "You can understand what I say. Is that correct?"

I nodded affirmative again. He caught on quick. "Yes," I said. Verbalizing couldn't hurt.

"You met with Blackstone. Do you know what happened to him?"

The time had come sooner than I expected. Dread pooled in my stomach. The thought of giving this stranger bad news reminded me too much of the dark days after the world found out about my father's crimes. Because of me.

It may not be as drastic, but I was still going to alter this man's life forever. Not only had their leader died, Blackstone had been their only hope of ever leaving this Mention. All I had to do was figure out how to convey the news so he would understand.

And I had to. There was no excuse not to, and the sooner I dropped that bomb, the better for everyone. Especially for my peace of mind. Although I had to admit to myself that the only reason I was willing to say anything was I knew these people were pacifists. Not everyone had a problem with killing the messenger.

Mason was pacing just far enough away to give me privacy. He was alert, his eyes roaming the area, keeping watch over the group of Outsiders still setting up camp, Tellar's soldiers, and our own teammates. But I could tell he took extra time watching over me. My heart hitched a little in my chest.

But I didn't have all the time in the world to make a breakthrough. Something had to work. I leaned closer, and I looked the man in the eye, focusing, concentrating as hard as I could. Would he understand if I tried hard enough? Blackstone managed it with me, and had transferred other abilities to me. Surely this was one of them. And I couldn't handle keeping this secret any longer. I already had enough of them.

"There was an accident," I explained with supreme effort.

"What happened?" Dusty Blond responded.

I couldn't believe it. It actually worked! "I'm sorry to inform you that Blackstone is no longer with us," I said, giving him the news immediately. Better to rip off that bandage right away. Playing games or trying to soften the blow wouldn't be doing him any favors.

The man gasped, drawing back, a pained expression on his face. "Please tell me you are mistaken." His voice was broken. My pulse sped up in response. I didn't want to hurt him. I didn't want to hurt anyone. But once again, the things I had to say were the instrument of pain for so many.

The need to comfort him nearly overwhelmed me. Living in the slums, I learned pretty quick that I couldn't show a moment's weakness. Empathy, sympathy, compassion - all those could be used to trap me. Made me vulnerable. But the desire to put my arms around the stranger standing before me, wrecked and hurt, and hold him, crashed over me.

It was a struggle, but I shook it off. There was no way for me to explain that kind of gesture to my team. Even if Ginger was out of my line of sight, she would be watching. Waiting for another opportunity to twist my actions. And that one wasn't easily explained away by me.

"There is no mistake. I'm sorry for your loss." I hesitated, giving him time to process. But I couldn't stay much longer. "He did something while I was there. To my head. I can speak with you because of it, but there are other changes. There is no time to explain, but please know that you have a friend in this camp, and I will help you. I promise."

I didn't know why I told him so much, why I made him a promise, but it had to do with Blackstone. Like he was taking over, forcing me to reach out and put myself into a position of weakness. It was terrifying, but at the same time, peaceful. Somewhere inside of me, I was certain none of the Outsiders would hurt me the way everyone else in my life had.

It was creepy, truth be told. But it also felt good.

Mason stopped his pacing and raised his eyebrows at me. My time had run out. I had to head back to my side of the camp before he busted a vein trying to watch everyone, everywhere, as if our lives depended on it. Sometimes it did, but today, not so much. I felt bad about not telling him what was going on with me. But everything was so new with him.

Could I trust him with this? With anything? Questions that I had no answers to and wished Blackstone's memories could help me with.

"Thank you. I understand. I will ensure our people hear the news." He seemed so humble.

"Yeah, no problem." Even though I was positive it was going to cause problems. "What's your name?"

"My name is Ro. I am the oldest of the last generation of Outsiders born onto this planet, Blackstone's successor."

"Okay." That was more information than I expected. But something about the quality of his tone struck me. Oh. He hadn't said all of that out loud. That information came to me silently, thanks to Blackstone's alterations. "My name is Bailey, Ro. If any of you get into trouble, call my name or ask for me and don't stop asking until somebody comes and gets me. All right? I'll do what I can to ease the tension."

There I went again, inserting myself into something I had no business being a part of. It was nearly impossible to control myself. But we were responsible for their new fate and, try as I might, that obligated me as much as any deathbed promise. Then again, I needed to wrap things up as much to keep from promising too much as getting back to my team.

"They have always been suspicious of us," Ro explained. He was treating me as an ally. This man trusted me and we had only just met. No wonder so many of them had died in this Mention. "We have been here a long time, too long, and yet they still see us as the outsiders. It is their name for us."

I couldn't handle how serious, how deep our conversation was. Time to lighten the mood. Deflect this man's growing connection with me. "Well, that's because you're all so pretty. Seriously, have you seen their fish eyes or not?"

Ro had lost somebody important to him, but my joking eased his mind enough that he gave me a genuine smile. I suspected my newfound abilities to sense what was coming from those around me was stronger among Blackstone's people. "There is something about your eyes, too. Better. Special."

Relief filled me. He was playing along. Maybe he could

sense what I needed, too. The conversation had been too intense for me. And the Outsiders were the type to give people what they needed. "Flattery will get you everywhere, my friend. I'm going to head out now. Remember what I said. You need me, you call my name."

He bowed his head in gratitude. I really wanted to hug him. I bet his kind did that kind of thing all the time - and then my memory supplied me with the meaning of different types of embraces. Wow. So much to know about these people. Would there ever be an end to Blackstone's memories?

I shook my head to clear away the clamor, and without another word, I turned and walked off. No way could I handle more of this, and my struggle to make my words understandable to Ro had left me with a splitting headache. Besides, I would see them again when I checked on them later.

Unfortunately, later was when the trouble started.

CHAPTER THIRTEEN
The Aggressor

THE CAMPSITE WAS GROWING crowded. Each evening when we stopped, more locals had joined us. They didn't hike with us, and I wasn't sure if they were different people each time or camp followers. They all looked too similar and my team didn't interact with them, per Nash's orders.

Mason took off into the trees to wash up in one of the many pools of water the locals ensured were nearby each time we stopped for the day. There were too many people around for me to join him. Normally I would go out to the hot springs with Ginger for safety, but there wasn't a power in the Mention that could force me to do such a thing.

Instead, I'd have to wait until I could find where the other women washed up. I didn't want a repeat of what happened the last time I bathed by myself. A shudder wracked my body at that thought.

The sink was back in the tent. I used it to wash off up before checking my pack and shaking out my clean clothes.

It didn't take long to inventory my personal items or check the team goods I carried now that I was back to pulling my normal load. Bored, I stepped outside the tent.

I looked around for Mason, hoping he was back already. Neither one of us had any duties at the moment, and soon enough Tyler would take off to spend time with Javilin. Alone time was becoming an addiction. Not that I minded.

Ah, there he was. Mason entered the clearing, his hair wet. I bet he was all squeaky clean. My pulse quickened. Damn. What a man.

Something across the camp caught my eye. A sudden increase in the activity where the Outsiders had erected their tents drew my attention. The dark patterns of Javilin's uniformed men stood out among the muted colors the Outsider wore. My skin prickled with concern. There was no reason for them to be there.

A sharp cry cut through the sound of the crowd. My gaze snapped to the source - a couple of the soldiers were harassing the women. The poor things were trying to protect themselves from the grabbing hands, ducking and retreating.

How dare they? Fury filled me. I couldn't let something like that pass, and I didn't care what the culture was like. Nobody was going to harass a helpless woman while I was around. Especially when they didn't have the capacity to fight off their attackers.

Mason strode to my side. "I can show you where the women using the river are at, if you want to get cleaned up."

"I'd love to, but there are some people who need saving,

and you look like just the guy to do it."

Mason raised his brow. I jerked my head towards the Outsiders and watched his face as he took it all in. The disgust that followed his quick assessment filled me with relief and pride. That was exactly what I had hoped for.

"Damn. All right, I get it. So much for Nash's order to keep away from the locals."

We weren't supposed to make any aggressive moves without Nash's prior knowledge and permission, either, but that wouldn't hold either of us back if needed. He would never agree to us taking sides against Tellar's soldiers, but that meant little to me. Blackstone's people were in trouble and unable to protect themselves. That was all that mattered.

Mason and I headed back to the other side of camp. On our way, we caught Tyler's attention. He tracked where we were going. His eyes narrowed. And then, after a brief exchange with Javilin, he joined us.

"Rescue mission?" Tyler asked. "Nash is going to be pissed."

"But that's not going to stop you from backing us." I grinned. It felt good to have somebody willing to stand by my side.

"What can I say? I'm bored."

I laughed, then turned back towards our destination. We trotted over to the unfolding scene.

Women in pastel dresses were squealing as the men tried to intervene by blocking the soldiers with their bodies. They did a good job, considering they didn't believe in violence. But it wasn't enough. Those soldiers weren't going to take no for an answer.

We would have to make them stop. Mason reached out and grabbed one soldier by the back of his stiff leather armor and yanked him off of a pretty little brunette with light blue eyes that matched her fuzzy dress, tossing him aside. Everything about her looked soft, and I could understand why a rough man might want to embrace somebody like her. But she wasn't willing, and that was what mattered.

"What the hell?" the soldier demanded furiously. "Back off, man. She's mine!"

Mason growled, shaking the guy as his buddies became aware that something was going on. Before they reached us, I stepped forward and away from Mason and Tyler, drawing their focus.

Most of my team had picked up enough of their language to communicate our basic needs. Hopefully Tyler and Mason wouldn't realize how much more I understood than that.

"She doesn't want you," I snapped. "What kind of man forces himself on a lady like her? Find one of your camp followers and leave her alone."

The soldier took a step closer to me, but Mason loomed in front of him, bristling and threatening. He didn't need to understand the soldier's words to see the threat.

Elation filled me. I loved having backup.

A few of the other soldiers, intent on their desires, slowly realized what was happening. They stopped their offensive groping and gathered around us.

"What if I don't care what you think?" one yelled. "I can take what I want."

"Not tonight you can't," I retorted, enraged by the misogynistic jerks that lived on this backward pile of cockroach droppings they called a planet. "How about you get out of here before I show you exactly what happens to a man who pisses me off?"

Then the fury I carried with me, that grew with each injustice I witnessed, boiled over. But it was more, overwhelming me to the point a switch flipped in my head, setting me in motion. It couldn't have been Blackstone's influence, because he was a pacifist. But whatever the reason, I pulled out my knife and had it against the punk soldier's throat before he knew what happened.

The two other soldiers came at me as I held the man hostage. Mason and Tyler kicked into gear, taking them on. Tyler's fist slammed into one soldier's face as Mason took on the beefier of the two, grappling with him as he tried to plow forward to get at me.

They exchanged blows, but then backed off when they realized they couldn't get through my team to reach me. It would be hard to get at their comrade before I nicked an artery. I wasn't sure if they knew how much of a threat I was because of their narrow-minded views about women, but everyone was pretty sure my knife could do substantial damage - too fast to stop.

"Apologize," I demanded. "Then tell your friends to back off, and I might let you go." I pressed my knife against his skin harder. It had to hurt, but I was careful not to break the skin. I had no idea what their idea of an Unforgivable Offense was, but I didn't want to find out the hard way that there was a taboo about spilling blood. But at the very least their masculinity would require payback to save face. Not that I would let that stop me.

That was when Javilin showed up. Before I could even draw a nervous breath, he ordered away the other soldiers, who immediately stood down and departed. After a tense moment, I removed my knife from the jerk's throat and stepped back, sliding between Mason and Tyler.

Javilin's muscles rippled as he strode over to my former hostage and got right in his face. "Get over to our side of the camp and don't come here again or I'll string you up myself. I told these people that they had to travel with us and as such, they are under my protection. Do you understand me, soldier?" My nemesis stiffened. He turned towards me, but Javilin cut him off before he could say a thing. "Keep away from the newcomers, too. I'll kill you myself if you screw this up."

The three offenders took off. My respect for Javilin rose as I witnessed the control he had over his men. The soldiers didn't look back even once. Not even to threaten me with retribution or cast significant dirty looks.

That didn't mean my hostage wouldn't come after me at some point, but it was impressive to see his commanding officer make him toe the line. I should have guessed Tyler wouldn't have spent so much time with somebody who was unworthy of him.

Javilin tuned to face us. "I apologize for what just happened. Tyler, please explain that I will make sure this won't happen again and that your friends can relax and enjoy their evening."

I let Tyler translate, inaccurately, and then the three of

us walked back to our tent.

"What the hell were you thinking?" Mason growled. "He could have flipped you over his shoulder. You had to stand on a rock to reach him!"

"I don't know," I admitted. The two guys turned to stare at me in disbelief. "Look, I'm sorry. But that pig was hurting her. I'm sick of this Mention and I'm really sick of the men here."

Tyler snorted. "Some aren't so bad," he said, his eyes sliding away from us. I turned to follow his gaze and caught sight of Javilin's tent. "In fact, I think I should thank Javilin for all his help."

"Yeah, see if you can soothe those ruffled feathers," Mason replied. "Make his protection worthwhile and maybe we won't blow this entire mission."

I tried not to let his words hurt my feelings. Besides, he was right. What I had just done was extremely foolish and could have messed up everything. There was no way Nash would keep me on the team after we got back to Earth Prime if I had.

"I hear and obey," Tyler quipped as he took off, anticipation written all over his face.

Mason and I moved off together, back to the tent. "You're lucky Nash wasn't there to see. Or Ginger. I don't know what's going on with you two, but I have eyes. She'd use this to her advantage without hesitation."

I gulped around the lump in my throat. I hadn't even thought of that. "Nash would understand." But my uncertainty was plain in my voice. He probably wouldn't. Nash was an outstanding leader, but he wasn't going to take my side if I destroyed our chances of striking it rich.

"Look, you need to watch your step. No more rescue missions. Got it?"

He was so forceful, I almost turned around and ran away. But I realized it meant he cared what happened to me, and my resentment softened. "Yeah, I get it." I ducked into the tent, Mason close behind. "And thank you. I couldn't stand to see those soldiers hurting defenseless women."

He grunted as he secured the ties to keep the tent flap closed. But then he turned and the look in his glittering eyes softened. "Any time, Bailey." His arms slipped around me, tugging me against his body. My knees weakened as he leaned down and kissed me, hard and fast. "Now, how about you let me help you use this fancy sink to wash off since I'm not letting you out of my sight while your actions are still fresh in those soldiers' minds?"

Heat flooded my veins. "You don't mind?"

Mason's hands unzipped my vest. "Not at all. You still need to get rid of the dust from the day. Then I can show you how much I like your clean, sweet little body." He slipped off my undershirt and tugged at my pants as I kicked off my boots. In a flash, my pants joined the rest of my clothes in a pile on the floor.

"Fine by me," I said, breathless with anticipation.

Mason's chuckle was like music to my ears. It felt so good to have his hands all over my body, the warm washcloth stroking over my skin, cleaning and pleasing in equal measure. There had never been a time in my life where I had been with someone who wanted me as much as Mason did. And it felt good, my own desire heightened by his.

I let myself go, responding to Mason, keeping my focus on him and what we were doing. I didn't want any stray thoughts to trigger memories that belonged to Blackstone and distract me from the naughty ideas running through my head. Or the pleasure crashing over me.

CHAPTER FOURTEEN
Lost In A Memory

I SHIFTED UNCOMFORTABLY. MEDITATING usually came easy to me, a habit of long practice. It got me ready to use my compass, but it wasn't working this morning.

Images of the Outsiders, their women looking frightened and the men using their bodies to block the soldiers from harming them, only to be knocked aside, kept running through my mind. Every fiber of my being wanted to leap out of the tent and chase them down. But I had promised to stay inside until Mason returned. He was concerned Javilin's protection had worn off after our altercation the day before.

Pursing my lips, I took a deep breath, held it for several seconds, and then let it out slowly, blowing away all my stress, worry, and even all my happiness. Everything had to go to promote the emptiness that I needed.

My hands moved almost of their own accord across the screen. I tapped in a few equations, but it was really just a simple exercise. Nothing was happening. There was still darkness when I looked into the viewer.

I rested my arms on my knees and then closed my eyes. If my memories were getting clearer and stronger because of Blackstone, then maybe I could take advantage of that. Use his gifts to remind myself of all the tricks of the trade I had learned while in training.

Focusing on navigation, I opened my mind to receive the memories I hoped would give me ideas about our situation. The Corps took their training seriously, but there was so much to learn that nobody could retain everything. But if the Blackstone Effect resurrected every single vivid detail, I might be able to find something of use.

An image of the Corps headquarters drifted into my mind. I hadn't been there in years, not since I applied to join. The sight of the building in my memory, surrounded by crowds of gateway jumpers heading to their destinations, reminded me about how scared I had been, how determined I was to start a life on my own terms.

I was pulled farther into the memory - the dome covering the entire Corps complex rippling faintly overhead, the smell of the asphalt in the heat and too many bodies in close proximity stinging my nose, the sound of my nervous pulse thumping in my ears.

The tent faded around me, and all that was left was me lost in the memory of signing my life away. It was a memory dating before my education as a navigator - and therefore not helpful in my current circumstances.

But no matter what I did, I couldn't back away from the torrent of images pouring through my mind, couldn't disengage. The struggle to control the Blackstone Effect hurt my head, slamming me with a migraine. Before my pain got so bad I'd end up screaming, I let go and dove into the past instead.

"Name?" The intake clerk was a crusty old soldier, one of the many veterans of the wars that worked for the Corps when they came back to civilian life in the slums. He was there in front of me, clear and in high definition, as if I was experiencing it in real time again.

"Bailey Hawke, sir," I answered. It didn't hurt to show respect. Not that it would get me anything but the goodwill of a man who had zero connections. If he had any, he would have gotten a better job. Not that he even noticed.

The old man grunted and scanned my I.D. chip. I had to fight to get my connection to my father removed from my file. It was the only thing my sister had ever helped me do. Being the daughter-in-law to the President of Earth Prime had its perks. Apparently, she could move mountains.

I held my breath, but whatever popped up on the clerk's screen gave no indication that I was related to the Baby Killer. I knew exactly how things went down when people learned that bit of information about me, but the vet only validated my finger and DNA prints and then shuffled me along to the next station.

Things were moving faster now that I didn't have to stand in line behind a thousand other applicants. "Position?" This vet was a woman. She must have seen battle because half of her face looked like it had been melted off. My father came back whole and healthy from the war, but most veterans weren't that fortunate.

"Navigator," I responded. None of the workers were chatty, but that didn't surprise me. The Corps was a serious and often deadly place to work. It didn't exactly inspire people to have a good time.

Most people who signed on came from the slums, which were basically hell on Earth. Nobody appreciated a friendly gesture, because that usually turned into a stab in the back. No matter how long I lived there, I couldn't seem to get used to it. But it was something I had to deal with on a daily basis.

The woman raised her eyebrow, the burned part of her face twisting in response. I couldn't tell what she was thinking, but I got the feeling she was scornful of my choice of jobs. Good thing that was my business, and not hers.

She scanned my I.D. and enrolled me in the navigator program. There were uniforms stacked on a table nearby. She jerked her thumb in their direction and told me to check in with stores and have them give me the gear I needed. Although I wouldn't get my compass until later.

Three days later, to be exact. My hands shook as I collected clothing in my size. I had just finished the last of my tests. Nobody would tell me my score. I had to wait until they called me in and then either issued me a compass or kicked me out into the general population to try for another, less skilled position.

"Hawke!"

My jaw clenched as I turned. I hated when they used my name like that. The last thing I wanted was for anyone to hear it and make a connection between me and my father. It wasn't exactly the most common name.

"Yes, sir?" I queried.

A slender man with ice gray eyes looked down at me. The look on his face gave nothing away, and neither did his words. "Come with me."

I followed in his footsteps, heart pounding in my chest. I wondered if anyone could see me shaking, or if it that was just a feeling I had inside. The last thing I wanted was to show any signs of weakness.

We walked through the cement quad in between the classroom buildings. They were monstrous, tall and wide and able to educate thousands at a time. The sheer size of the main Corps training complex dwarfed us, and it took almost an hour to get to where we were going once we boarded the light rail.

Finally we arrived at a building made of glass and steel, strangely beautiful, especially when compared to the concrete buildings in the complex. My heart pounded harder when I saw the words above the doors: "Instinct - Knowledge - Imagination."

I must have made it. I was now at the headquarters for the Navigation department. Surely there was no way they would have brought me into their headquarters if I had washed out.

"Welcome back, Mr. Rackam. The room is ready for you." A pretty little bit of a thing was sitting behind the counter in the lobby, smiling openly and welcoming everyone through the door, but especially us. We got her undivided attention. That alone would have told me Mr. Rackam was an Important Person.

"Thank you, Monica," he said. I remembered being

impressed at the time. It wasn't every day that a higher up knew the names of random support staff, especially vacant-eyed brunettes.

He led me into the elevator and we shot up to the top floor. I was nervous and surreptitiously ran my damp palms down the sides of my pants. I wasn't dressed for a visit over a hundred stories into the air. It was my best outfit, but the small part of me that still remembered what it was like to live among the elite knew it wasn't appropriate attire for the top floor.

I often wished that I had the comfortable assurance that the others in the slums had regarding their attire. Nothing was as important as survival, including the opinions of others. At least they had clothes that hadn't fallen to rags, and that was better than most.

We left the elevator and hurried down several hallways, all lined with windows offering a stunning view of the Corps complex that Rackam didn't slow enough for me to take in or enjoy. Typical. Would it really kill those people to slow down for one second so the rest of the world could enjoy what they took for granted?

Apparently not.

"Please take a seat," Rackam said. His cold eyes took in my appearance, looking me over, but I couldn't tell what drew his focus.

The room was set up with one large, long table with at least twenty chairs. I selected a chair that faced the wall of windows so I could take in the view.

"I'll be back in a moment."

Rackam took his leave, and I soaked in the warm

afternoon light, golden from the ultraviolet shield dome over the complex. It changed the concrete buildings into a buttery-soft paradise from where I was sitting. It didn't look like the hell it really was. I had only gone through testing, but I already sported several bruises from the harsh training methods, a blend of boot camp and torture.

I wasn't sure how long my eyes had been closed before I became aware that they were, and I struggled to open them. By that point, I hadn't slept for about two days. The accommodations they provided for us weren't private or secure. I awoke on the first night being groped by a man with breath that smelled of stale alcohol. Fortunately, my time living in the slums prepared me. I never heard what happened to him or where he went, but whatever and wherever, he had a knife puncture in his gut to remember me by.

Thankfully, I was still alone. I cleared my throat and sat straighter in the chair. Only a few seconds later Rackam was back with two women. They nodded curtly to me in greeting, and then the three of them sat across from me.

"First, I wanted to congratulate you on passing all of your entrance exams. You have impressive scores and the three of us wanted to meet with you to discuss your plans for the future." Rackam sounded serious, even bland, but once his words sank in, I realized I was being praised.

"Thank you, sir. I was planning on being a navigator with a secondary subset as a tracker out in the field."

Rackam nodded. "That is what you signed on for, but we have other positions available for those with the aptitude. We wanted to get to know you a little better to see if you might be a good fit."

A young man trotted into the room and handed Rackam a fat file folder. My I.D. number was written along the side and a bar code beneath it. It was thicker than the one I had turned into the Corps. The one my sister had helped me scrub.

My heart started pounding when Rackam flipped it open and I saw my picture on one side, and a stack of sheets on the other. I knew what a permanent file looked like. The last time I saw mine, I was assured that all traces of my connection to my family would be erased. But when Rackam's eyes narrowed, and he lifted cold eyes to meet mine, I realized it was a complete file, nothing expunged.

I recognized that look. People usually fell into two major categories. The ones who hated me because of my father, and the ones who wanted to get closer to me because of my father. Both types were sick in their own way.

Rackam looked like he hated me. My DNA had just ruined the Special Job I had waiting for me.

He looked up at the young man, who mirrored the look of disgust. The women leaned closer to the file, jerked back after glancing it over, and then departed. I never even got to hear their names.

It was all so familiar, but also unexpected. My cleared records had worked so far. Now I was trying not to drown in my disappointment as I waited to hear what was about to happen next.

"I was unaware of your lineage, Hawke. Fully expunging your record is impossible. Our counterintelligence agents will always find what you are trying to hide. But for people with your connections, that won't always stop you." His eyes glittered, scorn written on his face. "You may stay and join a team going into the portals. I worked with your father and I owe his daughter that much. But you're no longer welcome in this building."

It didn't even hurt. I was so used to that kind of crap that I just let the tiny seed of hope that had taken root inside of me die a cold death. I wasn't going to be a part of something important and special. Instead, I would be sent out into the unknown to see if I survived. Which was fine. It was nothing less than I expected.

And even if I wasn't going to be important to the Corps, I was going to be the most important person on my team. Nobody would walk out on me, even if they gave me that look. Never again.

Drawing my will around me, strengthening my resolve to never let them see me hurt by their words or attitudes, I stood. The young man walked over to stand next to, and slightly behind, my position. Well then, apparently I had gained myself an escort. How exciting. Look at me, I was practically famous.

I pushed that bitter thought out of my head and waited for Rackam to leave the room before I followed a short while later. I was disappointed. My curiosity would never be satisfied. I would never know what types of jobs they had for a special case like me. For the special jumpers without fathers like mine, that is.

My feet dragged as I shuffled out of the conference room and entered the hallway with the massive wall of windows. Determination filled me. I wasn't welcome, but I was going to take my time and soak in the view.

"I didn't know General Hawke had another daughter," the younger man said. He was in a different kind of uniform. I later found out that it was worn by the special security force that protected the important people who ran the Corps.

"Yeah, well, you and everyone else. It's not something I like to throw out there," I replied. It was easier to avoid discovery when I didn't have to hide from investigators.

He didn't answer me. After a few more steps, he said, "Rackam isn't the only one who owes your father his life."

One eyebrow shot up. Interesting. Not sure what he wanted to say, or which category he fell into, I made a noncommittal noise to acknowledge his words.

The aide looked up and down the long, empty hallway, then leaned in closer. "Listen, I don't have much time, but I've been in a lot of meetings over the last few months. You're lucky you are being kicked out. The special projects have the kind of facilities that, once you enter, you never leave. This is a mercy."

He was reassuring me? That was uncommon. I walked a few more feet before digging deeper. "Why are you telling me this?"

"Because I knew your father. I was one of his personal aides. I can't condone what happened, but it didn't erase all the good he did, either."

A complex, nuanced view of my father's actions wasn't common, either. No wonder this guy had made his way up in the ranks. They liked their officers to have critical thinking skills.

"Yeah," I acknowledged, even though I didn't agree. If he had been haunted by what I saw in that secret room, he wouldn't give my dad an ounce of credit.

He pressed the button for the elevator. "One more thing. When you go out into the Mentions, never skip."

My forehead wrinkled with confusion. I had yet to hear that term used and had no idea what it meant. I hadn't even begun my actual navigation classes.

"Why?"

"Most people mess it up and never return. You have the ability to do it successfully. That's not what you need to worry about. If you skip, and they find out you can do it, it won't matter who your father is. You'll be sent to their special projects section and end up as a brain in a jar."

I thought he was exaggerating, or using some kind of slang. Then again, if the rumors I had heard over the years were even remotely accurate, then he was being serious. They did occasionally preserve knowledge by removing a brain and connecting it to industrial-size computers.

"I'll keep that in mind. What's so hard about skipping, anyway?" I didn't ask what it was. That I could find out later.

The elevator doors opened. I glanced out the windows before stepping inside, my last look of what life was like for those lucky few who didn't have a father like mine. And had enough money to keep themselves out of the slums.

"They drill navigators in the math and science they need to get to and from Earth. Most people can't manage that much, but of those who can, most can't grasp the sequences needed to start from an entirely different place in the Multiverse. I checked out your results when I was sent for your classified file. Nobody has ever tested that high. You're pretty special. Rackam's actions would surprise me if I didn't know better."

"Yeah? What's that about?" Nothing was ever as it seemed, but this just got a lot more interesting.

"I was there when your dad pulled him out of the ditch. His guts were hanging out everywhere. General Hawke cut through the fighting and got him to safety, then forced the medics to heal him." Most died on the battlefields because there weren't enough medics and too many available bodies to worry about replacing them. "Rackam's putting on a big show to get you kicked out, but he's doing it to save you. He doesn't like owing a serial killer any favors."

I nodded curtly. The ground rushed closer and closer while the elevator hurtled towards the bottom floor. Towards my reality. My father had, apparently, just saved my life.

The pit building in my stomach ever since I saw that file folder grew even bigger. I didn't want to owe the Baby Killer anything, either.

My father didn't even know me. The last time I saw him was the morning I called the police. All the babies scared me. They weren't moving, and there was something wrong with their faces. But here he was, influencing my life in ways I never expected. Or wanted.

The nausea grew acute. I sucked in a deep breath as we walked out of the building, my escort still with me. "Take this," he said, holding out a folded piece of paper. "It might save you someday. There's no way a brain like yours is going to stay within the lines. I've seen your test results - you aren't made that way. This might keep you alive when you do break the rules."

He spoke as if it were inevitable. I took the sheet of paper he handed me and glanced at it for a second, then folded it up and stuffed it in my pocket.

"Thanks," I croaked around the lump in my throat.

"Good luck," he said, and then returned to the building, leaving me by myself.

None too soon. I raced away, as far as I could get, my boots slapping the concrete as I bolted. The vast distances and wide-open spaces forced me to veer into a small alley between two buildings. Thankfully, there was a refuse container there, which I held onto while I heaved up every drop of the crappy soup they had fed us over the last two days.

General Atticus Hawke. Hero. He saved a lot of lives. And he fought beside his troops. They all would have died for him at one point. Now, who knew what their loyalties would lead them to do?

Maybe save the daughter they never even knew he had.

After all of my moralistic denouncements of my father or anything he could give, not that there was anything left once the government seized his assets, I couldn't handle it if my determination crumbled in the face of the very real thought that I might lose my freedom. Or my life.

But there was no way I was going to accept help from anyone who owed my father, either. I tugged the folded paper out of my pocket, and without another thought, I tossed it into the refuse bin. I shut the lid and hit the starter button. The accumulated trash, my vomit, and the paper that he said would someday save me all went up in flames.

CHAPTER FIFTEEN
Trustworthy

REALITY RETURNED, AND I was still sitting in the tent, clutching my compass to my chest. I didn't have a photographic memory, but I remembered some things so well I would never forget them. Not any part of them. But the pathways Blackstone opened up in my neural network were forging new lines of communication within me. Stronger and clearer.

And I saw it. That damned paper the special security officer gave me. In my haste, before I ensured I couldn't be tempted to use the information connected to my father by burning it, I had glanced at the paper.

I saw what he had written on it. Thanks to Blackstone, I could actually read it in my mind.

The helpful stranger was right. It was going to save me. And my team. Now I knew how to get off the Mention that defied our instruments. And we would make it. It was easy, really. All I needed was a little imagination. And a whole lot of luck.

With a burst of energy, I hopped up and tucked my compass under my shirt. Then I went looking for Tyler. He was the closest thing I had to a friend, besides Mason, who was on duty. He was also catering to Javilin, trying to ensure my actions hadn't caused irreparable damage. Although Javilin seemed like he wanted to keep us happy just as much.

Was Mason my friend? He and I were sleeping together, and he wanted us in an exclusive sexual partnership, but what else did that mean? Would he be loyal? Take my side, no matter what?

Not that Tyler and I were that close yet. But we were definitely friends, and our bond had grown, especially since we got to this Mention. I was sure of it, even if I couldn't figure out how to classify what I had with Mason.

The sad thing was, everything I felt had been unfamiliar to me until Blackstone pushed his memories into my mind. He had loved at one point in his life - deeply. I wasn't sure if I'd get to the same place in my life, though. The people were different where he came from. More trustworthy and loyal. As much as I liked Mason, did that really guarantee he would be there for me when I needed him most?

There was something about Blackstone's memory that was strange, though. The feelings had existed, were still there inside of my head, sinking deeper and deeper along with everything else he had transferred to me. But I couldn't see anything else. There was no image to go along with the emotions.

I had no idea who she or he was, but the agony of

fierce love was there, blanketing everything. From the place where I viewed his love with my borrowed memories, I could tell it was simply too painful to think about. So I didn't. For my own peace of mind.

And I tried to ignore how I felt about Mason, too. I still wasn't ready to trust him. Even though he was adamant that he wanted to be exclusive, I still had no idea if he would choose me if it came down to the wire. Only time would tell. And time would also reveal what he was doing with me, even though he knew full well whose daughter I was.

"Watch it," a voice snarled. My body jerked in response, but it was soon apparent that he wasn't talking to me. A soldier knocked into a stack of pans in the cook's tent, making a crashing sound that echoed around the canyon.

To be safe, I looked around, making sure nobody was tracking my movements. Fortunately, the slimy jerks who I had confronted when they attacked the Outsiders hadn't even noticed me. Good thing, since they easily could have come after me in my distraction.

I shook off my preoccupation and acknowledged it was yet another way to avoid the actual issue at hand. Introducing the idea of skipping to my teammates. My heart nearly skipped a beat just thinking about it. But I was positive I could do it. And so was the Corps, even if they wanted to stop me because I was the Baby Killer's Spawn.

No. I wouldn't think about that. Stress always made me prone to dark thoughts. And the more I fell prey to them, the more memories came at me. And with my new abilities to not only recall details but essentially live them over again in high definition, I had to derail my train of thought before I fell apart.

My searching eyes finally found Tyler, who was in the soldier's camp despite the familiar form of Javilin was absent from the area. I sighed with relief. It would be easier to get him alone to talk that way.

I jerked my chin up in greeting and Tyler hopped to and did a quick hop-step jog to where I was standing. He looked so relaxed. Almost carefree. Hopefully that would make him receptive to what I had to say.

"What's up? Do we have a meeting?" he asked.

"Nah, I just wanted to talk. Do you have time to go for a walk with me?" I studied Tyler. He looked different. If I didn't know better, I would have said he was glowing.

Tyler nodded and fell into step beside me. We skirted around the soldiers sitting near the fire, eating or repairing their equipment and the rips in their clothes. They were taking the opportunity, since we would spend the next several days in one place. We all needed to preserve the game we hunted for more travel rations. The locals went after a large animal that looked like bison, and the meat was pretty good. I also saw plenty of deer in the forest, but the big beasts had more meat and were bigger targets.

Soon, we were in the trees, out of sight and mostly out of earshot. Not that any of the locals spoke our language. Unless Tyler taught Javilin more than I knew.

"What's going on?"

I took a moment to glance around and ensure we weren't being followed. "I have something I wanted to run by you," I explained. Nerves made my voice quieter than usual. I needed his support, but what I was going to suggest wasn't exactly regulation. "Something to do with my calculations."

Tyler laughed. "Me? I'm just the biologist. I couldn't help you if I tried. I didn't even come close to scoring high enough to be allowed to take the navigator test, much less get issued a compass of my own."

I shook my head and grinned back. "Don't worry about it, Tyler. I'm not talking to you because I need help with my math. Actually, I wanted your opinion as a friend."

It came as a surprise when Tyler's eyes narrowed with confusion. It occurred to me that while we were friendly, Tyler didn't actually consider me a friend. I looked away, trying to hide how hurt I was. And how embarrassed.

We spent a lot of time together, teasing and laughing. How did I misread the signs? And how was it possible that I was so blind? What an idiot.

I hurried to cover my mistake. "Or as an ally, I ought to say. Ginger's way too hostile for me, and Mason never lets me get a word in edge-wise."

Tyler's expression changed. He looked more comfortable with my revised characterization of our relationship. I tucked away my feelings of humiliation, hoping to keep a blush off my face.

But it worked. He took it as I hoped and moved on to lighter, more superficial things. "I bet you never get a chance to talk. He's hot as hell and ready all day long. Not that you can blame him. A man like him would probably die if he didn't release all that pent-up energy somehow."

He leered, and I laughed, a familiar exchange. In that

moment, our usual pattern reasserted itself and we moved into familiar territory. Where Tyler could laugh and enjoy my company but not have to put more into it than that. And where he didn't have to put out more effort.

I kept up the banter as we searched out a fallen log or flat boulder where we could sit. Joking about Mason or Javilin and their sex drives was far easier than trying to figure out if me reading Tyler wrong meant I was also reading Mason wrong.

Kids from the slums grew into suspicious adults. We couldn't trust easily and even as children we had a series of interactions more like temporary allies than friends. I was an idiot to step outside that just because Tyler had put a sink in our tent, or liked to joke around during our down time.

But soon enough we found a place to sit, and I steered the conversation to what I really wanted to talk about. "I want this to stay between you and me, okay? I'm just speculating here, and I don't want anyone to pitch a fit and get all worked up for nothing."

Tyler nodded and made the age old gesture of trust - he took his index finger and made an "x" on his chest. *Cross my heart.*

"Promise. Now spill."

I looked around one more time to make sure nobody has followed us and then leaned in so he could hear me, but nobody else would be able to, even if they managed to avoid my searching eyes. With only a slight pause to indicate the seriousness of what I was about to say, I finally blurted what was on my mind. "I'm thinking about skipping when we leave."

Tyler gaped at me. "You mean, take off once we get back?"

Of course Tyler would go there. "No, I mean skip to another dimension when we leave this one. Bypass Earth Prime. There's something about this planet that's blocking me. I thought the best way to get out of here is to skip and then recalculate once we get to where we're going."

"You're insane!" He jumped to his feet and loomed over me. "No way. I don't care how good you are, none of us would ever be on board for something like that. You know how often people disappear. We can't do it." His voice shook with anger.

He also looked scared. Then he gripped my arms, yanking me to my feet. My cursed freezing response took effect, and I simply stared up at him, a lump in my throat and heartbeat thundering in my ears. Then he shook me, waiting for me to respond. My shock made it hard to react. Nothing went the way I thought it would.

"Okay, Tyler. You're right." My voice quivered, and the dryness in my mouth made it difficult to speak. "I was just thinking about different ways to make it out of here sooner."

"No way. It's not worth the risk and you know it."

"Yeah, okay. I don't know what I was thinking. Temporary insanity or something."

Tyler latched onto my retraction and went with it. "Lame." His arms dropped, releasing me from his bruising grip. "Look, I need to get back. Javilin should be done soon and we're going to a hot spring he knows about. I'll tell you where it is when we get back."

"Sounds great. I could use a break. I'm so tired, I'm thinking crazy thoughts."

Tyler snorted. He accepted that comment, allowing it to soothe his concerns. We headed back to camp. I'd never mention it again. I didn't want Tyler to think I was still contemplating it. I couldn't afford him tattling on me to Nash, not with Ginger already playing sides.

Besides, Tyler knew me best out of everyone, except Nash. If he couldn't handle the news, nobody could. There really wasn't anyone left to tell, not even Mason. Not with how Tyler responded. And I should have expected it. Man, I really had fooled myself in a lot of ways. Too hopeful to be realistic.

Fine, then. It might have been easier with some support, but now I knew better. I'd just have to do it without them knowing.

My head was pounding, a migraine overtaking me. It was so bad that when Mason had gotten off his watch, I sent him to enjoy the hot springs Tyler was talking about so I could stay in the tent and try to rest it off.

Oh, who was I kidding? I was hiding. Hiding from the truth I only just realized. That it was all my fault.

Tyler wasn't my friend, he was a guy who liked to joke around with me when we were out in the Mentions. He had my back when we were attacked. They all did.

But I couldn't fool myself any longer. Not after Tyler's behavior. It hurt, but it was also humiliating. How could I not get it? And what about Will? I was just beginning to like the guy when he turned his loyalty to Ginger and never looked back.

Then there was Ginger. I didn't even know where to start, how to stop the swirling thoughts and memories, but one thing was clear to me. That was my fault, too. If I was normal, she'd treat me the same as Abilene. Sure, she was jealous and an attention hog, but at the end of the day, she didn't hate other women. Just me.

I was so cut off and cold that none of them would care if I dropped off the face of the planet. As long as they weren't relying on me to get them back to Earth Prime. Even worse, that was exactly what I had wanted. So, go me. Success.

My feet kicked at my sleeping roll, trying to smooth the wrinkled fabric under my feet. I hated lumpy blankets. Frustrated, I sat up and then smoothed the bedroll down until it lay neatly and centered on my side of the tent. There.

With a groan, I banged my fist into the ground, angry at myself. I thought I was so smart. But really, I was the dumbest one of all.

"She's causing problems, Nash. We need to get out of here, fast, and then dump her. We can't afford to be at her mercy any longer," I heard Will say through the thin, sturdy fabric of the tent wall nearest to me.

I froze. Did he not know how close he was standing? That I could overhear?

It was the middle of the night. Maybe he thought I was asleep, or didn't realize where he was. Or maybe he didn't care if I heard. But, no. That would be dumb. Will wouldn't jeopardize his rank unless he thought I wasn't around to stick up for myself.

"She stays," Nash snapped." I don't like you any more than I like her this jump, so back the hell off. We can reevaluate the team when we're at base camp. Until then, you better have her back and keep her safe or none of it matters."

"That's the problem," Logan added. A bolt of acid clawed its way through me, shocked that he was there, and joined in. "We need to keep her safe, and she knows it. She doesn't care about any of us. Her goals aren't our goals. Did you see how she went into the camp of those strangers? She could have started a war, and Mason's such a fool, he would have started it right along with her."

I didn't know Ginger had gotten to him. Or maybe I should keep it real. It was possible that Logan had always resented me. I wouldn't be surprised. But it revealed Ginger's tactic for Mason: he was obsessed with me and lost his judgment.

"Mason isn't a fool. But you are if you don't realize Ginger's playing you and Will the way you think Bailey's playing him. I'm not blind. I know my team and you better get it together or I'll take you out myself. Right now, all I want is to finish this damn jump and get the hell out. I need Bailey to get home, but I don't need you. Don't overplay your hand. Got it?" Nash sounded furious as he defended me. But it hurt, hurt deep, when his defense wasn't about who I was. It was about what I could do.

Stupid, stupid, stupid. And I had set that up. I wanted everyone to need me, to force them to stay when they found out how broken I was. Everyone else had abandoned me - this way, I could guarantee they'd watch my back. So much for being a genius.

"Yeah, we got it," Logan replied. "But something needs to be done about her. Bailey only cares about herself. She won't even interact with us and you know that's basic, Nash. She just stares at us as if we don't matter. Like she doesn't even see us. And I hate when her face goes blank like that. It's like we don't matter to her. She thinks she's better than we are."

But I didn't. If only they really knew me, knew what I thought, knew what was keeping me up that night. Then they'd know I was so much worse than they could ever imagine. As screwed up and unfair as this whole situation was, they were still much better than I was.

Something inside me snapped. My fist struck out, slamming into my sleeping bag with silent violence. I was the Baby Killer's Spawn. I hated myself more than they could ever hate me.

And maybe I needed to take a step back and remember that. I was my father's daughter. No good could come from having a relationship with them, anyway. They'd only betray me in the end.

"Go on, get back to your patrol. I'm beat. And don't let me hear you talk about this again," Nash ordered.

I heard the scuffling of boots as they walked away. After my ears could only hear the rustle and murmur of the locals, I realized my whole body was still tense. I forced myself to relax.

It didn't work. My body was still as stiff as a board as

my reasoning played through my mind, as if I were there making the decision to be a navigator again. I had to accept things were the way they were for a reason.

And it had always been that way. There was never anyone I could trust. So I made it through my classes and I was the most valuable position. And that was all that mattered.

But telling myself that didn't work. It did matter. So much that my entire body felt like it had been hollowed out and filled with pain.

Maybe that was why I cared so much about Mason. I wanted a relationship. But no, that wasn't true either. It could be that Blackstone connected to my brain and expanded what was already there until it was no longer recognizable.

There was no denying it. I was different, and there was no going back. My eyes were open. I was the author of my own pain. And damned if there was anything I could do about it.

CHAPTER SIXTEEN
Decision

"YOU'RE DIFFERENT TODAY," MASON said as we ate breakfast by the campfire near the edge of the clearing. We only had another day left before the meat was done drying for our trail provisions, and we could head out again. I couldn't wait to free myself of the constant, small fires billowing smoke all up and down the bare side of the field.

"Nah, I'm just tired." How could I explain what I had gone through? It wasn't something that Tyler had done, or even the rest of the team. It was me, and there wasn't anything really different about me.

"It's more than that. What happened?" Mason sheathed his weapons, his cleaning and sharpening regimen finished. He slipped next to where I sat on a fallen log the perfect distance from the flames.

The constant din of a camp full of soldiers and the local camp followers suddenly filled my ears, my awareness of who may be watching. Or listening.

"I think this trip is wearing on me more than the others." My eyes flickered over the ever-present people. There were far fewer bodies crowded together in the clearing than in the slums, but their watchfulness was bothering me. "Hey, I need to wash my clothes. Want to come with me? We can talk more."

Maybe I could trust him, even a little. So far Mason had kept my secret, and I had yet to hear him say anything against me. In fact, he was enough on my side that Ginger got her harem of men to bash him to Nash, hoping to undermine Mason's position.

He reached out his hand, slipping my plate from my grip and into the bin set aside for washing by a low-ranked soldier. "I'm always up for some time alone with you."

My gaze met his. There was a familiar glitter as he stared down at me, and the corners of my mouth slowly rose into a smile. His obvious attraction to me heightened the compulsion I felt whenever I was near him, leaving me breathless with mounting excitement.

Mason held out his hand, and I slid mine into his grip as he helped me to my feet. "There's a nice spot back on the trees, if you're up for a short hike," I suggested.

"Sounds good." He cleared his throat as I turned away. "Shouldn't we get our clothes first?"

I giggled. Sure, my clothes needed cleaning, but Mason made all the thoughts and memories and increasing awareness of those around me disappear. All that was left was my growing desire. But my practical side reasserted itself. "Right. It would be silly to head out without them."

He chuckled. "Allow me." Mason ducked into our tent and collected our bundles of laundry and the soap we used to cleanse them without polluting the water. The Corps wouldn't hear of damaging the environments of the pristine Mentions ripe for the plucking.

I stepped closer to gather my bundle from his arms when he rejoined me, but he ignored the gesture. Instead, he tucked my clothes into a sack with his and slung it across his shoulders.

It was oddly disconcerting to have somebody else casually help me out like that. I never even occurred to me that he would take care of anything that was my responsibility. But I should have. Relationships were so hard.

My eyes were growing used to the shadows of the forest. The weak light filtering through the eternal cloud cover helped, but was too weak to truly illuminate the pathways. It was second nature to pull out the small lantern provided by the locals and shed enough light to keep us from stumbling into any problem areas.

"Tyler said this area has been settled for a long time." I matched Mason's pace as we walked together, the path wide enough for the two of us. "That's why we don't see many predators."

"He's good at his job," Mason replied. "My last team's biologist must have lied to the team lead because that man didn't have a clue."

That happened sometimes. The Corps classes weren't easy, but some people were good at taking tests. Once they hit the Mentions, everything fell apart. "Was it bad?"

"Yeah. Half the team walked right into hyena territory."

"Damn." I loathed hyenas. They were filthy scavengers, but deadly to a weaker animal. And humans fell into that category all too often.

"I planned to leave anyway, but that shut everything down." We came to the river and turned north for a short distance to reach the hot springs outlet. Mason tossed down the clothing and handed me the soap so I could get started. "Fortunately, your team had a spot."

It was sad Abilene had died, but death was the most common way for a position to open on an elite team. And ours was one of the best.

"Well, I'm glad you're here." I tossed my clothes down on the river bank after I rinsed and wrung them out. I heaved a sigh and pushed myself back, off of my heels, and onto my butt.

"It's worked out better than I thought." Mason shook his clothes in the water to rinse them, his muscles rippling in his arms.

I hesitated, but then decided I needed to give even the smallest part of an explanation for my recent preoccupation. "I finally figured out how to get us out of here, but it's going to take a little more effort than usual. I'm not sure how to present that to Nash yet."

As a lie, I would say it wasn't as bad as some of the others I've told. There was no way I'd tell anyone I was skipping. Not now that Tyler freaked out. But I had to say something, and it was at least close enough to the truth that it didn't bother me too badly.

Hopefully, he wouldn't notice my fib. I closed my eyes and twisted my body and stretched, arching my back, working out the kinks I earned while washing my clothes in the stream. But my movements also thrust out my breasts. Maybe it would serve as a distraction.

And damned if it didn't work. My lips curled into a smile when I felt Mason's hands slide around my waist, then up to cup my breasts. His full lips nibbled my earlobe. He had dropped to his knees behind me, dragging me closer.

"Good thing I'm off duty," he murmured. "I haven't spent much time with you in days."

I tilted my head to give him better access to my neck. As I wanted, he nibbled his way down my neck.

"Tyler told me about some private hot springs. Want to check them out with me?" I asked, knowing the answer.

"Hell yeah. Let's go."

I laughed as I grabbed my clothes and spread them out on the bushes nearby to dry and then led Mason off into the trees. He followed, my uncertainties and unhappiness forgotten for the moment.

Maybe I was as manipulative as Ginger. Maybe not. The mechanics of a relationship were new to me, and I wasn't trying to control Mason. Only attract. And maybe distract, but just a little.

All I knew was that I would get out of this Mention as soon as possible before everything fell apart, and I was going to do it any way I could. Using any method I could. Some of those ways were more pleasurable than others.

It was more than an hour later before we were done with each other, drained and spent and luxuriating in the heated water. My head lay on Mason's arm, where he had rested it on the bank behind me.

"I'm glad you came with me the other night," I said. I wanted to let Mason know how much it meant to me that he had my back, but I didn't want to sound too serious or make him think I didn't know how to have a normal adult relationship. Or normal anything.

Some of the normal interactions still eluded me. I had no experience with the connections between a family, much less with a partner. I wasn't even sure if I really even knew what love was.

A wave of Blackstone's memories overwhelmed me, and there it was. A glowing, everlasting, agonizing warmth. That old man had given me everything, and he had loved before. Deeply, irrevocably.

Okay. Maybe I did know what love was, now that I had his memories. I just didn't know what to do about it. And if it was even acceptable. Certain things just didn't happen anymore. Not on my planet. Not with my people.

Not with the daughter of General Atticus Hawke.

My trip down memory lane, back to when I first joined the Corps, reminded me what the world thought about me. Mason was kinder to me than that, but I wondered how he would feel once we were back on Earth Prime and I was no longer his only other choice of sex partners or worse, his only ticket home.

That had always played a part in the feelings of my teammates. They were obligated to me if they wanted to get back home. I thought I knew what I was doing when I set out to manipulate that dynamic on my behalf. Now? Not so much.

"I've got your back."

"Thanks. I can't stand to see those weaker than us being abused. There were plenty of willing women for those soldiers, even if they aren't as pretty as the Outsiders."

Mason sat up, his arm sliding from behind my head. He turned towards me, eyes serious. "I don't like it either. But it's the way of the world. Theirs and ours." He rested his hand on my cheek, softening his words. "You need to keep focused. We're on Tellar's side, and that's it. We get our agreement, exploit the hell out of these people, and die rich."

"True. That's the goal." But I wasn't sure if I could live with that, regardless of my contract with the Corps. Or my obligations to my team.

In the privacy of my mind, I admitted to myself that it had never been enough for me. And I was wondering if I could stuff the genie back in the bottle now that I let him out. Even worse, my genie was telling me that I had to save the Outsiders.

I suspected my genie was named Blackstone. I tried pushing back against the constant, developing changes in my perspective, resenting the alterations that divided my loyalty and broke down the barriers I had erected to hide my vulnerably side.

But I couldn't do it anymore. The alterations in my thinking were successful at yanking me out of where I had been for the last fifteen years of my life because I always knew there was more. A higher purpose. A sense that maybe the way I looked at things, my desire to be accepted and care for others, to protect the weak, wasn't wrong.

And if it wasn't? Then I was right. And if I was right, I needed to keep fighting, not stop. Not back off and let events play out the way the Corps wanted them to.

To cover my silence, I snuggled into Mason's side, relaxing into his strength. Would he think I was a freak? Maybe. He had a hardcore, realistic side that never wavered.

I always thought the way things were on Earth Prime made people strong. The harsh reality, brute strength, playing politics. But in the end, true strength came from relationships. Ginger did her duty with the men in on our team, and it opened a door between them. Trust. Intimacy. Connection.

She barely had to give any of them a push to turn their backs on me. She has the strength of numbers despite being such a terrible person. Ginger wasn't always nice to the guys, but they didn't care as long as their needs were being filled.

No, I always knew there was something wrong with me. And that was fine, whatever. Everyone has issues. Maybe not as bad as mine, but it wasn't a contest. Nobody was going to win a prize. Certainly not me.

But I thought my damage was in who I was. In how I couldn't relax, enjoy myself, make myself available to others the way everyone else did. Not back at the Corps camp, and not out in the Mentions. Now I realized it was all a part of the same damage.

The explanation was simple. I was blind to it. The root of my problems was that I wouldn't let any in. Nothing touched me. I thought it was a strength, but it was my biggest weakness. I didn't have a leg to stand on with anyone. Nobody was going to back a crazy, dangerous plan to get home.

Not even with Mason. Not yet. We had barely begun to form our bond. I would have to hope what I had already given him would be enough when the time came.

"You ready to go back?" Mason asked.

I groaned. It had felt so good to be with him, the locals and Outsiders and our team all at a distance. Far enough that I wasn't bombarded with random stray thoughts from them. But I nodded my answer, and we climbed out of the hot spring.

On the other hand, our time together had made me feel so good. Clean and ready for the next step.

Water dripped off Mason's muscular body. I got the urge to lick a drop off of his chest, so I did. He liked that. Then he returned the favor.

Instead of returning to camp, Mason and I spent another hour near the hot springs. And I was ready for what came next. Where my primary purpose diverged with theirs and I followed a higher calling. Greater than the one given to me by the Corps, who in the end only cared about their own goals.

A shiver ran through me. Was that how my father started along his path? He told the media that he had a higher purpose, and nothing he did was wrong. He didn't need a moral imperative because his calling, his plan, was right. That meant everything he did was justified.

Well. Here's hoping I didn't have to kill anyone to get my way.

That thought made me stumble, and Mason reached out to steady me. But it was too late to stop the very real, incredible thought that popped into mind. I would do it. I'd kill if needed. I already had, in self defense.

But this was more, a new realization, an acceptance of something that might look like my father's path, but wasn't. I couldn't do it if I thought it was. But for once in my life, it was clear to me that I was more than my genetics, that my life was my own. And so were my choices.

Just as Mason reminded me, I had to be willing to do anything to accomplish my purpose. And this time, it felt right. Because it was greater than the Corps' desire for riches. Or my desire for riches. It was greater than the need to go home to Earth Prime the way they wanted me to, and not the way I needed to.

The shield I had placed between myself and Blackstone's alterations disintegrated. What he had given me was a gift, after all. Something that made me figure out who I was and what I wanted to do.

I had to save those weaker than me. They needed me. It was a tragedy that I was too little, too scared to save those babies from my dad. But as Blackstone's memories and feelings and abilities settled into my bones, there to stay, I embraced the thought that there was still something I could do for other people right now.

The Outsiders needed me. And I was going to take them home. Skipping dimensions would get the rest of my team home, too. I no longer care about their objections. Regardless of how they felt, of what the Corps demanded, I'd find a way to do it.

My pace quickened as I was filled with resolve.

CHAPTER SEVENTEEN
Fast Talk

"TAKE ME TO YOUR leader," I said. The irony was not lost on me, but I was in a mood. I think I've heard it called slap-happy, whatever that originally meant.

The older man led me further into the Outsider side of the camp. I had waited until nearly everyone was asleep, except Tyler, who was on duty that night.

Despite having a truce with Tellar's people, Nash still had us on a guard duty every night, although we were doing it discreetly. Javilin had to know, but I doubted he cared. Knowing the soldier's mentality, he probably would have thought we were weak and foolish if we didn't. And we would have been.

Not that Tyler would approve, but I knew he wouldn't care as much about my being around the Outsiders as anyone else on my team. Even Mason, who I left snoozing after some interesting nighttime acrobatics in our tent.

"Please wait here. I will get him," the man said. I

stopped where I was, near their communal fire. It was important to come across as cooperative and respectful if I was going to convince them of my sincerity.

My gaze wandered around. The Outsider campsite was lit up with torches implanted in the ground by each of the colorful, if subdued tents. There were many variations, and after studying them a bit longer, I realized they made a pleasing pattern that wasn't immediately apparent. They had a depth to them that took a while to process, much like their people.

Unfortunately for them, it made them stand out. Something other than the lack of bug eyes marked them as foreign, and foreign meant dangerous.

Ro walked towards me with an open, curious look on his face. It hurt my heart, like I was looking into the face of a doomed child. My doomed child.

"Good evening," I said, even though it was almost midnight. It was getting easier to project the meaning of my words into his mind as I spoke, although it still gave me a slight headache."I apologize for the late hour, but I would like to speak with you. Is there somewhere we can be private?"

Ro nodded and led me towards the outer edge of their camp. There was a small rock outcropping, which we used as a bench. It was closer to the trees than I would prefer, since I had no way of knowing if any of the guards were passing by, but we would probably be okay if I kept my voice down.

"I didn't expect to see you so soon, lovely lady," Ro said.

"Well, I couldn't keep myself away I guess." I quirked my mouth into a rueful smile. "Unfortunately, this isn't a social visit. We need to discuss what's going to happen to you when we get back to Tellar's compound."

Ro wasn't as oblivious as his open and honest nature made him seem. "If Blackstone never made it back with our plaque, we were illegally living on that land. I fear this will be the last of us."

He said it without deep emotion. I would have thought he didn't really care, except there was something in his eyes that told me otherwise. And a wave of emotion, as if carried by a gentle breeze, carried his concern and sorrow to me, where it touched my heart. Blackstone strikes again.

"Not if I can help it," I assured him. Ro looked surprised. "I'll get you home. I have a way to do it, but I need your help."

I could see the struggle going on inside of Ro. "We have no power left," he admitted. There were shades of agony and defeat in those words. I didn't let that stop me, even though I felt them as though they were mine, and I wanted to sink into the ground under the burden of it.

"I don't need your power. But I do need your support. I'm going to tell my leader that the only way to get us back to Earth Prime is to use your power to bolster my own, using my compass. You'll have to pretend, but it will give you all a reason to be there."

"Why would you do this thing?" he asked. Did the Outsiders have as much of a prohibition against lying as they did violence?

"It's the only way to work with my team. We are not in sync the way your people are. But you can trust me. I am here to help you and I can't do that without your cooperation."

How did I make him understand he could trust me? It was a huge ask. But then an idea came to me. I reached out my hands and lay them across his. His eyes met mine, confusion and curiosity making them glitter in the flames of the torches.

I focused on my emotions, my thoughts, and all my best wishes for them. Then I imagined them flowing down my arms and through my hands, into his. I didn't have the implants Blackstone did, but they were designed to enhance an ability that was already there. I would have to hope it made my intentions known without the metal in my body.

"Yes," Ro murmured. "I see. I understand. We can do this thing for you."

Was I crazy, or did that really just work? Blackstone had really done some serious alterations to how my mind worked.

"I'm warning you, though. It'll be a hard sell because Nash doesn't have any experience with people who have powers directed by the mind. There were always rumors on our planet, but nobody could ever prove it. At least not officially. But that doesn't matter, because I'll be able to convince him."

Could I? Really? But it had to happen, so I would do everything I could to ensure Nash did what I needed him to do. Ro remained silent, so I continued.

"Nash doesn't have a choice. If my team wants out of here, they have to comply with any demand I make that won't kill us. That's the law."

I didn't know why I was babbling. I was telling him too much, things he didn't need to know about the plans I had made. They sounded less formed and a lot crazier when I said them out loud.

"But we will be able to return home after we reach your planet?" he asked.

"No. I'm not taking you to Earth Prime. I'm going to tell them that's where we are going, but we are stopping by your planet first. It's the only one I can get to, and that's only because Blackstone had been here for so long. He read the stars. Besides, it's the least I can do."

I didn't tell him that if I took them to Earth Prime, they would never leave. Any people who could hop dimensions the way we did were dangerous. The Corps would study the Outsiders until they were nothing but biological residue.

My body jerked as a sudden snapping sound startled me. I couldn't tell if it was an animal or a person, but something large had just snapped a twig. Probably by stepping on it.

I jumped up and ran into the trees in the direction where the sound came from. I searched frantically in the darkness for the source. But I didn't see anyone and couldn't find any tracks.

As I turned back towards camp to explain my abrupt departure to Ro, I caught a bright flare out of the corner of my eye. I slipped back behind some undergrowth to hide my position and shortly after, Ginger stalked by, close enough to touch.

My stomach plummeted. I knew it. I knew somebody had heard me. But how much? And why did it have to be Ginger?

My boots pounded the dirt as I followed her, trying to come up with a plan. My mind raced faster than my feet, and I was running hard. I had to catch her before she made it to Nash.

Ginger jogged around the outside edge of the entire camp, staying just behind the tree line. Obviously she didn't want anyone to see where she had been when she broke cover, thinking I had no clue she had been eavesdropping. It worked out for me because that meant when I caught up to her, we would still be private.

She whirled around. I wasn't covering the noise of my pursuit since I was trying to get her attention, anyway. "What the hell, Bailey? Why are you following me?"

"Oh, right. Like you weren't just spying on me. Why the hell do you think I'm following you?"

The flash of triumph in Ginger's eyes was so bright it was plain as day, even though we were in the dark forest. Or maybe it was the new abilities I inherited from Blackstone. Which gave me an idea.

"It's too late for you," she snapped. "I'm telling Nash and he'll take punitive measures until it's time to jump home."

A navigator had a lot of leeway out in the Mentions,

but we weren't gods. The leader of the team could do any number of things to keep us in line, up to and including torture. It kept us from getting too big for their britches. How else could they control somebody who held the lives of everyone else in their hands?

There were stories from the early days when jumpers were left behind deliberately, or dropped into a canyon as they crossed through a gateway, or blackmailed with the threat of those types of things. Now, there were repercussions.

"Look, it doesn't have to be this way," I panted. "If you would just let me explain, I think you'll understand and -"

But Ginger cut me off. "No more words, you little idiot. What you want to do is wrong. You're insane! And you betrayed your duty to the Corps. Even worse, to us! Will and Logan aren't blinded by your mewling little facade anymore. Nash knows better, too. I don't care how much you play up your Daddy's Little Girl role with him. You're such a pathetic freak! Nothing you say will change my mind."

She was right. About all of it. I was still reaping the effects of my behavior, my efforts to protect myself. But she was also wrong, because I knew there was still something I could do to change her mind.

I leaped closer and grasped her arm right above her wrist. She tried to rip away from me, but I held on and mustered together whatever it was Blackstone did to me until I was able to push some of it into her through our connection.

The way I had done in the Outsider camp. The way Blackstone had done to me when we first met. He had me telling him everything. Things I normally never would have. And he did it by making me feel like I could trust him. That we were friends.

"Listen to me," I ordered. My voice felt fuller, somehow bigger than normal, and Ginger stopped trying to pull back. She froze, staring at me with wide eyes. "The Outsiders are harmless. They won't hurt anyone and they deserve our protection."

"But why? We don't know them, and we don't owe them anything. Our job is to work with Tellar."

Damn. No matter how convincing I could make myself, who Ginger was inside wasn't going to change, regardless of the abilities I had. I needed to think of something else.

"You're right, Ginger. You have no duty to them, but you have a duty to your team. The only way we'll get out of here and back to Earth Prime is if we help the Outsiders. They have powers of the mind that we need."

"You told that man it was a lie."

"No, Ginger, I wouldn't lie about navigating. You know I would never lie about that. We are going to go home, to Earth Prime, and the only way we're going to make it is if we stick together. If we use the Outsiders. We exploit people all the time - you know that. I told Ro what he needed to hear because I needed his people. Do you understand now?"

I put everything I had into persuading her. And it worked. I could tell it did. I let go of her arm, and Ginger stepped back. Then her face cleared from the dreamy look, and she narrowed her eyes at me.

"I'll let this one slide, Bailey, but you better watch your back. If you do one thing wrong, anything at all, I'm going to make sure you'll end up in the slums with something to remember me by."

Oh, and I believed her, too. But it didn't have any effect. I wouldn't think about her threats until it was time to take her on. For now, I had enough to do with keeping the Outsiders safe and walking the fine line between saving those who needed saving and treason.

I didn't respond. Ginger sneered at me with a little huff and then headed back to camp. I stayed in the trees until the shaking stopped. Then I made my way back to the Outsider's campsite. A smile replaced the fear on my face when I saw Ro.

"We're good," I assured him. "I'm going to talk to my leader tomorrow, and we'll figure out a way to take care of you. They'll all know we need you in order to leave, and if there's one thing you can count on, it's their desire to make it home, rich or not."

Ro nodded. I knew he didn't understand what we were doing on the planet. It wasn't altruistic or exploratory the way his people had viewed the Multiverse. We were like locusts, fire ants, cockroaches. Creatures with overwhelming numbers and a need to feed them all. To feed our greed. Regardless of how anyone else felt about it.

I took my leave and walked back through the trees and into our camp. When I didn't see Ginger, acid poured into my stomach, unsure I really was successful. I hoped I was, and it was enough to keep me from Nash's wrath.

CHAPTER EIGHTEEN
Ambush

WE WERE FINALLY ON the move again. The camp followers were scattered, either heading back to their villages or following along behind us at a slower pace. After our break to hunt and dry meat for our journey, my legs were reminding me that I should have kept up with my usual morning jogs.

Up ahead, I spotted a brightening under the canopy of the forest. The terrain shifted, and the trees thinned. Soon there was nothing but dust and mounds of cinder rocks and mountains made from the last volcanic eruption. Giant, smooth stones moved from previous ice ages mixed in with wavy and streaked volcanic glass.

"That's glass mountain," Javilin said. "Be careful of what you touch, it will draw blood."

He wasn't kidding. There was a giant pile of boulders and chunks made entirely of volcanic glass. It sparkled and shone in the watery sunlight breaking through the clouds here and there. If this Mention ever had a clear, sunny day, it would be stunning.

Logan was our geologist - he had been like a kid in a candy store for over a week, but this was something more. He couldn't contain himself. His hand snaked out and gently patted one large boulder of black glass, twice as tall as he was. When he pulled back, his palm was red with blood.

Ginger made clucking noises and cooed at him and took care of his wounds. It was a bit over the top, but Logan lapped it up. Will didn't look thrilled, but he didn't say anything about it.

She better watch out, or else she'd get a lot more than she bargained for. Ginger might even be the one who had to watch her back around Nash, who would punish her a lot quicker than he'd punish me. Her games were all about making me the bad guy, but it was starting to cause tension and jealousy among his team.

We continued to make our way through the rocky trails, winding their way through mounds of the broken planet. There were two large piles of boulders on either side of our pathway, three times as tall as any of the men in our group.

Rocks and scalding hot water rained down on the front of the company as soon as they marched through the narrowed pathway. Shouts rose around us and in a flash, our team had our weapons out and assessed the situation.

Nash gestured to me and Will, and we grabbed all the packs up and ran back towards where the Outsiders marched at the end of the line. We were supposed to hide our tech, but I grabbed Ro and dragged him along with me. And where he went, so did the other Outsiders.

"Come on, come on, we've got to get you out of the way," I shouted as I urged him along. "Somebody might get hurt protecting you, and I don't want you caught up in the fight." I almost wanted to speak in a baby voice. Not that I didn't respect Ro and his people. I did. But they seemed so childish to me in their helplessness.

Will looked pissed, but I didn't care. I wasn't ever going to win his approval, and I couldn't leave them behind. They were more important to me than he was no matter what my Corps contract said.

We stashed our packs and then I told Ro to keep walking the other way, at a quick pace, until they reached the last campsite. It wasn't that far, and I would know where to find them.

It was also hidden from the heavily traveled pathways in the forest. They might be okay if they stayed out of sight. In case we lost.

Will and I sprinted back towards the action. I had to be careful to assess the danger because once again, I might have to turn around and run away. It was so frustrating. Even though they knew I had to remain safe, my team still thought of me as a lightweight. Useless for anything except a ticket home. A non-combatant.

It was humiliating. And I could kick some serious butt. I practiced all the time. Mason was showing me new and dirtier tricks than I had ever learned before. But no. My first priority was to keep myself safe.

The soldiers seemed to have things pretty well in hand

when we returned. Will ran to join our teammates, who were cutting through groups of three or four raggedy, skinny locals in huge swaths. If they knew anything about tactics, they would have blocked our retreat. But they didn't.

There was a debate once, back when they formed the Corps, about whether we should stay out of planetary politics. To remain above and aside, and to let things unfold naturally on the worlds we discovered.

But it wasn't expedient, and we might not have gotten what we wanted. So philosophies like the Prime Directive and the Hippocratic Oath remained on the cutting room floor. We would fight, and kill, anyone who stood in the way of what we wanted. And it wasn't just what we could do. It was what we had to do.

I ran to join them. There weren't many of the enemy combatants left. If you could call them that. They were so thin, and dressed in rags, and I couldn't tell if some of them were children or just small due to lack of nutrition. They were obviously poor and starved.

Even the slums on Earth Prime didn't produce such wretched human beings. At least, not anymore. Not once they figured out that healthy humans worked harder and working humans didn't have enough time to plan a rebellion.

Mason was in his element. He twisted and leaped and sliced those people into ribbons. Something inside of me that belonged to Blackstone, and a much younger me, wanted to cry out and stop him. The rest of me admired how amazing he looked when he was protecting his teammates.

A filthy woman blocked my path. I wasn't sure where

she came from, but she was there, right there, and I knew what I was supposed to do. She was wide open, and it would have been easy to plunge my knife into her chest. I was required to. But my new neural pathways existed. They connected the old me to the new me, and the practical me was lost.

Will threw himself in front of me. He hated me. I knew he did - anger and hatred poured off of him in waves. But he also needed me, and despite his resentment, protected me anyway.

The woman fell to the dirt at our feet. "Get the hell out of here, Bailey," he growled fiercely. The woman tried to protect herself, and her farming implement sliced deeply into his arm before she died.

I backed up and turned around. There wasn't anyone behind me. Of course there wasn't. They didn't understand tactics. So, like I always did, I ran.

This time I didn't feel guilty. This time, it felt right. Blackstone's alterations were a part of me. I didn't feel any shame for running away from the slaughter of peasants.

"What happened?" Tyler asked. He was was gathering more bandages from where I had directed the Outsider's to set up a supply tent. Since they were back in the cleared area where we had camped the night before, I also had them erect tents for the wounded, build up fires and boil water, and so on. When the soldiers and my team came our way, we were ready to help them.

It was the very least any of us could do, since we were worthless in combat situations. I tried to feel shame, but

I couldn't. I knew I wouldn't be able to blindly follow the tenants of the Corps any longer. Even if we only got a meager stipend from this earth-copy, I wasn't going to participate in another jump. Not if I had to hurt people. Not anymore.

"I don't know, man," I replied. "She was so frail and dirty. You could see she was hungry. I could feel how desperate she was and couldn't do it."

"Damn it, Bailey, you know better. That will get you killed. And then what would the rest of us do? You can't afford to be that selfish. We can't afford it, either. How would you feel if we were trapped here forever with no chance of ever getting home because you felt sorry for a woman with a dirty face? She was trying to kill us. That's all that matters in a fight."

He was right. I knew he was right. I had said the same things to myself, but it didn't matter. Blackstone had taken me over.

No, he didn't. It was me. It was always me, the little girl, the girl who blew up her life to save the dead babies. Too bad the dead didn't need saving.

"None of them stood a chance, even if I didn't help. It was a bunch of weak peasants fighting strong and healthy soldiers. But that's fine, I guess, it's okay if we kill them, too, even though it's obvious they're just trying to survive. You've seen what some of those soldiers do to the people here. They destroy everything in their path, and for no reason. It isn't about survival for them, so why are we taking part?"

"Screw you, Bailey. Javilin was walking in front. He's

got burns all over his right side, burns I'm not sure won't get infected. They could kill him if that happens, and you're feeling sorry for the people who attacked us? We did nothing to them. None of the soldiers did."

Tyler was panting, his angry breath heaving in his chest, and I just stood there, staring at him, incapable of answering. Because he was right, and I knew he was right, and I didn't yet understand how I felt about it all. Or why I could no longer act. Knowing my mind was betraying me, but accepting it was me, just me, only me, who made that decision.

"I'm sorry," I said, but Tyler huffed in disgust and then stormed off. It wasn't even because Tyler was in love with Javilin. He was right, anyway.

I watched him go, pushing my pain and confusion aside. Feeling that cursed blank look on my face. The one that separated me from everyone else. They thought it meant that I didn't care about anything. I knew it meant I cared too much. Life bites.

By some miracle, I avoided any actual conversation with my team over the next several hours. After we cleaned and bandaged the wounds, tallied up the dead (peasants thirty, soldiers zero), burned the bodies, and dusted off the residue of our efforts, we turned in for the night.

Nash had me and Ginger split the watch until early morning when the fighters took over. Then around midday, after we all had a chance to recover, we headed out again. Javilin sent ahead a scout, but there wasn't anyone else waiting for us at the ambush site.

There was a sense of finality to our movements. It was

finally time to see what that stupid symbol on the map meant. Then I could convince Nash I needed the Outsiders, and that it was time to go back to Earth Prime. Yeah, there would be a skip. But he wouldn't know it.

During that last leg of our journey, we were attacked four more times. Apparently, the people in Tellar's territory were desperate. I wished there was something I could do, but they needed the kind of help I wasn't in a position to offer. They could have been a strong and healthy community. There were enough resources. But like in most Mentions, the locals were abused and ignored instead.

And we helped cut them down. There were so many conflicting priorities pressing in on me that the stress was getting to me. I had a headache I couldn't shake.

The thing was, I felt bad for them and emphasized with them, but I hated what they were doing. To them, their violence meant death. Their own death. We could have helped them, but instead, they kept attacking in the most pathetic guerrilla warfare tactics known to man - on any planet.

We kept killing them, and they kept coming. Finally, after two especially brutal days, the suicide missions stopped.

"I can't wait to get there," I heard Ginger say. She and Will and Logan were all walking close to each other. Will's arm was bandaged from wrist to shoulder, but he was going to be fine. That fact didn't stop Ginger from cooing and catering to his every need.

"I know the first thing I want to do as soon as the tent's up," Logan said. His hand slid over Ginger's backside. I was pretty sure Will didn't see because there was no change in his expression. "There's a river or hot spring out there with my name on it." Yeah, right. Sure he wanted a bath.

Mason tugged on a strand of hair that had slipped out of my clip. "Hey, what's going on inside of that head of yours?" he asked.

I turned to look at him and gave him my best attempt at a smile. He was so patient with me. It was really quite amazing, especially since we started off as rocky as we did and I had been so standoffish lately.

"I'm working on the equations I'll need to get us out of here," I said. In a way that was true, but mostly because me, plus the Outsiders, equaled our escape route.

Even though what variable would guarantee success was beyond me. I was willing to take some of it blind, but Blackstone had enough knowledge and memory to plug in some of the information, and away we'd skip.

"Damn, I always did like the smart ones," Mason said. The look in his eyes made me lose a step, and I stumbled. He grinned as he steadied me.

We heard a shout from the front of the line. Everyone stopped, and Nash trotted up front to see what happened. After several minutes, he sent Tyler back to our position. He jerked his head to the side. We congregated a distance away from the locals to hear what he had to say.

"We're finally here. It's a narrow opening, so Javilin is going to send out scouts. Then we'll follow after. They haven't worked it for years - they have no use for the metal inside. They can access iron closer to the main camp."

Once the scouts returned, we rejoined Javilin and

his men. My teammates fell into the usual lineup and we entered the cave.

Later that night, we sat around the main campfire, mostly numb.

"I'm going to live off planet," Logan said. "I know most of the elite stay on Earth Prime, but I like fresh air and sunshine too much. Hell, I might even buy up an entire continent so I can play at making my own environment."

"Not me," Ginger said. "I'm going to get the biggest penthouse in the Vatican that I can. I'm thinking about getting into politics."

I snorted to myself. Sleeping with politicians wasn't nearly the same thing as getting into politics, but whatever. I'm sure Ginger would get exactly what she wanted.

"Come on, Mason," Will said. "What are you going to do now that we're rich beyond our wildest dreams?"

Mason leaned back and thought it over. Will hadn't asked me, and I was glad. I had no idea what to say. I was still focused on how to skip us out of the Mention, especially important now that we found that rarest of metals, home-grown on this planet.

It was a shock to all of us when my compass went wild, setting off notice that meant we had discovered the coveted metal highest on the Corps priority list. It should have detected it the second we landed in this Mention. But like everything else, something about this place had screwed up what should have been straightforward. Like the constant cloud cover, making it impossible to plot the return trip to Earth Prime.

We needed to get back as quick as we could, but there was no way I could do it in a place that messed with my compass enough that it couldn't even tell north. Our trip would be difficult, but this particular area made it impossible. We'd all have to wait until we got back to Tellar's compound. Or an area like it.

The precious metal that made up most of our tech was everywhere in the abandoned mine. The locals had no use for it, but that one mine had more of that metal in a single place than had ever been discovered anywhere else.

There was no native scientific name for it, but ever since we learned about it decades before, we called it filthy tech. As in, the metal that made the tech also made us filthy rich.

Walking into that cave with Javilin was such an easy, typical thing. We were a little tired and ready to end the day after a string of peasant attacks, but once we saw that telltale glow and my compass went off, none of us were tired anymore.

We hit the mother lode. Our trips were finally over. Now it was up to me to get everyone back to Earth Prime so we could enjoy the fruits of our labor. If labor meant walking into a cave and discovering the endless stash of the most sought-after metal in the Multiverse.

"I'll probably get some land off-planet, too," Mason said. "I hate Earth Prime. It's a filthy cesspool and I want to get away."

We all nodded. The choices were between power and stay, or peace and leave. No in-between. Not once we had the kind of money that put us on the radar. It was understandable.

Before anyone realized I never got my turn, Nash showed up. "Bailey, you and I need to talk."

Ginger perked up. So did Will. Maybe they knew something I didn't. They acted like it was the best day of their lives, and besides the fact we were all now suddenly rich, there was nothing to make them feel that way except me getting into trouble.

I studied Nash. Did he look like trouble? Yes.

Biting back my concern, I got up and hopped over to where Nash was standing. I gave him a cheeky grin, but it died on my face when he looked at me with that gruff, distant look he usually reserved for the Mention natives he was about to enslave. Not a good thought.

We walked off into dark evening. The cloud cover blocked all the stars again, so the darkness surrounding the circle of light from our torches was like a wall.

"What can I do for you?" I asked. My usual cheerfulness had been crushed by the flick of his eyelid.

"Care to explain to me what you did the other day during the ambush? What the hell was on your mind, kid?" he asked. Frustration poured off of him, but also a blank spot, like there was something missing from his emotions. Blackstone's gifts on the fritz, maybe.

"I did what I always do. I ran. I'm sick of it, but I do it anyway."

"Bullshit. You ran, but you took the Outsiders with you. They aren't your responsibility. You jeopardized our entire mission to drag along a bunch of pacifist freaks?"

"No! Nash, we need them. You know they have strange abilities. You've seen some of them. Their people learned to enhance the power of their minds. Well, I can use that to boost the read I'm getting here. This Mention is blocking my compass, Nash. I keep drawing a blank. But with their help, we can get out of here. We need them." I stopped once I began repeating myself.

Nash's face caught the light from a torch. He looked shocked. His source obviously didn't tell him the lie I had already begun to believe. That we needed the Outsiders.

Well, maybe it wasn't a lie. We did need them, just not the way I kept telling everyone. If I left them behind, I couldn't function. I wasn't sure where the compass would land us after that.

"Why the hell didn't you tell me?" There was no lessening in Nash's affront. He was still mad at me, and more than just for saving the Outsiders. And I didn't know why.

"I just figured it out. I'm sorry. There was no time to tell you, I swear."

"What about that woman? The one who attacked you? You didn't fight her at all."

He got me on that one. It was dereliction of duty to let anyone strike me without a fight. I was the essential personnel. "Will took care of her. I didn't need to do a thing."

"I hired you to navigate, but you know damn well I also hired you because you can fight. You're always training just in case you need to defend yourself and you just stood there. Will said you weren't frozen - that you did it on purpose."

I hated how mad he was at me. I didn't know what to

do. Nash had always been so supportive. He cared about me. Even when I screwed up, he was there to teach me, guide me into being the person I wanted to be. Not just a part of the team like anyone else.

"She was so weak," I said.

"I don't care. There are plenty of non-combatant navigators out there and I hired you instead. I don't want dead weight, even navigator dead weight. You get your act together or you're gone. And I'll file the papers before we file the mining contracts."

"No! I'm still a part of this team. That money is mine, too." My heart was thundering in my chest. Nash could tell them I didn't earn my share. He didn't have total power over me and my percentage, but it was hard to fight.

Especially when the rest of my team wasn't on my side. And I needed that money, bad. I couldn't do this anymore.

"Yeah? Well, next time, act like it. If I hear you aren't pulling your weight or fighting, then I'm cutting you out."

I swallowed around the lump of bitter acid in my throat as Nash walked away. I couldn't process what was happening. He always had my back. He always listened to me. And here I was, in danger of losing every dime I should have from that trip, the untold riches that would get us all out of the slums forever.

Nash meant it. The connection we had was gone. I felt no tug of affection from him at all.

Turning, I trudged towards the rock outcropping, headed for the stream. I needed a moment alone, and I wanted to splash some water on my face. I slipped on a pocket of gravel, looked down to find a safe place to plant my feet and regain my balance.

Looked up and met Ginger's triumphant stare.

I couldn't look away. She finally broke eye contact and sauntered off. Her message was clear.

She was the reason. She broke my relationship with the man I looked up to like a father. Even worse, she severed the tie he had to me. And I didn't have a clue what to do about it.

CHAPTER NINETEEN
Disaster

"A PENNY FOR YOUR thoughts," Mason said. He tugged on my hair, which I was letting air dry. Not like there were any hair dryers anywhere in this Mention. He had caught up to me at the edge of camp after I got back from taking a freezing cold bath in a little stream. I missed the hot springs.

"I've got so much going on in my head, I'm not sure what to do first. It's like I can't make any decisions anymore outside how to get home."

Mason reached out and lightly grabbed my arm. "Come on a walk with me. We can talk it over."

Our eyes locked, and I realized he knew something was going on with me. He looked worried. I nodded, and he led me away from the camp after I tossed my bathing supplies near my tent.

"I'm in trouble with Nash," I said. "It's pretty bad. He threatened to keep me from collecting on my percentage for this Mention."

"That's bullshit. He can't keep you from that."

"Technically, he can. You know that. We've worked together for five jumps, so we have a history he can cite in the filing. Yeah, I can fight it, but his clout will be more than mine once we hit Earth Prime. He's pissed I didn't kill any of the peasants."

Mason rubbed his scalp where his buzz cut stuck up a little in the back, cursing under his breath. "Do you think he'll go through with it?"

"I might be able to convince him we're good. As long as no more weakling 'rebels' show up asking to be killed, because I just can't do it. It's like I've come to the end of my rope. It's over for me. Even if I don't get any of the money, I have to retire. I'm not any good."

"The hell if you aren't. Navigators can sign on as non-combatants. You can change your profile after we get back. Not like you'll need to, because you're going to get your money, even if I have to talk to Nash myself. I can file a countersuit."

I stopped. We were in the shade of a large boulder, and a slight breeze kept the humidity at bay. "You would do that for me?" I asked.

Tears filled my eyes. I never had anyone volunteer to do anything on my behalf before. In my experience, people only looked out for themselves. When it comes down to it, they matter more to themselves than anyone else does.

To be fair, some of the elite stick together. Although nobody could tell based on the Hawkes.

"Of course I would. It won't cost me anything, and you've more than earned your share. We won't even be able to get off this rock without you, and we all know there's something wrong here jacking with your compass. No matter how crazy your teammates seem to be on this trip, they still have faith in your ability. That right there tells me all I need to know to back you with the Corps."

I pretended to study the horizon while I desperately tried to keep the moisture in my eyes from overflowing. Fortunately for my dignity, a rabbit, or something that looked enough like a rabbit yet twice the size, bounded across our path.

Mason whipped out an arrow and killed it without hesitation. I was impressed as hell with his hunting skill. I didn't think there was anything that man couldn't do. He was a Bain all right. The downfall of my solitary existence. I had fallen for him, and hard.

He trotted off to collect his prey, and I swiped at my eyes to dry them. "Damn, that thing's huge," I called to him when he got a little closer. "That can feed all of us by itself."

Will was still cooking for the team. The soldiers cooked in their individual units while on the road, and we followed suit. We were still on the lookout for fresh meat despite dried provisions, and some of the plants and veggies Logan said were healthy. They weren't too hard to find once we knew where to look.

Some things looked the same in every dimension. Even with the slight differences between planets, a carrot always looked like a carrot.

It took a while for Mason to get back to me. I realized after a few moments that he was giving me time to settle down. That sweet gesture was almost enough to start the tears again. Man. Something was seriously wrong with me now that the damned brain of Blackstone merged with mine.

"Tell me what's going on with you," Mason said. We made our way towards the stream so we could field dress the rabbit, since we weren't going back to camp right away.

While he set up and cleaned the carcass, I wandered around, looking at the different stones along the bank. I wasn't anything near as experienced a geologist as Logan, but I still knew what pretty was when I saw it.

I picked up a black rock that had dusty sparkles inside. It looked like a blurry, starry night. I popped it into the pouch attached to my belt.

At the Corps camp, I had a small rock collection locked up in my valuables box. I didn't have much else to store in there, and I had been collecting rocks as mementos since I was little. The only other thing I had in there was a picture of my mother.

It was the old-fashioned kind, printed out on a sheet of plastic and laminated. I never looked at it. I put my rocks in the box and then the Corps locked it back up for me.

Suddenly it was all too much for me. I should have confided in Mason, but I was still worried he wouldn't be able to accept what I wanted to do. So I improvised.

"I need the Outsiders to help me. They have this thing they do with their brains. It taps into the extrasensory areas."

Mason nodded. Some of the Mentions had people who developed their brains in the way the humans on Earth

Prime were still trying to figure out. Some of the more powerful ones were brought back to study. Their minds worked only a little different from ours, and the scientists wanted to figure out a way to make it work for us, too. Anything to give us an advantage.

If they knew what Blackstone did to me, they would want to know. They might even decide that dissecting my brain would help, which is why I wasn't going to tell anyone about it.

The interesting thing, at least to me, was that the part of the brain I used when I was navigating was the same area where those people's brainpower came from. If I had to stand up in front of a disciplinary committee at Corps headquarters for demanding the help of the Outsiders, the science behind my claims would seem reasonable.

"You need to pitch that to Nash."

"I know. But there are obstacles. Like Ginger," I replied. "She hates me. She's trying her best to screw me over with the rest of the team, and it's working. I need to get us out of here before it's so bad nobody will back me."

"Why don't you talk to her? Play on her greed. She can't get back and cash-in until you get her there. Make her put it in writing."

I huffed a laugh under my breath. That wasn't a bad idea. "I can try. But it's Nash I'm worried about the most. I don't get why he's so mad at me. We've always gotten along and now it's like he can't trust me."

Mason washed his hands off in the stream. He stood and studied me intently, from head to toe. "You're an idiot sometimes, Bailey. So you're going to have to take my word for it. He's got more going on in his head than you realize, and if you talk to him now that he's calmed down, he'll listen."

There was something in his voice that I didn't understand. Like he knew more than he was telling me. I reached out with my jacked-up brain, and I could feel a barrier there, stopping me from seeing what he was thinking. It had to be natural. And I didn't want to break through. If Mason was keeping something private, then fine. I'd wait.

"All right. When we get back, I'll speak with him."

Mason tied the rabbit to his sling, and we walked back to camp. He asked Tyler where Nash was, and I headed that way while Mason went to meet with Will to give him the rabbit.

It took me a solid half an hour hike before I got to where the landscape softened and trees showed back up. I wasn't sure why Nash went so far out, but I figured it must have been for a good reason.

By the time I got there, I wished I never tried.

I heard them before I saw them, but I didn't understand what was happening until they came into view. They couldn't see me from where I stood in the trees, behind a tall bush that had little spikes on it and berries that looked sweet and plump but were poisonous.

Nash was there with Ginger. And they were engaged in the type of activity that I wished I could burn out of my mind. But because of the new Blackstone changes, I was never going to be able to forget.

"Tell me you don't want her," Ginger demanded as they copulated.

"I don't. I'm with you, Ginger. And I love it." Nash grunted as she moaned loudly, but I knew it wasn't in pain.

No, I was the one in pain. But I was frozen to the spot, unable to turn and run the way I desperately wanted to.

"Say it. Tell me you don't want her."

"I. Don't." Nash growled. "Shut up, Ginger, you hear me? Just shut the hell up."

"No! I want to hear it. Who don't you want, Nash? Who will never share your bed?"

"Bailey," he ground out. But the worst part wasn't that he was telling her he would never be with me. No. I could hear it in his voice. He wanted me. He said it again. "Bailey."

And Ginger loved it, loved that this man was wishing he could have something I denied him and that she was with him instead, even if it meant pretending to be me.

Me.

I almost threw up. My legs were numb and I couldn't move them. *Please, please let this end.*

Ginger cried out her triumph as they finished. Nash said my name again. And again. Then collapsed forward onto her, his head drooping forward near her neck, resting on her shoulder.

"That's right, Nash," Ginger panted. "You will never have sex with Bailey. Because she would never let you. She thinks she's better than us. But I'll always be here for you. And I can do anything for you."

Nash pulled back and rolled away. "Go away, Ginger."

She smiled, smug and victorious. Then she stretched, groaning as she pushed herself up. She grabbed Nash's shirt and used it to wipe the sweat from her body before tossing it back down beside him. "Something to remember me by."

I hated her. Bile rose in my throat and as she turned towards me, I froze for another reason. I didn't want her to see me.

"Get the hell away from me," Nash growled.

"Sure thing, boss man," Ginger said, mimicking my voice exactly. I almost screamed out loud when Nash grabbed her ankle to stop her from walking off. "Oh, yeah. That's what you like," she purred.

Instead of leaving, of stopping the torture as I remained trapped in a horrified, frozen body, they started up again.

"Do you like that, baby?" he asked.

"Yes, daddy. I love it."

"Come on, Bailey. Give me what I want."

Finally, mercifully, I summoned the strength to turn my back, tears filling my eyes as Ginger called him daddy and Nash called her by my name.

Bailey.

Once I couldn't see them any longer, it was like a spell had released me from its grip and I was able to run, fast, faster, crying and choking in horror as I heard Nash shouting my name in the distance.

I had no idea I could throw up that much. Everything I have ever eaten must have wanted to take a bow because I couldn't stop heaving for almost five minutes. Right when I thought it might be over, I could hear Ginger squealing and Nash's shouts play over and over in my mind, and I started heaving again. I couldn't tell any longer whether the tears were from the pain in my abdomen, or in my heart and mind.

Nash calling her Bailey. Ginger calling him daddy.

I simply couldn't handle it. Nash was my mentor. I looked up to him. I even loved him. But that wasn't love. Whatever I saw was warped.

It hurt he was having sex with Ginger, who I knew full well was manipulating him, and he should have known better. But wanting me like that, pretending she was me, acting out a role like that was devastating and I wasn't sure if I would ever get over that.

He told Will and Logan that she was playing them. And that they needed to get their priorities straight. Was he watching my back when he said that, or his own? Was he trying to get rid of the competition?

Ever since I joined his team, I wished he were my real father. But now I knew even men I could respect and admire could be warped monsters. For the first time in my life, I finally understood why so many people could love my father the way they had.

They didn't see his monster face. They only saw the upright man. The rest was hidden from them and they never pushed aside the veil.

I couldn't blame them. Too much pain was there. The private lives of the people we love and admire should be sealed away, locked up in chains, and labeled "Here Be Dragons."

When I looked at Nash from now on, what would I see? His rough, handsome face? His hand rubbing the scar on his chin? The reluctant humor in his eyes when I got sassy?

No. No, all I could see were Ginger and Nash together, her calling him daddy.

I finally stopped heaving when I managed to cut off the flow of thoughts. When I stopped thinking about anything, forcing my over-full mind to quit racing and fluttering and pushing and functioning at peak capacity. I was grateful I learned to meditate. Because that was exactly what I needed to do.

It was what I needed to feel. As if my brain were empty and unfocused, open wide and humming faintly. No noise. No thoughts. No memory.

I leaned down by the small creek at the edge of our camp and rinsed out my mouth. Then I splashed water on my face and neck. It was cool and soothing. I pulled out a bandage from the pack I kept around my waist and I soaked it in the cool water and dabbed my eyes. They hurt so much, it felt like I had been crying for centuries.

It took me an hour to get back to camp. I couldn't seem to push myself, so I trudged slowly until I got there. Then I slipped quietly into the tent and crept into my bedroll. I was exhausted, and I needed to sleep.

Using my canteen, I poured more water onto the damp bandage and laid it across my eyes so they wouldn't be swollen in the morning. I didn't want anyone to ask me questions. And even more importantly, I didn't want Ginger to suspect I knew, that I may have seen something. The glitter in her eyes at the end told me she had sensed somebody was nearby. She always had been an exhibitionist.

Thankfully, Mason was on patrol. He would ask how it went and I couldn't face anyone in that moment, much less talk about it. I just wanted to embrace the numb bliss of sleep.

"How did it go?" Mason asked. His voice woke me from a fretful set of nebulous, nightmarish images that haunted my dreams. I was relieved to be awake, even though I could barely open my eyes when I removed the dried fabric draped across my face.

The interior was dim, but Mason had lit a lamp. We were alone in the tent. Tyler slept by Javilin's side every night, and it gave us the privacy I cherished.

"I don't want to talk about it," I replied. A wave of nausea crashed over me, like it was carrying every nightmare I ever had with it.

"What the hell happened?" Mason asked. He dragged me out from under my bedroll and studied my face. I shifted my gaze away. "Come on Bailey, I need to know."

"He was with Ginger," I said. I wasn't sure if I could go on. Mason pulled me to my feet and tugged me against his chest, enveloping me in a soothing warmth. He waited silently until I could speak again. "They were having sex, and it was the worst thing I've ever seen."

"Why?" There was something in his voice that told me he might already know. And if he did, why didn't he tell me?

"Because he was calling her by my name and she kept egging him on. It was sick. She called him daddy."

It might have sounded ridiculous to anyone else, but

Mason knew who my father was. This wasn't just a bit of harmless endearments or playacting. His arms tightened. "I'm sorry you witnessed that. I didn't know they were together or else I would have kept you away."

"You knew about them?" I was in hell. Life was misery. I pushed away and glared at him. "You knew there was some crazy jacked-up stuff going on and didn't tell me?"

"No. I knew Nash wanted you. He never stops looking at you when you're around. I didn't know that Ginger realized, but I should have. Women like that always seem to know. Did they see you?"

I shook my head. "I think Ginger realized somebody was there, but there was no way she could know who it was. I'm going to act like I have no idea what she's talking about if she makes any of her snide comments, fishing for confirmation."

Mason nodded gravely. "Good idea. You can't let her think she's the one in control. It'll puff up her ego and we can't afford for her to get even braver than she already is."

He was right. "Yeah."

The problem was, I didn't know the first thing about how to fight a woman like Ginger. While she manipulated every weakness she could, I was struggling because I wanted to protect those society considered weak. My brain had never worked that way, never looked for ways to directly attack another person outside of the self-defense fighting techniques I practiced regularly.

She took, and hurt, and used every flaw, every blind spot or obsession as a tool to control the people around her. Ginger was so good at it, people loved her for it. Did everything they could think up to please her in return.

Will and Logan were bending over backward to do what they thought would please her. As if anybody ever could. A person like Ginger was never happy. And maybe that was why they kept trying to achieve the impossible. She knew how to get them to do her bidding.

But not me. I wasted all my time trying to protect myself, or help others when I could. That left me with no examples in my past to help me understand what to do now.

At the moment, I had no idea how I was going to get up and face the day with my heart so damned broken. I thought I had protected myself, but here I was. The relationship I thought was so important, so good and nurturing, was nothing but a sham. And a complete wreck.

Mason studied me critically before speaking. "You did good with your eyes. They aren't puffy and you look well rested. Now, get up and get out there for breakfast or else it'll look like you're hiding. At least to her mind. She's going to be looking for any sign and frankly, I don't think you're going to hold up against her."

"Gee, thanks for the vote of confidence."

"Bailey, you just lost the one father figure you ever had. You're fragile, even if you don't want to admit it. But you need to keep it together until you have a chance to get Nash back on your side. You're going to have to give him something, Bailey, something that will make him think you're worth being loyal to. Make him want to help and protect you even if you don't call him daddy."

The interactions of men and women, as seen by

Mason Bain. Everything a transaction, give and take and manipulate. No. Not Mason. Ginger.

But Mason knew how she was, and he was on my side. I couldn't afford to lose my faith in him. It wasn't right that I was projecting my thoughts about her onto him.

"So, what do I do, Mason?" I asked bitterly. He was trying to help, but everything about this situation sickened me. "Should I play the bad girl, just like Ginger? Do my part, if any of them even want me anymore?"

The thought of doing anything with my teammates, which had always made me uncomfortable, now made me feel sick. Every part of me rejected the idea and brought the nausea back. And the thought of a man I cared about like Mason suggesting I do so? Every fiber of my being rebelled.

"No, Bailey. I would never ask you to do something you didn't want." He slid his arms around me and held on. I didn't deserve such kindness and understanding. "You need to remind him that you're the good girl, because that's the only one he can respect. Now come on, it's time to eat."

CHAPTER TWENTY
A Different Enemy

IT TOOK ME TEN minutes to gather myself together to face
Ginger and Nash. But as we prepared to join the others,
a drum started beating an alarm sequence. Mason and I
grabbed up our weapons and ran out of the tent.

Frantic thoughts raced through my mind. I didn't want
anyone to get hurt. Or anything bad to happen to anyone.
But I was glad we all had something to do, and I could
avoid seeing Ginger and Nash interacting over breakfast as
if nothing happened between them.

I wasn't proud of it. But that was how I felt.

It was still pre-dawn, and in that perpetual cloud cover,
the sun wasn't even close to breaking through the darkness.
We all ate before sunrise anyway, and it was probably the
most lax time of day. Whoever was attacking, they knew us
better than the pathetic peasants rebelling all along the trail
and getting slaughtered.

Our team met up at our campfire and then we headed
west to our assigned post, previously agreed upon with

Javilin. His burns were still bothering him, but from what I had seen during practice drills, it wasn't slowing him down. His soldiers were still a solid fighting force. The noises of battle came from the northwest, so it was likely our team was going to see some action.

What if I failed in my duties? I couldn't stop the barrage of memories and guilt over how hard it had been for me to stand against the peasants - and my failure to do so. Was it going to be like that with a genuine threat?

But no. It couldn't be. I had to prove to Nash I could pull my weight, and I wasn't the person Ginger was trying to make me out to be. I needed that damned money if I was ever going to get away from people like her.

From people like Nash.

I readied an arrow and kept my eyes peeled. Soon enough, a band of men came at us out of the darkness. That they had made it that far set off alarm bells in my head. The fact they were dressed in battle leather and had weapons instead of farming tools took care of the rest of my misgivings, though, and I let the arrow fly.

Got him in the neck. Nash was positioned far enough behind me that he could observe my actions. A wave of approval came from his direction - Blackstone's gift telling me that I was back in his good graces.

At least, until Ginger got a hold of him again. But I would keep performing to the highest of standards and do everything that was expected of me. That should cover me for a while.

Now all I needed to do was get to him first whenever an opportunity arose for Ginger to play her games and manipulate his perception. Or maybe I could figure out a way to get to her first, and divert her. I snorted. Doubtful, but the thought remained.

I continued to shoot arrows at regular intervals and even took down several more of our enemy. Apparently, Blackstone's fiddling with my mind didn't apply to soldiers. I felt no qualms as I mowed them down.

Ginger took out a few herself. She and I both used distance weapons. Abilene, our strategist until her death, used a sword, and she was better at it than any of the men on the team. I missed her in that moment more than ever before. She and I had never gotten along, but that woman was a true artist with a blade.

Our team won the battle in our part of the camp, and soon after the sounds of fighting died everywhere else. We checked in with Javilin. I was pleased to see Ro was there, and that his people made it through without injury or getting in the way.

One local reported to Javilin that the Outsiders had stayed where they were told and the enemy soldiers skipped right over them. There was something honorable about that, but I pushed that thought aside. Our enemy could be honorable, but that didn't mean they weren't still our enemy.

Several local soldiers were hurt, and a few had even died. A grim sign that we were against a more seasoned and skilled set of enemies. They were definitely trained, although they dragged their dead away during the retreat, so Javilin couldn't identify them.

All the uniforms held the insignia of their lord in the

leather straps that crisscrossed their chests, both for Tellar's men and our enemy. By dragging their injured and dead away, they kept us from observing valuable intelligence. Like who to be on the lookout for in the coming days.

"Good job, Bailey," Nash said as we left Javilin's command tent. It felt like an apology. Ginger was standing behind him a few feet away, and she looked furious. I didn't smile, but I wanted to. It was a victory against her jealousy and hate, and I would take what I could get.

"No problem, my liege," I said, giving him a flamboyant bow. His eyes crinkled with amusement the way they normally did when we interacted. Not wanting to ruin the progress I had made, I grinned back and then practically ran over to my tent to drop off my weapons and clean myself up.

I did it. I had looked into Nash's face without hesitation. Even though the entire time, all I could see was the image of him hovering over Ginger, calling her by my name.

But Ginger was watching. And despite how awful her presence made me feel, I mustered up enough strength to act like nothing ever happened. She would never guess I saw them together, or how I felt about it.

As long as I kept my emotions in check and hid my reactions, they would never know. It was difficult enough to do that I felt some pride in being able to pull off that brief confrontation.

I'd have to try with her one more time. Maybe use Blackstone's gifts again. Figure out how to convince her to hold off and then never see each other again once we got back to Earth Prime. Anything to get through these last days and be rid of her forever.

Ultimately, it came down to survival. And I simply couldn't let her win.

"Ginger," I called. She kept walking like she didn't hear me, but I knew she did. And she knew I knew - but didn't care.

Her actions, her body language, all made it clear. There was no way she was going to give me the time of day, no matter what. She hated me, and it wasn't going to change.

I quickened my pace and caught up to her at the edge of the creek we had been using to clean and repair our weapons. The sun had gone down after a long day of fighting and cleanup, and they built up the fires so we could see. Fortunately, nobody else was around.

Ginger threw down the arrows she was carrying and spun around to glare at me. "What the hell do you want, Bailey? I'm busy."

"Look, I need to talk to you. I know we don't see eye to eye on a lot of things, but we're going home soon, and I want it to be as pleasant as possible. There's no reason to fight anymore, not when we're all richer than we've ever imagined."

Ginger snorted. "Get bent, Bailey. You want to get together and braid each other's hair or something? We can become best friends and go out to bars and pick up a soldier or two? Oh, wait, that's right, you're damaged. You can't function like a normal woman. You've always left all the work up to me and now, after all this time, you want to be friends? What the hell?"

There was no way I would ever change her mind about

those things. My argument against them evaporated, and my hopes went with it.

Then I remembered I could try using my new brain. Reaching out with all the power I suspected was inside of me, I threw my hope and forgiveness at her. As if I was trying to transfer it over to her. Like I was trying to shove sunlight into a bag. Impossible - but maybe not, with the help of Blackstone.

"I'll do my part," I promised. "I swear. I want to make it out of here, and I need the Outsiders to help me. And I need my team to back me. Don't you want to go home now? I don't want to wait here a year or more, and then hope we get there. Let's work together. I'll take on some of your work. I'll watch your duty stations. Whatever. I know I owe you and I'm willing to do what it takes to show you I'm sorry."

"You're scared," she said. And she wasn't wrong. Maybe some of that leaked through the emotions I was trying to make her feel. Or maybe it was just that obvious.

"I know."

"Yeah, you're scared you've already lost. And you have." Whatever I had been trying to push into her failed to withstand the rush of superiority and triumph. "Forget it, Bailey. None of your promises are going to get you anywhere with me. I won. You hear that? I won! And I know it was you the other day when I was with Nash, you pervert. You were there. You know I won."

After what I saw, I wasn't so sure I was the one with a problem. But that kind of thought wasn't going to help me. Instead, I stepped forward, reaching for her. But the firelight cast deep shadows, and I didn't see a few of her arrows had rolled a little down the slope, too. I stepped on two of them and they broke.

"Oh, crap. I'm sorry," I said.

That really didn't matter. Ginger exploded.

"What the hell is wrong with you? Now you're breaking my weapons and coming over here pretending to want to be friends and you just don't get it - I won. You think I'm an idiot? I know what you're doing. You think I'm going to be grateful to you and lay off. Be friends just because we're rich. Well, too bad, Bailey. Your stupid little games aren't going to work on me."

It looked like she wanted to punch me, but instead, she ran off into the darkness outside of the circle of campfires. The glimmer of an emotion, out there somewhere in the gloom, came to me. A thought, an emotion, a motive. It filtered through my frantic pleas and suddenly I realized that the soldiers, our enemy, were still out there, waiting for their next chance.

"No! Ginger, stop. Please." I called to her, screamed her name, trying to stop her. But she kept running. The sounds of her departure disappeared quickly.

I had to stop her. It was too dangerous, and I was the reason she was so pissed off that she didn't follow procedure. And with the way she made my teammates feel about me, what would happen if they found out I was the reason she ran off?

The trees obscured my view, and the echoes from her pounding feet had already faded. I couldn't tell where she was, and I wasn't sure where I should go. But I ran for a while anyway, until I was out of breath.

As a precaution, I stayed away from the area where those feelings had come from, knowing there was a warning there for me as well. It was where the enemy was waiting, patient and watchful.

It was hard to know how to handle her, but it was my duty and I knew it. So, I kept looking.

My heart thundered in my ears, pounding against my skull like a refrain, *stop her, stop her, stop her*. Didn't Ginger know that our new enemies had to be somewhere out there, close and waiting to spring on anyone who came too close?

Why couldn't she just listen to me? I already knew she would never lay off, no matter what I did. And all I wanted was a truce, to lay off long enough for me to get us all out of the worst Mention to navigate that I'd ever seen.

I slowed to a walk and strained my ears, trying to hear her. The snap of a stick, the shift of rocks down a slope. As if I conjured it, I did hear a snapping sound, but it was so much louder than I had imagined. The crashing of rocks boomed louder than I expected, too.

The screaming was so close and horrifying. I froze. My body shuddered violently as my scalp prickled, imagining what must be happening.

Graphic images and thoughts bombarded me. They were trained soldiers. We killed several of their men, and they were likely burying them. But they would have left traps. Done something to protect themselves.

I was shaking, trying to push the images out of my head, uncertain if it was my imagination or if I was picking up on the thoughts of the men Ginger ran into. I felt so bad for her while a jumble of pictures came into my head, horrifying images of her body broken under a cache of large boulders, dark smears of blood on her body and the forest floor.

My heart settled down, but the shaking continued. It was in shock, a wave of freezing cold settling into my bones. Hot tears poured down my face, regretting Ginger's last moments, regretting my role in them. Feeling sad and scared and angry and there, right there in the deepest part of me, relief.

I truly was a monster.

CHAPTER TWENTY-ONE
Ro's Invitation

I THINK THE WORST part was trying to wrangle all of my emotions together without going insane. My head was no longer mine alone and apparently, neither was my heart. Or my sense of right and wrong.

Ginger dying was tragic.

Right.

But. It also helped me out. And recognizing that fact?

Wrong.

Right?

My thoughts kept going back and forth, shaming me. I knew that I had to look out for myself because nobody else would. That was actually one of the tenets of the Corps. So why did I feel so bad for being so glad I didn't have to deal with Ginger and her games on top of trying to figure out how to get everyone off planet?

Twenty-four hours later, and I was still trying to work through it. I kept away from the rest of the team except Mason, who knew how she treated me but didn't pressure me to figure out how I should be feeling. Nash had taken the guys to search for her body, excusing me from helping so I could work out our return trip.

I kicked a rock from my path, sending it skittering down the slope until it landed in the water. I impressed myself with my aim, considering we were almost back at Tellar's castle and we were once again surrounded by trees and thick underbrush, obstacles that blocked a clear and easy pathway to the stream.

Then I kicked another rock, mad at myself for thinking about something so frivolous when I was supposed to be doing a little soul-searching. It landed almost on top of where the other rock went into the water. It was like fate was torturing me.

"Madam? May I speak with you?"

I turned and saw Ro standing off to the side. If he had a hat, he would likely have it in hand, a picture of humility and hesitancy.

"Sure. You don't need to ask my permission or anything. Come on over." I walked up the slope and he met me halfway.

"You seemed conflicted. Blackstone used to focus the same way, and we left him to work it out on his own by his request. We tried not to interrupt."

That was good to know. Maybe Blackstone wasn't on one side, with me on the other. Maybe we were both struggling in the middle. "That's sweet of you, but I really could use a break from my thoughts."

"I'm sorry about your friend," Ro said. He looked genuinely upset, even though I knew full well Ginger treated him and the others as if they were scum.

At the moment, I realized that I was never going to have the higher thoughts I admired in others or feel the way I should. I wasn't an angel, but I was beginning to think that Ro was.

"Thank you. It's hard to lose a teammate like that. I feel guilty that she stormed off during an argument and ended up running straight into a trap."

There was something about Ro that made me want to pour out all my secrets in hopes that he could help me. It wasn't right to burden somebody else, but it was almost like he was pulling information from me the way Blackstone did back when Rader held me captive.

We were at the edge of camp, still visible to the others but in the tree's shade, away from the clearing. "I can see his memories, you know," I said. I threw it out there just like that, like I was telling Ro for the fiftieth time that I hated how overcast the sky was, or that mud often sticks to the bottom of my shoes when I step in puddles.

Ro nodded. He was such a placid man. It was soothing. And maybe a tad annoying. I didn't know what I wanted. Maybe for him to condemn me the way I felt I should.

"That is one of the abilities the ceremony imbues into our Magus class."

"So, you're telling me you guys are magicians?" I gaped at Ro, blinking and wondering what happened to my normal life.

"Of course not," he laughed. "But it seems like magic at times. No, the mind is a powerful tool, and many of our people have the ability to use it. For centuries, it was a dangerous and often deadly expansion and we almost stopped doing it entirely. Some of our scientist noted that the success rate was higher for some families than others, so they were the ones we concentrated on."

It was more than I had ever heard him say before. Maybe it was because he trusted me now. Or it could be he enjoyed sharing the history of his people even if he was born elsewhere and didn't know it firsthand.

"Do you have many in the Magus class?" I asked. It was because I wanted to know, although the Corps would want that information included in my report. Not like I'd add that. I was going to talk about the Outsiders as little as possible.

"Anyone could try, but unless they had the correct connections in their synapses, they failed. It is an elite class. We have families who have abilities that work better than others, and some can't do any of it at all." Ro held out his hand to graciously help me over a loose mound of rocks blocking our path as we entered deeper into the forest.

"You are the children of the people who could use those powers, but you don't have them yourselves." Why did I bring that up? I wasn't trying to hurt him.

"The Blackstone family is our most powerful, but none of us descends from his clan. They can utilize their brains to engage every one of the Magus abilities. I'm not sure the rest of us even know everything they can do, but I know enough that I can help you if you want."

I stopped and turned to search his face. Then I reached out with my mind, much like I had when I set up his ability to understand my language in a way I still didn't understand, and he was like an open book. He really meant his offer.

"You would do that? Help me figure this out?"

He wanted to get home, but I realized he meant to help me further, for no benefit to himself, with no expectation of a return. That was something I wasn't used to. Not at all.

"Yes, I will be happy to. I will also confer with the others and see if they also know anything that can help, and we can discuss this later. Perhaps you would like to join our camp for dinner tonight? I came to invite you anyway, but now I see there is a deeper purpose that we can help fulfill."

"Thank you. I would love to join you. Would you like me to bring anything?" Something inside of me remembered what was expected of me. For years my old nanny had stayed with me, I think paid for by my sister or her husband. She had instilled in me all the rules and duties of the elite, despite living in the slums - and nothing my sister ever did indicated that she would relocate me.

My nanny fulfilled her duty without kindness or mercy. Still, I was grateful. I knew what happened to little girls who didn't have anyone to look out for them at all.

"No, this is our way of thanking you for your attempt to take us to our home."

"Well, it will be my pleasure. I'll come by just after sundown."

"We'll be looking forward to it."

Ro turned and headed off, but I called to him to stop. There was something I had been wondering for a while. "What do you call yourselves?" I asked. "Tellar's people call you the Outsiders, but what name do you have for your race? For the people from your planet?"

"Humans, of course," he answered, and then left.

Although the two of us were conversing, we were speaking different languages. I could project my meaning to him, and easily heard the meaning in what he said, without any effort or headache.

When he had answered me, I consciously tried to hear the actual words he was saying rather than the translation, and even though I knew the word sounded different in his language, that was what I got from it.

Human. Figures. They were still a part of the Multiverse of earth carbon copies. Despite the differences we've all seen in the vids or out in the Mentions, we all still bled the same shade of red.

The methods used by the Corps made certain we saw plenty of blood, so I knew that for a fact.

They really knew how to make a girl feel welcome. Every one of the Outsiders made a special dish. They were fabulous, but I only ate one bite of each and even then I thought I'd eventually explode.

There was this one dessert that almost made me cry because I couldn't eat any more of it than the tiny amount I managed at the end. I didn't have any baggies to sneak some back to my tent, either.

"I've spoken with my people, and came up with as much information as we could to help you," Ro said. "I've asked Res to come and visit with you. She has the best memory and can tell you our history."

"Well, that sounds like a good start." I leaned back and tried to breathe around my engorged stomach. Ro soon introduced me to a lovely woman several decades older than I, though my Blackstone memories still saw her as a toddler.

"I'm honored to meet you," Res said as she greeted me.

"No, the honor is all mine. Come and sit by me and you can tell me all the things I need to know."

Res moved to sit beside me. She looked at Ro, who nodded encouragingly. "It was a thousand years ago, during our people's renaissance, that we learned about the power words," Res said. I shifted where I sat on the fallen log so I could see her better. "Men were seeking a way to create precious metals from base, inexpensive materials."

Ah, the old "turning lead into gold" search. Humans have always wanted to strike it rich.

"And they chose to use words?" I asked. I couldn't figure out how anyone could possibly think that would help them. In my experience, words usually caused harm.

"No, it was an accident of fate. One of the alchemists had a daughter who enjoyed singing. She had a broad range, and could go low as well as high. She was working on a new piece of music and wandering around her father's shop when the discovery was made. Her voice channeled his equipment, and he made the discovery."

I knew I shouldn't let it annoy me, but it made me angry that the father, rather than the daughter, was credited with the discovery even though everyone knew she was the one who was singing. That was so typical. "What happened? Did lead turn into gold?"

Res laughed. Ro and a few of the others sitting nearby looked amused. It was not in a cruel way, and I took no offense.

"No, of course not. There is no point in turning lead into gold. It takes too much effort and costs too much to make it worthwhile. No, the first burst of directed power blew a hole in the wall. It took many experiments and a lot of effort and thought from our elders before they finally realized it was the mind that controlled the power, and not the voice."

"Why did Blackstone's implant extend down his arm and around his hand? I mean, if it was the voice, wouldn't he have needed his implant in his throat?"

"Her voice was just a tool. Her father led the studies on how to expand the mind, how to utilize its gifts. They founded the first of the Magus families. Their name was Blackstone."

I nodded. I actually recognized the story once Res began speaking. It was like I was being reminded about a childhood story I was told at my mother's knee. Except I never knew my mother. And the woman who came to mind was nobody related to me. It was all Blackstone's memories.

Maybe they could help me with some practical things. "Do you think you could help me direct the power, even though none of you have gone through the ceremony? I know this planet has messed with your lives, and I'm sorry for it. But can you help me stop these moments where Blackstone's memories overtake mine?"

Ro nodded affirmative, and Res continued. "The Outsiders represent all the Magus families. When we first came to this planet, they thought we would have the best chance if we had access to every gift and power our people possessed." She sighed in unison with me. I couldn't help it.

What a life. Trapped in a place that stopped them from ever getting home, even the ones with the implants and training. "I appreciate your help. I know this has to be hard for you."

"We are honored to help. I'll get my friend Peto to see you now. He is the one from the family Barrus. They are the ones who had the best control over memory and telepathy."

Res left to get her Outsider friend. I had a flash in my mind's eye, and I recognized him when he arrived.

It was Peto, along with Res and Ro, that spent the next several hours with me, teaching me how to control the power in my mind. At least, the one power that kept taking over, so I had memories that sucked me in so exclusively, they may as well have been blackouts.

That was downright dangerous. What if that happened during a battle with the newer, stronger enemy that had already killed several of our own group, both the locals and Ginger? Or in the middle of a jump through the Gateway? That would be such a disaster. Deadly, even.

I was exhausted and sweating by the time we were done working through their mental exercises. But it was worth it to learn how to build a wall inside my mind. Or I guess it was more like a faucet, which I could turn on and off, but also allow greater or lessor flows of information and memory.

It was control. For the first time since Blackstone had filled my mind with too much of everything, I could choose what I would see. And how much of it.

When I got back to the tent that night, I slept like a rock. I even missed spending time with Mason, who came, slept, and then left before I woke. I was no longer on rotation - Nash always ended the trips by assigning me to focus on our ticket out of the Mention. So Mason let me sleep.

CHAPTER TWENTY-TWO
The Plan

"NASH WANTS US TO meet this morning," Tyler said. He was never around anymore, and I was beginning to miss him. I was glad for the private time with Mason, but I never saw Tyler during the day, either, and as much as I liked the Outsiders, they didn't know me.

Not that Tyler really knew me, either. But we came from the same place, and when we were out in the Mentions, sometimes that was all we really needed.

"Let me grab my pack and I'll walk with you," I suggested. Tyler waited for me to grab the pouch I kept on my belt, my compass, and my knives. I carried them everywhere with me, especially since I wanted to input any of the bits and pieces of calculations that came to me.

"What's up with Mason?" Tyler asked. He had a twinkle in his eye. I could feel curiosity and something else, something that felt sunny and clear and hopeful. I think he was happy for me, but Tyler was focused on his own situation and it made everything else seem better.

"Seems to be going well. He's kind of possessive."

Tyler laughed. "I noticed. But I think that's a good thing. It keeps the rest of the guys away. You're a throwback, Bailey. I know people look down on that, but it's okay. I would be a throwback, too."

I thought that over while we walked around the edge of camp towards one of the border fires our team used as the center of our patrols. It was located a ways back from our home camp, which was in the middle of the troops near where Javilin pitched his tent.

"I guess. I've always been told it's wrong to be selfish."

"It is. But is it really selfish to be selective? None of the guys are required to service their teammates. Nobody expects us to be up for anything at any time. Yeah, maybe it's old-fashioned to be selective, but is that really a bad thing?"

I was shocked. I always felt like there was something wrong with what they expected of us, but most women didn't care. Being available to our teammates promoted loyalty and was a part of the duties expected by the Corps. If I didn't take part, technically I could be written up for dereliction of duty.

But that didn't make it right. Apparently, I wasn't the only one who thought that way.

"Maybe not. And as uncomfortable as it is, I'm glad things are the way they are so I don't have to deal with Will and Logan."

They were still giving me nasty looks. Ginger's games had worked on them, and since I wasn't willing to be used by either of them, there wasn't anything I could do to counteract her poison.

It was a good thing we all struck it rich or else I would have to start over and find a new team. A team that might expect me to participate fully because there was no Nash to protect me.

Oh. Nash probably allowed me to avoid the physical aspects of my duties because he wanted me for himself. In a strange and perverted way, he helped protect me. I shivered.

"Come on, you two," Nash bellowed. "Light a fire under it and get your butts over here. We've got some planning to do."

Everyone else was there, so we trotted the remaining distance. Mason called out a greeting. Logan and Nash nodded my way, but curtly. Will didn't even look at me. He acted like I wasn't even there. That was fine by me.

"We've got a new duty roster," Nash announced. "The rebels are out there and a few camp followers have heard some of their plans. They're planning an attack in a few days, and it's the real soldiers this time. Now, I don't know about you, but now that I've struck it rich, I don't want to lose any more of our teammates. I want out, and fast, with the rest of us intact."

That was when every eye turned towards me. I knew what they were thinking.

"I can get us out of here," I promised. "But I have to wait two days before there will be enough pressure to use the force of the tectonic shift to boost the power I need to get my compass to work. Then I can show you the location for the portal."

Nash unrolled his copy of the map Javilin gave him. It had the filthy tech metal marked in four different places, and we were told each held more of the metal than the mine we saw on our tour of Tellar's territory. That mine alone was enough incentive for us to get home safely as quick as possible.

We already had our treaty with Tellar and the Corps would send in the countless hoards from the slums to work the mines. They had officers and scientists to run operations all over the planet. Eventually, this Mention would be just another Corps business.

I didn't even bother to think that over. It was going to happen, and I had agreed to it. Nothing Tellar had done made me feel bad for him. And the peasants probably would be better off.

Nash handed me the map, and I projected the picture I had in my mind over the top of the landmarks mapped out, studying it closely. Then I groaned.

"Damned if that isn't a little too close to the enemy camps. We'll have to go in quietly and with some back-up." I sighed.

Nash swore ferociously. "Bailey, you know we can't tell the soldiers when we're leaving. Tyler's already on lock-down." That meant if Tyler told Javilin anything, he'd lose his portion.

"I know that, boss man, but I need to be in the right location for this to work. It has to do with rock density, gravity, and lithostatic pressure. There isn't enough time for me to teach you what you need to know in order for you to understand what I'm saying."

I spoke with confidence because I knew I was right, but I also knew my attitude was often seen as ego or a superiority complex. If they had any idea about who I really was, they would know I never thought I was better than they were. They could have memorized the same information I did. Eventually. No, I knew full well how little I was worth.

"Tell me what you need," Nash said. He always cut to the chase.

"I need all of you ready to go before sunrise two days from now. It'll take a couple of hours to hike where we're going. We also need backup. The Outsiders use portals, too, but they use a different method. I've been talking to their leader a lot over the last few weeks. If I can get them to agree to come with us, I can use their method of materializing the gateway to enhance ours. I need the extra boost to get out."

"What's in it for them?" he asked suspiciously. Rightfully so, even though that part was a complete fabrication. I didn't need the Outsiders at all.

"If we can get Javilin to agree to let them go with a marker from Tellar saying they can live on their lands, they'll do it. That's the only thing that motivates them." It was a lie, but one that would make sense to them.

"I don't know Bailey, that's a lot of non-combatants to take care of, and we're going to be right up on the enemy in that location."

"It can't be helped. Besides, the Outsiders can protect themselves if attacked. They'll be fine. And if not, it's on them."

Nash nodded. That was also something he understood.

"You get them to agree, I'll push for the marker. I can figure out an excuse as to why we want them to have it."

The other guys nodded curtly. There was something in Tyler's stance that told me something was up, but I would talk to him later.

"All right then, now that we mapped our escape route out, let's take a look at our new duty roster," Nash said. I pushed aside my conflicting emotions to concentrate on what he was saying. It was important. It also helped me push aside the thought that lying was the very last thing a person should do on a team run by Nash.

CHAPTER TWENTY-THREE
Important Lies

"I KNOW WHERE WE need to go to get out of here," I informed Ro.

His dusty blond hair was sticking up in back, making him look younger than he was. I think. I wasn't actually sure how old he was. Probably older than I thought, since most of my feelings about him and the Outsiders were based on Blackstone's memories. That meant I saw them as children to be protected. Children who had been robbed of their legacy.

Children who I wanted to save beyond all reason. In the end, I didn't think it was just Blackstone's memories doing that to me. There was the part of me who wanted to save those babies so long ago that was screaming to finally, finally be on time to rescue them.

And something else, something new. Like my connection to other people was different, deeper, and I understood them better. The Outsiders were good, solid, peaceful. It wasn't something they did. It was who they were. And I wanted to keep that kind of person safe.

"Is there anything you need from us?" he asked. It was like he read my mind. He may have, except I knew the Mention kept him and his brethren from receiving the mind-expanding actualization that people like Blackstone went through to unlock the power in their minds. The same as what he used on my mind.

Maybe I was broadcasting. I had only begun to understand what my brain was capable of and how to use it. "I need to get to a certain location where the tectonic pressures have built up enough energy that I can tap into it and use it to launch us beyond the fields keeping me from seeing through my compass."

Ro studied me, his eyes narrowed, lip twisted as he thought. It made me grin when he said, "I have no idea what you're talking about. But I believe you. How can we help you get there?"

"I need you to play along with me. I'm going to make sure my team knows we have to take you to the location with us. They must believe that your help is vital to our success. That we need you to get out of here. But I'm afraid they won't believe the story if I'm the only one telling it. I need you to lie, Ro, to get us all home. And I hate to ask something like that but it's the sad reality. I need you to lie."

Outsiders objected to telling lies, but it seemed Blackstone personally had no issues with it. As long as it was for the greater good. There were memories and emotions that proved it.

I had spent weeks mediating and playing through

various scenes of his life. They were a practical people, and I had a good enough argument to convince Blackstone. But would it be enough for Ro? There were nuances to the Other's mentality I didn't yet comprehend, and I wasn't sure yet if Ro had the same philosophical bent as his deceased leader.

"I will do what you need," he agreed, immediately relieving my anxiety about what I was asking him to do. "I know Blackstone has given to you in a way he could not give to us. There are times when we speak I see him looking at me through your eyes. I am still loyal to him, and now to you. Tell me what I need to say and it will be done."

For a moment, I couldn't speak - it was such a quick response and had thrown me off. I patted his arm to express my thanks.

It made me uncomfortable to think that somebody could see that I wasn't myself anymore. That there was somebody else there with me, a person who had taken an important place in my decisions and actions.

I didn't want Nash or my team to know, or else they'd never trust me again. And I needed their trust to get us all out of here. "Make sure everyone is ready to go by tomorrow," I said, regaining control over my voice. "The spot isn't too far from here but we're running out of time."

My compass told me a lot of things. The tech used to make it was still beyond our understanding, although we were able to use most of it. I spent a lot of time exploring different areas in the device, the extra functions we were never taught and the headings. Pushing buttons I probably shouldn't, in order to see what I could discover.

One of those things buried in the device was a map of the planet I was standing on. Whichever one I was standing on, earth-copies included. There was a setting with the telltale concentric circles that showed tectonic pressure. I was pretty sure I could predict earthquakes with the thing.

But all that energy, the pent up pressure of a planet - that was power. Deep and mighty, and it should push my compass over whatever obstacle had been strangling its abilities. To a place where it could open a gateway portal through a Mention that had turned into a trap when we first arrived.

The Corps would come back to this place no matter what. There was too much filthy tech metal to ignore. Better minds than mine would figure out a stable gateway, and then they could exploit this planet the way they always did.

But once I was out, I was out. They wouldn't be getting any help from me. I was beyond ignoring the harm the Corps did. Just because it was always that way they've done things didn't mean it always had to stay that way.

Not if I could help it. And thanks to my memory of a note handed to me by a well-meaning man back at the Corps headquarters, I not only figured out a way to get off planet but also how to get back to Earth Prime while skipping. And his warning gave me guidance on how to avoid ending up locked away for being able to do it.

I spent a little more time with Ro and Res, and then I headed out. I needed enough sleep to have a clear mind. Success or failure, whatever way it went down, it was going to happen in only two more days.

"Can I talk to you?" Tyler asked.

I looked up from my knives, the main ones and the one I always kept hidden beneath a bandage on my leg. I was sharpening them, honing their edges. We were about to face the enemy, or at least get really close to their position. There was likely going to be a skirmish, or worse. I needed them as backup for my arrows.

"Sure," I said, laying my things aside. Tyler looked nervous. He was chewing his bottom lip, but the emotion I got from him was actually as close to joy as I had ever felt. How many times have I misread people?

Tyler looked around. I followed his line of sight, but I didn't see anyone nearby.

"Look, I know I'm on lock down and I'm not going to say anything to Javilin or anyone else. I know how this works and I'm okay with it. But I can't leave." Tyler's hands were shaking, but I could sense it was excitement, not fear. "I wanted to tell you because I won't be coming back with you, and I know you calculate how long the portal lasts. I already spoke with Nash and he's agreed to file my claim for me."

Members of the teams who strike it rich fulfill their contract with the Corps. Immediately. Once they discover the riches, their obligation was complete. Only the leader and the navigator had duties they were required to perform after that point, although we all kept watch and continued to keep each other safe or else how would any of us make it back?

But even without having to wait until after the Mention

claims are filed and the earth-copy surveyed, team members can choose to step off. They didn't have to report back. The leader would file the claims, and the Corps would wire the money into the accounts we had set up when we first signed on with the hopes they would someday overflow with money.

Claims were a part of the leader's remaining obligation, if asked by their team. People occasionally stayed behind, but that usually occurred on nicer, more advanced planets. And only if the leader was trustworthy. It was pretty rare, though. But Nash wouldn't screw over a productive member of the team.

Good for Tyler, although I wished he was telling me because that meant we weren't likely to ever see each other again. And that he wanted to say goodbye. Because he would miss me.

But it was really just about logistics. I was reminded once again that my barriers and habits kept even those I considered my friends separated from me. It hadn't even occurred to him that I'd miss him.

Or to care how I felt about it at all. We were teammates and allies, but not friends. And I had done that to myself.

"Sure, no problem, Tyler. I'm happy you found a place you want to stay. It's been an honor and a privilege to work with you."

Tyler paused. He had been digging little holes in the dirt with a stick he had found. "Thanks, Bailey. I feel the same way." To my relief, I could tell he actually meant that. He shook my hand, and then Tyler glanced around once more. "I heard you're taking the Outsiders with you. Are you sure that's wise?"

"Yeah, it's fine. They can defend themselves, you know. They don't believe in attacking or even fighting back if they think the situation calls for some kind of sacrifice, but I needed them to get the gateway open. I told them I'd open a portal for them to get home in exchange for their help."

"Can you really do that?" he asked. It showed how little he knew me that he would even ask me that question. I might be a liar, but only when it was in everyone's best interests. And leaving the Outsiders behind was in nobody's best interests. Besides, I was the best navigator in the Corps. I could do it. Now that I knew how.

"Yes, of course I can." I tried not to sound insulted, but I heard the sour note and Tyler gave a little huff, amused by my reaction.

"Oh yeah? What about the team, then?" he asked. I knew he was suspicious because I was foolish enough to try to confide in him before. "Are you going to get them home, too?"

I was glad he phrased his question that way, because that meant I could answer without lying. He wanted to know if I was thinking of skipping, but he didn't actually say that.

"Definitely," I assured him. "Getting them to Earth Prime is my first priority."

And it was. It just wasn't going to be our first stop. I didn't care anymore what people thought about skipping. It was based on fear, and navigators not understanding how things worked. I had always had a better understanding than any other navigator I had ever met. But once my mind was expanded by Blackstone, it turned out to be a cakewalk. I knew exactly what to do. And once I put all the pieces together, I knew exactly how to find home.

Tyler eyeballed me for a minute, but finally decided that I told him the truth. I made sure of it by broadcasting trust.

"That's great. All right then," he said. "I'll see you tomorrow. Make sure you get plenty of rest. We don't want you making any stupid mistakes."

"You got it." I gave a snappy salute. Tyler tossed the stick he was still holding into the nearest campfire and headed off.

I wanted to say something memorable, something that told Tyler how happy I was for him. That we really had a friendship. But instead, I watched as he walked away, his joy still leaking from him like little bursts of sunshine.

It was better that I let him go. I couldn't change things at that point, and I wouldn't even if I could. Because to miss me would put a dim spot on the sun of his happiness and he really was my friend. At least from where I stood. So I turned back to my weapons and finished sharpening them.

CHAPTER TWENTY-FOUR
Gateway Jumpers

I HAD EVERYTHING I owned packed and strapped to my body or in the pack slung around my back. We were ready to leave. Loaded down so we could head out in that predawn gloom.

Nash looked my way. I could tell he was about to ask me about the Outsiders, but they showed up at that moment, walking silently and loaded down with their own belongings and weapons. It was an impressive display, over thirty strong men and women of various ages showing up without a sound.

"We're ready when you are," Ro said with a slight smile on his face. Maybe he realized how Nash and the others felt. It was plain to me my teammates were reassessing their initial opinion of the Outsiders. It was probably obvious to Ro as well.

I deferred to Mason and Nash, who were standing together. Mason winked at me, and I let my lips twitch upward in response.

"Are all your people here?" Nash asked. Ro nodded his response. "Then let's go. Javilin has some idea about what's happening, but Tyler will explain the rest after. Let's move before the guard comes around again."

We followed Nash, his arm raising and then dropping forward in the traditional gesture for the start of a journey. For a jump through a portal. My teammates fell into line in the usual order, which meant I walked in front of Will and Logan. I was uncomfortable having them behind my back where I couldn't see them, but at least I could rely on my new hyperactive sixth sense to warn me about any potential attacks.

Not only did my new skills help me stay on guard, the Outsiders were right behind my team. I knew beyond the shadow of a doubt that Ro and Res, and any of the Outsiders within reach, would have my back. Not just because I was their ticket off the planet that had kept them and their parents prisoner, but because for whatever reason, they cared about me. Bailey. Not the vessel carrying Blackstone's memories and abilities and gifts, although they cared about that too.

Without any of that, they still cared about me. Maybe I had failed with my teammates, but the Outsiders were my friends.

I wasn't quite sure what to do with that. It made me nervous, and I worried about them, but something about that kind of support made me feel stronger. Lighter. Capable. I had no experience with true friendship, but it felt wonderful.

It was three hours later when we stopped for breakfast.

We wanted to eat to retain our strength and stamina, and because of the intelligence provided by the camp followers, we knew we were entering enemy territory after only another two hours. Nobody liked fighting on a full stomach. In fact, it often caused problems.

"You have everything under control?" Nash asked.

I studied him before answering. He was around my father's age, and I had always wished he were my dad. Now, I could barely stand to look at him. The image of him and Ginger was burned into my mind and I wasn't able to separate that from what I saw at that moment. A man who wanted to go home, rubbing the scar on his chin like usual, asking me for the truth.

"I do. I know exactly what I'm doing. You'll be sitting pretty in your favorite bar back on Earth Prime in no time. After you file our claims, that is."

Nash let out a small laugh. "Too right. Okay, wrap it up and let's get going. We need to push it if we're going to get there in time."

We picked up the pace for the next couple of hours, and then, as if we crossed a visible border, Mason and a few of the Outsiders fanned out in unison and trotted in front. They were keeping an eye out for traps, like the one they caught Ginger in on the night she died.

Mason had a small metal cylinder he held discreetly, the only tech he brought with him. I didn't think Nash approved it, but I bet he was glad Mason had it. It identified anything not natural. There wasn't a tripwire that could hide from that thing, thankfully. Especially since we had to halt four times in the next twenty minutes to disarm them.

Even though our vanguard fanned out, we kept our group tight. The area we were going to was heavily forested, and it helped our advance team keep our path clear.

It was eerily quiet, our group making only a small whispering sound as our clothes occasionally brushed against branches and foliage. I watched my feet carefully so I wouldn't step on any sticks and break them, or send rocks skittering down the slope that jutted sharply to our right side.

The clearing I had marked on the map was almost dead center on the fault line. That was the best place for such a large crowd to gather around. It took a lot of power to hold a gateway open long enough for seven people to jump through, and that was on a normal jump. If we could call any jump normal. But it was especially true for a jump on a planet that fought us like this Mention did.

"Mason, you and the two lead Outsiders head out and scout near the last known enemy location. I need eyes out at least two clicks. Be on the lookout for any activity. I don't want any uninvited guests coming to the party."

The strange new threesome, Mason, Ro, and Res, took off. Meanwhile, I marked out where the Outsiders should stand, and where my team would go. I explained to Nash that they needed to group together near the portal while the Outsiders remained on the opposite side.

He thought it was because they were staying behind, and of course he would think that. He wouldn't know we skipped until we got to the planet belonging to the Outsiders. Hopefully, he wouldn't kill me until after I opened the portal to Earth Prime, and he knew he could make it home. By that point, I hoped he'd let me live. I had already angered him beyond reason once. He rarely gave second chances.

I pulled out my compass, centered myself, and then pressed my thumb to the screen. Some of the Outsiders gasped when they saw it change. From their point of view, it probably looked like a miniature explosion. But what was left when the burst of light dissipated was bigger and more sturdy than how my compass started out.

"Five minutes, boss," I announced.

At first, it surprised me we didn't feel any rumbling beneath our feet. But then I remembered from our classes that earthquakes hit once the tectonic pressure became too much. It wasn't a slow set of shakes - it was sudden and violent. The still earth meant nothing. The pressure was still there.

I typed equations into my compass, getting ready to key in the sequence that would connect it to the power of the planet itself. I was pretty certain no human had ever used a compass in that fashion.

At least, not an Earth Prime human. The ones we stole the tech from so long ago invented the compass and many of our other stolen tools. They had to know everything their inventions were capable of, unlike us.

But there was something intuitive, almost natural about the compass. Like it could develop right alongside my understanding of the forces it tapped into. That it developed tech by itself as I came up with it. So in the end, I wasn't sure if even the Techs had ever done what I was about to do.

I started humming. There were certain tones, added to how I held my mouth and shifted my tongue. That would help the process. Music was math, and math ruled the Multiverse. The unnamed girl who had discovered the Magus way of using their brains came to mind. She did it by singing, too.

The compass responded. I pressed various buttons in a hurry, and out of the corner of my eye I caught sight of Mason and the Outsiders running back. They reported in to Nash and he looked concerned enough that I could see it from where I stood and didn't even need Blackstone's gifts to do it.

I knew then, in the way a person knows the hurricane was about to land, that inevitably, the rebels would come, here and now. Of course they would. It always came down to timing.

The ground began to shake. It wasn't bad enough that it knocked anyone over, but it was enough to throw us all off balance and a few of the older Outsider women staggered.

I stopped humming and instead formed whole syllables, nonsense words that meant nothing, even to my translation gift. Swirling, ever enlarging, concentric circles on the map indicating the pressure was building. The ground was shaking with fore-shocks, and then we heard a roar coming from the center of the planet. I frantically input the last of my calculation. I needed to channel the energy before the ground split and swallowed us whole.

My body was shaking, the compass was shaking, but it wasn't the ground that was making it happen. Somehow I had become a part of the equation, and I was opening the portal with my entire being as much as I was operating a compass.

But it wasn't working. The portal still wasn't opening. There was still another step, and in that moment, I realized I had no idea what it was.

I had failed. How was that possible? I had checked and rechecked and validated until it felt like somebody had squeezed my brain until all the knowledge in the universe had flowed through.

My head snapped up when I heard Ro yell my name.

"What was his name?" he shouted over the rumbling.

I knew what he meant. It was always there, a part of who I was once Blackstone had changed me, but I had never thought about it consciously. It felt foreign on my tongue, yet as familiar to me as my own name when the words left my lips.

"Kastor Magus," I shouted, trying to lift my voice above the rumbling of a planet that didn't want to let us go. "Blackstone."

At the mention of his name, I realized why it was never used. Kastor was Blackstone's personal name, the precious sense of self that he held onto through all those years. He also used it to focus his power. The word, the tone, the phrase. It focused the power I was trying to channel and unleashed it when I needed it the most.

The ground stopped rumbling and stilled, but a noise like a freight train thundered all around and a burst of light, the excess energy, exploded around the clearing. For the first time in all the times I created a portal gateway, I could see it. My new mental pathways gave me a new way of seeing. It glowed, it ripped, it tore through the dimensions and opened a door.

"Jump!" I screamed. Nash went first. Mason, Ro, and Res stayed where they were, watching the surrounding trees, keeping us safe. I stepped aside, and Will and Logan leaped through. On the way home, I always went last, except for the strategist. Mason stayed a short distance away to protect me, to ensure the gateway remained open long enough without external interruptions.

But it was okay. Mason trusted me. He believed in me. And he was trained to do exactly what I said when I was navigating. So instead of telling him it was time for him to leap, I turned to the Outsiders instead.

I gestured to them, my body shaking, gripping the compass with all my strength, forcing the power through it like a conduit, my brain practically pulsing in my skull. I needed the rest of them to go through and do it quickly. One after another, they leaped into the unknown at my direction. Trusting me, believing in me.

The last few of the Outsiders finally made it through until all that was left were Ro and Res. At my nod, they launched themselves into the portal, into their home world, their duty finally done. I gestured at Mason to let him know it was time.

That was when the rebels broke through the trees into the clearing.

Mason ran straight at me. Not to the gateway where I directed him, but at me. Before I knew what was happening, before I could react, he lifted me off of my feet and threw me at the portal, launching me through the other side.

But the second the compass passed through the gateway, it lost contact with the tectonic power on the planet. With an instantaneous, violent snap like sharp thunder, the portal closed. It disappeared immediately, and my connection to the Mention was gone.

So was Mason.

CHAPTER TWENTY-FIVE
First Contact

I WAS SCREAMING WHEN I landed.

As if I were connected to the portal, the energy a part of my being, I knew the second the gateway slammed shut. The Multiverse healed itself, the dimensions once again divided, leaving us jumpers on one side.

Except I was here, Mason was there, and there was no going back. The convergence of all that power took time, and I had no idea when I could go back for him. My hands shook as my compass reverted to its natural form. I would find a way to get him, though. Of course I would. Even if there were too many enemy soldiers for him to have fought off.

Nash helped me up. He handed me a scrap of fabric and I wiped the tears off of my face. I needed to focus. My work was not yet done. Nash and my teammates had to be sent back to Earth Prime before they realized the meadow we had landed in didn't have a giant dome protecting it.

That the trees along the outskirts weren't hiding a massive city teeming with people.

We weren't home, and I had to make sure they never knew that. To get them out before they strung me up for dooming them to another Mention because they wouldn't believe me when I told them I knew how to get them home even if I had skipped. It had to happen soon, or I would never get Mason back.

"Where are we?" Nash asked. He looked around, trying to get his bearings. We obviously weren't at what we jokingly called the "Welcome Center" back at the Corps Headquarters. But I had prepared for that question.

"I don't know," I replied, keeping my voice even. "Something happened back there and we aren't where I was aiming." That last part was a lie, but it worked as an explanation. We were exactly where I intended us to be.

"Where's Mason?" Logan growled. Will still wouldn't even look at me, much less say anything. He blamed me for Ginger. I was just lucky he restrained himself.

"He engaged the enemy," I replied. Unfortunately, the words caused me to choke up. With a supreme force of will, I pushed through, knowing none of the men on my team cared about how I felt. I didn't need a sixth sense to figure that out, either. "He pushed me through first and it closed the portal."

"Can you get him back?" Nash asked, the look on his face sending an icy bolt of terror down my spine. When did he decide I was the type of person to conveniently strand a teammate? Much less one I had a relationship with? But he looked like he believed I did.

"I need to spend a few days here to figure it out, since this is where the portal opened. There's no way I'd lose a man after all these jumps." To my relief, Nash relaxed just enough to let me know he was hearing me. Ginger hadn't fully turned him. "As soon as I get my bearings, I'll open a gateway and get you to the right place on the planet. Give me a few minutes."

It wasn't unheard of to do a jump from one side of Earth Prime to another. It was unusual for me - I always hit my target. That was one of the reasons why I was the best.

Nash raised his eyebrow at me. I shrugged and busied myself with prepping the compass, opening it back up and checking the settings. He didn't know it, but most of my attention was on the tracking maps. I had shifted the portal to send the Outsiders separately, and I needed to get my team to Earth Prime before they showed up.

The Outsiders would land only a short distance away. Not far enough to be hidden from my team. It was all I could do being tied to one location in the other Mention to use the tectonic pressures. The rest of their jump used something other than "distance," but I didn't know what else to call it when I sent them twenty minutes into the future.

I didn't even really understand how I did it. It just fell into place when I said Blackstone's name, the formulas flooding my mind and guiding my fingers to push the right buttons on my compass. My original plan was to land the Outsiders farther away, where my team couldn't see them. But that was impossible.

But I had to find a way. Bringing earth-copy humans

to Earth Prime was considered treason. Only the Corps could do that, and even they needed permission from the President.

If the Outsiders had landed anywhere near us in time or space, Nash would have carried out the punishment immediately or else he'd have been found guilty of the same crime. The penalty for treason was, as it always had been, death.

Fortunately, my compass was humming and working great. With a few strokes, a portal appeared. It was night on Earth Prime and we could see it clearly in front of us, a dark spot calling to us under the shimmer of the domes.

"I'll follow in a few days," I lied. "I need to get Mason back."

Nash nodded, accepting my explanations. He wouldn't try to argue with me, and he had other duties to attend to. Most important was to file our claims as soon as possible.

We all got a share, even Ginger. Hers would go to her designated heirs. If she didn't have any, it would revert to the Corps. If a dead jumper's share was redistributed to the teammates, some may be tempted to kill off the other members simply to get a larger portion.

Nash was the first to jump through. It was a relief to not have to think up any more lies. They would all leave without argument, knowing the portal wouldn't stay open forever. Logan went next. Will finally turned to look at me before he left.

"Watch your back, Bailey. I won't forget what you did."

His tone, the look on his face - I shivered as he leapt through the gateway. There was no telling what he would do to screw me over before I made it back. But there were more immediate things to think over at the moment. What he had in store for me would have to wait.

I closed the gateway and cleared the settings on my compass. I knew how to open a gateway home from anywhere in the Multiverse, and it was too dangerous to leave them where some local might actually figure out where we come from. Despite the contract being over, I was still honor bound to hide the coordinates.

Then I jogged to another position. I didn't want to be in the way when dozens of Outsiders landed.

It was like they appeared out of thin air. No wonder the humans in the other Mentions sometimes thought we were sorcerers. Even knowing how it worked the way I did, it was still indistinguishable from magic.

One by one they came through until Ro and Res were standing beside me. I purposefully didn't look closely at the portal because I was actually on the other side, shifting the time back twenty minutes, the effort keeping me too preoccupied to do anything to save Mason. What if looking at myself drove me insane or caused a paradox or any of the other things whispered about when the scientists debated time dilations?

But Mason was still there. He was about to be overrun by enemies. What would happen if I leaped back through? To help him? But it was already too late to find out. The gateway was closed before the thought finished crossing my mind.

"Is this it? Are we here? Are we home?" Res asked. She

seemed so excited, a little girl with her first puppy. A fifty-year-old little girl.

"Yes, this is it. You're here. I'm so happy for you," I said. And I was. I set aside my worry for Mason. He could take care of himself. There was a sharp incline on the far side of the clearing and he could make his way towards it, jump off, run. He'd make it because that was what strategists were good at doing. I needed to remember that or else I'd go insane with worry.

I gave Res a hug, and then Ro. He was shaking. "Now what?" he asked.

My focus now fully on the present, I laughed. I didn't know what to say. I racked my brain, fluttering through Blackstone's geographic memories, and I actually recognized the area.

It had been so long ago, but in my youth - no, in Blackstone's youth - he used to spend time here when he wanted to be alone. It was a small clearing tucked away behind the rolling hills where they built their capital city. Buildings designed to fit naturally into their world.

His people were all about harmony. I wasn't sure if my own brain could understand that without help. I still thought the golden glow of the ultraviolet shield in the Vatican was one of the most beautiful things I had ever seen. And they were the most unnatural things imaginable.

"Actually, we're close to the Magus center," I said. "I think we should start there."

They gathered together, an excited but subdued murmur of their conversations washing over me. Satisfaction at the successful implementation of my plan filled me when I realized they were Outsiders no more.

Something - a feeling, a sense, a noise - alerted me to another presence. I stiffened and clutched Ro's arm. "There's somebody coming. Stick together and stay quiet until I find out who it is."

Three men and a woman appeared through the distant trees, then walked slowly to where we were standing. I could sense their wariness at finding such a large group of random strangers gathered near their headquarters.

I stepped forward to meet them after gesturing for the others to remain where they were.

"My name is Bailey," I announced, projecting so they would understand me. "We didn't mean to startle you. I've brought my friends here with me today to return them to their homes. I would like to speak with the head Magus if you please." I used Blackstone's memories to help me ask for the right authority. The Magus clans would understand portal travel better than anyone else.

One man narrowed his dark eyes at me. "I am the current leader. You may address yourself to me."

Wow. How did I even begin? "I come from another world," I said in a rush. "I used a gateway so we could explore a new world and met a man named Blackstone. He said he was also from another planet and his people had been trapped there for many years. He and I couldn't understand each other so he did something to help my mind interpret his words."

They jumped a little when I said Blackstone's name,

but they remained still otherwise. "I need to speak with this man," the leader said.

"Unfortunately, he died shortly after I met him. But not before I promised to help send the children of his companions home. It took a lot of effort to break through the barrier around that dimension to get them here, but we finally made it."

"I see," he replied, eyes narrowed with suspicion. Not that I blamed him. It did sound like I was making things up. "Can you tell me the first name of the man you say you spoke with?"

"Kastor," I said. It still felt strange to use that name. In his memories, Blackstone hadn't been called by that name for years. And I had never thought of him that way.

Their leader raised one of his charcoal black brows. "Kastor? Are you sure that was his name?"

"As certain as I am of my own. He gave me his memories before he died." I wasn't certain I should have told them that, but trust overwhelmed me and I couldn't help it. It was like I was back in the tent when I first met Blackstone, and he had done something to make me blab everything.

They all turned to look at their leader. To say they looked disturbed would have been an understatement. "I understand," he said, giving no indication of what he thought of that. "Why don't you come back to our headquarters so we can discuss this further? We would love to help your friends reunite with their families."

I sensed no dishonesty from any of them. And I needed the help. I decided to go with the overwhelming urge to follow. I went back to speak with Ro, explaining what they wanted. It took no effort at all to get them to come along, their repressed excitement palpable.

CHAPTER TWENTY-SIX
Special

WE SPENT HOURS IN a large room with tables and chairs and refreshments. They treated us all well. I sat with the black-haired man at a small table. He told me his name was Sorcer, and he seemed very interested in anything I said. More than I would have expected. Then again, we had come through a portal and nobody knew anything about us.

"He said that they stopped trying to perform any of the ceremonies on their children, because it didn't work and was killing them," I explained. He had been debriefing me for over an hour. "They let their hopes for the alterations go and instead turned their focus onto trying to find a way home."

"Which they could not do." There was no condemnation in his voice. He was just stating a fact as he took notes.

"If planets can be anything, I'd say that one is pure

evil. I had my compass with me, and even with its help, I couldn't figure out a way to see past all the static. It was a combination of my tech, the math, and Blackstone's memories that helped me figure it out."

"What was stopping you?" Sorcer asked me. He was leaning forward, as if he wanted to pull all the information from me. Or that I wasn't speaking quickly enough for him.

"It was a time dilation. I've never had to address that before, but there's something about how time flows there that it altered the equations. Once I cleared that up, I hightailed it out of there. It took a lot of power, more than was available. I ended up tapping into a budding earthquake to get enough power. Even then I really only had the right coordinates to come here, rather than go home."

He didn't ask me where home was. I'd never have told him. Even back when Blackstone had me acting loopy and spilling my guts, there were some things I never said then, either. I'm sure he knew that.

"And they were provided by Blackstone?"

"His memories, the stars - he didn't betray you." My voice grew louder as I realized they could blame the old man for treason when he really took a calculated risk that paid off.

"No, we don't believe he did. Even as a young man at the start of his training, he could sense the very soul of a person. He trusted you. That means anything you did, it would be for our benefit."

Oh. Well, that was nice. "I wish my leader felt that way. Or any of my teammates. But I promised Blackstone to get the Outsiders home, no matter what. So I made it work."

I bit my lip, wondering if I should explain my comment about my team. Had it made me look bad?

"Yes, you did well. You did something our best Magus could not. And you did it blind." He didn't sound sarcastic.

"He didn't have the tech the way I do. It's not his fault. He probably could have helped me get back sooner if he hadn't died." A lump rose in my throat. The grief and loss I had felt because of our mind connection took me off guard. I didn't want to break down in front of them.

Sorcer jotted down a note. "Then you compensated for the time factor?"

"It was at the last second, but yes. And it only worked because time has to function normally here or else you wouldn't have been able to portal jump like we did. Then I figured out how to key the sequence home off of Blackstone's astronomy lessons and sent my team on their way."

Did I sound like I was bragging? I was filled with exaltation at the successful leap, but maybe to him, I sounded a tad snide. That would be just what I needed. Another group of people thinking that I believed I was better than them.

"You were correct about the time factor. I have my best people making calculations and interviewing the ones you brought back with you. We've been able to trace their families, but there is something you should know. Their parents or grandparents - the ones who made the trip - are still here. The time flux that caused so much trouble flows in swirls. You have landed here in what they would consider the past."

"That's crazy." It really was. And shouldn't that have blown up the universe or something? Wait. Nobody on that exploration team had come back. Maybe not.

"It does feel that way. The original team is here, and young, and have just signed on to train in our schools where we teach those who want to portal jump."

I stared at Sorcer blankly. Something fluttered in the back of my mind, and I realized that since I got to the Magus headquarters, there were no more of Blackstone's memories to guide me.

"I don't understand. Why can't I remember you, then?" I asked. I still felt no dishonesty or malice from Sorcer or any of the other Magus clans. But maybe it was their dampening field and not because I could believe in them.

"Our building has a dampening effect on certain powers used by the mind. It's a place of peace and reflection for many, especially the ones who have difficulty blocking out the thoughts of others. It extends to the place you landed, although it is weaker there. If we had stayed there longer, I'm certain you would have eventually recognized me."

Damn. I was flying blind. I thought if I couldn't trust them, I would know. A pit of acid opened in my stomach, and my heart started to pound. Did I just make a huge mistake?

Was I safe? Were any of us? With Blackstone's memories, if I met somebody dangerous from his past, I would know it and then respond accordingly. But not here. Did the block go away if I left? "Is it permanent?"

"Please do not distress yourself. You will be able to access the memories of the man who gifted them to you once you leave here.

"Then I want to leave," I blurted.

To give him credit, Sorcer didn't even hesitate. "I understand. Come, we'll finish our conversation in the shade of the trees. There is a cool breeze this evening."

Sorcer's casual response comforted me. He led me from the building and then past the pasture where I had opened the gateway. Farther still, until the prickling in my skin made me aware of the return of Blackstone's gifts.

"So the Outsiders - I mean, the ones who have returned, they are here before they would have been born?" I asked as we took a seat on a bench beneath an oak tree. It was common enough and identical to the ones I'd see on Earth Prime.

"Yes, that's exactly what I'm saying. We will reunite them with their families, although many of them are older than their parents."

That was insane. "Wait a second. If they know what comes next, that they'll be trapped in that Mention until they die, why would they even go on the journey? And if they don't, and their children aren't born, how could we come back to tell them?" My mind boggled, but Sorcer let out a laugh.

"They will go anyway. We've already secured their agreement. They know this will be a one way trip for them and are getting their affairs in order. They believe in what they do and want their children to have life. It will be many years before they depart, anyway. We have predicted this particular portal will open on a date three years hence."

Three years? Not a chance. I wasn't going to wait until

they left to go back for Mason. "What do you mean by predicting the portal?" I asked, latching onto another subject. But I didn't want to find out they waited that long for a reason that would also stop me from going sooner.

"Our power tears the fabric of the Multiverse. However, sometimes the portals are nearly open on their own and that is when we use them."

Some portals were easier to get to than others. But there were so many that the Corps assigned us the ones our compasses latched onto the best. The scientists probably had the same information as Blackstone's people, but with an infinite number to choose from, there was no need to wait years between jumps.

Did that mean Earth Prime was some kind of portal hub? And if all the copies technically were the same planet, then why didn't this one have the same number available?

And did that also mean that it wasn't our tech that gave us better access to portals, it was really us having more portals within reach? Would I have to wait three years before I could go get Mason?

My head felt faint as a mountain of emotions rocked me. No. I'd figure out a way. There was something strange about the Mention, and I was beginning to suspect it was enveloped in a swirling time flux, but I'd figure it out. Even if I had to wait three years to save him, three minutes after I left.

Sorcer's voice sounded faraway. "My dear, are you unwell?"

"I'll be all right," I murmured as memories of Mason flickered through my mind. Clear, full of detail, up close and personal thanks to the Blackstone effect.

"There are things we can do that will help you," Sorcer replied. "Techniques to control or even block the mind alterations until you can process them better."

"Are you sure I even can?" I asked. The anger and frustration I was trying to push aside added force to my words. These people were kind and helpful and even when I could access Blackstone's gifts again, they read as trustworthy. But they were content to wait years when I wanted to get back now.

"You have the ability. The mind transfer would not have worked otherwise. You have a special mind."

"I was the only one who was there," I blurted. "That's it. He first made me understand him and everyone around me. It hurt. But he said he couldn't do that to any of the Outsiders, that the damned planet blocked and stunted them. Then he died, but before he was lost, he put his hands on my head and forced it to work. It wasn't because I'm special. I was just convenient to a desperate man."

I stopped myself. There really wasn't anything else for me to say, anyway. If life had taught me anything, it was that I was only unique in bad ways. Even born to a family with status, I had spent most of my life in the slums. My father was the one who dominated my life, ruined it, and I hadn't even seen him since I was eight. Blackstone's gifts meant nothing about me.

"Bailey, the fact he could do anything at all tells us how unique you are. None of the people we have met exploring the portals can alter their minds the way we do. It was a miracle he succeeded, but most of all because he found you, somebody from another world who could take the alterations directly. Even here, with as many candidates as we have, almost none can do that."

His words sank in, pulling me out of the trap my memories held for me. "If you think you can help me control this, I'm willing to learn." And hopefully quick. I still needed to figure out how to get enough power to get Mason. Wherever he was. Whenever he was. These little mind trips weren't helpful if I couldn't control them.

I sighed. I turned my head towards the path breaking around the gentle roll of the hill, and caught the flicker of movement coming up the path. Soon, a man came into view, his features more apparent as he drew closer.

He had the same black hair and eyes as Sorcer, but he was not much older than I was. I could have dismissed the familiarity I felt as a family resemblance. But I would have recognized that face anywhere. I knew it better than my own, after all I had been through.

It was him. The man who clung to me as he lay dying in the dirt on a planet that had trapped his people for decades. It was Kastor.

Blackstone.

CHAPTER TWENTY-SEVEN
Blackstone

TIME SLOWED, AND I stood to my feet without a thought. My body went rigid. I couldn't move. Everything around me turned black. When I could see again, it wasn't Kastor walking up the path. It was an image floating behind my eyes. A memory belonging to him.

I saw myself, back when I first arrived in the Mention, dirty and bewildered and frozen. There was a look of panic on my face. Blackstone knew what Rader wanted to do to me. He would have been concerned for any woman caught by Rader or his brothers.

But it was more than that. He knew me. Blackstone remembered me, even after all those years being trapped in that Mention. He had met me on his planet, knew he would see me again someday. Waited on me, at the end of his life. The guarantee that his ultimate goal, to get their children home, would be fulfilled.

I should have known. They said the Outsiders had

come home to parents or grandparents younger than they were. The original team of explorers were all here, not yet having left.

Blackstone was one of them. I was standing on his planet, reliving his memories, and he was here with me, alive. My knees almost buckled when his thoughts and feelings overwhelmed me.

The memories took hold of me, pulled me along on a lightning-fast ride through his life.

He was sitting in the dirt. A small part of him wished he were standing when I accidentally walked into Rader's hidden camp where he was being held prisoner. A larger part wished I came for him sooner, when he was still young, when he was still strong.

Then he saved me. He helped me, gave me the gift to understand him, but along with it, a sense of familiarity. Closeness. We had known each other, trusted beyond all measure. A sense of that came through and I told him everything in that tent, more than I myself remembered.

The focus changed, and I was held in the moment that Mason approached him in the forest. Blackstone raising his hands, forgetting he held my weapons. Mason shouting at him to drop them. Blackstone calling back, telling Mason that he meant no harm.

His words, falling on deaf ears, meaningless to the man who had chased after him. Then Mason, cutting him down. Dragging him back.

Blackstone's palms cupping my head, held there by my hands on his. A touch, a connection, a last act of desperate love.

Memories faded and my eyes opened, once again standing beside Sorcer, watching Blackstone as he approached me. My eyes were afflicted with a strange double-vision, me looking out of my eyes, and also out of his.

Had I gone insane? I could see and understand both viewpoints at once. Humans weren't meant to do this, even the ones with special minds.

Then his voice, vital and vibrant and alive, speaking to me. "Good afternoon. I'm Kastor, a Blackstone Magus, at your service," he said. The sound of his name centered me, and I snapped back into reality, where I was just me, seeing from my own eyes, watching while Blackstone met me for the first time again.

I held out my hand, and he took it. There was an instant connection, as if we had known each other for years. He felt it too, a glitter of interest sparking to life in his eyes.

Fortunately, I was able to speak. "Bailey Hawke. But you can call me Bailey. I met some of your people on the other side of a portal and I promised Bla-" I stumbled on his name.

Oh, no. I couldn't say that, could I? Tell him that he made me promise to finish his mission as he lay dying?

I coughed. Then I uncapped my canteen and took a sip, grateful I still had it on me, using it as an excuse to avoid talking. I screwed the cap back on and used the back of my sleeve to dry my eyes. I pretended it was because I had coughed, but it was really because I was an emotional wreck, seeing him like this.

Sorcer had been observing us. "I'm afraid I must depart. I have instructed Kastor to not ask too many penetrating questions. Please, do not tell him too much about his future. We must avoid paradox."

I nodded my agreement. He departed, leaving me alone with Blackstone. He studied me, then gestured to the bench. "Please, let us sit. I can wait to speak until you recover."

The connection between us had to mean something. Us crossing each other's paths on different planets, in different parts of our lives. After another sip of water, I continued.

"I promised that I would help the children of your kind find their way home. But maybe while I'm here, somebody can help me figure out how to keep my brains from exploding because of these crazy gifts."

Blackstone laughed, his eyes twinkling. It was surreal to see him. To talk to him, and even touch him. I couldn't stay focused. Was I still on the verge of going insane?

Then again, I was exhausted. And they hadn't let me shower or change my clothes. Not that they were cruel. In fact, they seemed to be steeped in kindness. There were simply too many things going on. We hadn't stopped talking or debriefing for even a moment. Of course they didn't think about what a rumpled mess I was.

Sorcer hadn't noticed. But not me - I was keenly aware of what a disaster I looked. My hand drifted to my hair, but I jerked it back to my side. Touching it would bring attention to the mess.

Uncertain about what to do, feeling awkward after being left alone with this non-stranger, I leaned into the memories Blackstone had given me to see what it was like for Kastor to be meeting me for the first time.

It was an idiotic idea. I had no control over what I saw. Instead of getting a glimpse of his thoughts, I was bombarded with several flashes of memories. Walks, and combat training, and learning how to use my gifts. He was going to be an excellent teacher. Laughing, sharing meals, growing into trust and helping me calculate trajectories and time dilations.

But then one last memory, quick and disturbing, flashed through my mind.

One last shining memory rose behind my eyes, pulling me into the past that was my future. Me smiling up at Blackstone. Happy. And then he leaned down to kiss me.

No way. I shoved that thought right out of my mind and blocked the replay. I was positive I was about to punch him in that memory for daring to put a move on me, and I didn't want to disrupt our first meeting with future anger.

He was waiting for me. Patiently sitting on the bench, content to let me sort through the barrage of memories controlling my life. Somebody like him had to have gone through this, too. And learned to control it.

I tried not to think about it, but Blackstone was stunning. He looked like he was about thirty. His dark eyes glittered brightly and his black hair was in need of a haircut. He kept swiping it away, running his hand through the silky strands.

A picture rose in my mind. His hands, wrinkled and covered in clay, leaving behind dirty streaks after touching his hair. Which was white, not black, when I met him months ago, decades in his future.

Power radiated off of him, almost like a wave of light, touching me with its glowing warmth. "I can help you control the memories," he offered. His voice was gentle and kind. "That's why they called me here. I'm glad - you have traveled through a portal already. The stories you can tell..."

"What do I need to do? Ever since I arrived, I've been overwhelmed with all these thoughts and images." It was too much. I could feel the memories threatening to take over again. What if I couldn't get back out again?

"I can help you place a block. No more access to the memories, at least for now. Until you get used to what's happening. We're also worried that it will cause you trouble if you remember something that touches on a possible paradox because of your foreknowledge."

He was talking sense. Yes, he absolutely was. But I was more afraid of the possibility that I would go insane than letting slip too much information. I already felt halfway crazy.

My mind kept seeing this conversation from Blackstone's point of view. I almost cried out when I heard my words echoed back in misty memory before I even said them. "Yes, help me block them. I'm not sure what will happen to me if I don't. Now, if possible."

I heard the words as I spoke, but I remembered them, too. I wondered if I could have said something else before and changed it but didn't know despite already hearing the memories. At that thought, I broke out into a cold sweat and realized I was already half insane with what I already I knew.

Kastor placed his hands on either side of my head, the same way he had back in that damned hellhole Mention. Warmth from his palms soaked into my skin, and I leaned closer into the comfort. He hummed under his breath. It soothed me, and I relaxed.

"Feel the heat from my hands, sinking in deeper." The metal implants on his hands connected too, facilitating his actions. "Sense the shield, and take it from me. Place it between you and the new memories."

The funny thing was, it worked. I imagined a wall in my mind, and the rioting thoughts trapped behind it. Silence blanketed that part of my mind, and relief filled me.

"Thank you," I said as he pulled back, sensing I was done. "So very much."

"Anytime." The gentle breeze ruffled a few strands of my hair, and Blackstone tucked them behind my ear. It was a familiar gesture, like he had done it a thousand times before. But then he let his hands drop and leaned back. "Besides, this way we can speak more about your travels without your attention being drawn away by the past."

I chuckled, giddy with relief. "True."

"They have told me what they can, and I've met with some of the returnees. They are all being careful not to say too much, at least where explorers such as myself can hear."

"You don't want to know what happens?" I asked.

"I mean, you already know that none of you return." I don't know why I said it, but it was true. And I felt the compulsion to tell him everything, same as when I was a prisoner in Rader's tent. A morbid fascination crept over me. "Are you worried it will make you change your mind?"

Kastor Blackstone shook his head slowly. "I'm afraid we can't change the past, my dear, even the one that hasn't happened yet. Maybe we grow old and die, but we have children. And they come home. They are our hope and a future we won't give up. We can accept that, Bailey. We all must go when destiny calls."

I didn't know why I was so emotional. I kept telling myself that Blackstone had made me care about him with his mind powers and it wasn't real. But confronted with his younger self, I wondered if I was really tapping into something else entirely.

Maybe it was real. Maybe we became friends before he left. The trick Blackstone pulled back in the Mention could have been him sharing the mutual care and respect we had for each other in the future. Reminding me about the future we were about to have. He was somebody I learned to trust. After all I had been through, it would be tragic to lose that.

"I can't wrap my mind around this," I admitted. "I'm all tapped out of brain power."

"We can talk about you, instead. You're different in ways I haven't been able to discern, and infinitely fascinating."

What a shock it must have been to see me again, there at the end of his life. I could forgive him for the casual gestures and teasing in the present. He had to be grasping onto anything that would keep him from losing himself to a paradox, trying to avoid conclusions he could draw from just me sitting there beside him.

I understood how strange it must be for him. It was hard to settle into this new Mention. It seemed wrong to even call it that - it wasn't anything like the worlds we had visited before. That we had taken over. Any team visiting here would have left right away and never come back. Their technology was too advanced, knowledge too great.

That must be why Sorcer left us alone together. To allow us to figure out how to deal with each other without the pressure of an audience.

When Blackstone saw me, when he was old, he had to know his time was near. He took the chance of giving me his power in the end because he knew his life was over. Even though I was alien to him, he also knew it would work, because he met me in his past and I already had his gifts, which meant he succeeded.

What the hell. Time was entirely too confusing. "I'm not that interesting. In fact, you didn't act like you knew me," I said. "Maybe you forgot me."

Blackstone's laughter interrupted my attempt to deflect his intense attention. A blush crept into my cheeks.

"I'm sure I held that information back, but I never forget anything. And I could never forget you." The way he said it made me squirm.

The image of Mason's face broke into my thoughts and I almost started crying. This was too confusing. I was desperate to save him, yet I had been sitting there, laughing with Kastor. What was I supposed to do? I had to get to know this man beside me. His memories had helped me get out of that Mention. Now he can help me get back. No matter how awkward it was at first.

There had to be a way to find my way back to Mason. I promised myself I would. When I could. But for now, I had to deal with the new twists and turns dominating my life.

"Come with me. I'll show you to where you'll be staying. And I'm sure you would like to set your pack aside and wash away the stress of this situation."

I latched onto the change of subject. "That would be nice - and so would washing away all the dirt from the trip."

He laughed, then held out his arm. I humored him and placed my hand in his, and he used it to help me to my feet. But he didn't let go. Instead, he tucked my hand against his arm, like an old-fashioned knight, and set a leisurely pace.

"We will host you in the Blackstone compound," he said as we walked down the path back the way he had come. "Sorcer has requested it. We have the room, and our family is the strongest. If anyone can help you, it will be us."

He was stating facts, not bragging. It was easy to spot the difference. "What about going back for my lost teammate?" I asked. "I never leave a man behind. But I need help to adjust my compass so I can compensate for the time difference so we can go home."

A small village came into view, with low buildings

blending into the surrounding nature, along a cobbled stone street lined with trees and benches, fountains and displays of flowers.

"We will help you. To control your gifts, and to get home." He must have felt how scared that made me, because he rested his free hand on mine, holding it closer to his arm, surrounding it with his warmth. "You will be fine. I can already sense much of your destiny. You'll surprise yourself with how amazing you are."

I snorted. Yes, that was me, the Amazing Bailey Hawke. Daughter of a war hero who turned out to be a baby killer, and a woman I could only remember in one very distant memory. A small lady fading away under the onslaught of the monster, a mother who couldn't protect her child. The psycho and the weakling. Excellent lineage.

"Do you think you could teach me your method of travel? I think it can help me navigate. We had our brains jammed with theories and math, but there's more to it. I think if I could bring it all together, I might be able to figure it out."

Blackstone steered me up a small side path, lined with pretty cream-colored stones, soft like pumice or sandstone. And every ten or twelve steps, there was a dark glittering piece of obsidian set into the pathway, surrounded by clear stones that looked like rays of light shining out from the volcanic glass. Or maybe it was meant to indicate it was absorbing their light like a black hole.

There were hedges on each side of the path, and trees in the distance. I didn't see the huge stone castle until we came upon it after rounding the hill.

"I'll do everything I can to teach you what you need to know," he promised. "Now - welcome to Kastor Manor."

"They named it after you?"

Blackstone let out a bark of laughter. "No, it was not. I have done nothing to warrant such an honor. They named it after the first of my family to bear the Blackstone Magus title. When I was young, before the tests, I lived in his shadow. When I grew older, I was called by my last name, as many do when they attend school. I left it be."

There was something significant about what he was telling me, but I couldn't piece it together. But I knew his name was the right combination of sounds to help focus my compass when I opened the gateway to escape the Mention. It was the key.

If Kastor didn't hate his own name, he would have realized it was the ticket for them all to return home. How awful.

And maybe there was a lesson in that for me. Maybe I should stop being so upset when somebody called me Hawke. I had a lot to think about. But first, my new home.

The building before us was enormous. It was tall, probably at least five floors high, and it looked like they made it of the same cream-colored stones as the pathway, although I could tell they actually made it from a different material.

The front sparkled with rows of windows, tall and made from a thick crystal that refracted light. It was gorgeous. There was a chunk of obsidian set over each window, a part of the wall. There was also a giant, oval-shaped piece of the same black volcanic glass glittering darkly above the wooden door, which was painted white, like the trim around the windows.

"Beautiful," I gasped. "This is where I'm going to live?" It was a hell of a lot nicer than my little room in the slums.

Blackstone nodded. "The entire family lives here, but you won't be in the main quarters. There is more privacy in the workshops out back."

"I don't know what to say." Everything was so different. From my life in the slums, and especially from the Mentions. "I appreciate your help, and your hospitality."

If it had been anyone else, I would have slept with my knife under my pillow. But I still had enough access to the gifts we'd shielded in my head that I could get a clear read on his motives. And Sorcer's. They were going to help me because I helped them, above their typical desire to help others that I had noticed in the Outsiders. I had brought back their children. They felt they owed me a debt.

I could work with that. And I finally had the tools. My gifts, the compass, having a sense of time. All the pieces I needed to juggle. The only factor remaining was the power I would need to travel in time and through that damned barrier around the Mention to get to Mason.

But I was in a position to make it happen. It might take me three years to get there, but I was going to save him. Someday.

"Are you ready?" Blackstone asked.

"Yeah, I am. Let's go."

Author's Note

Thank you for joining me on Bailey's journey through the Gateway. I hope you enjoyed following her as she took on the locals, Ginger, and the overwhelming expansion of her mind.

She still has a lot of work to do before she goes back to save Mason, but she'll get there someday.

In the meantime, you can check out my other books at www.tjkellybooks.com or find me on Facebook, Instagram, TikTok, etc., as @AuthorTJKelly. Let me know what you think about the Gateway Jumpers!

More Information

Other Books By T.J. Kelly

Armageddon's Ward
Irregular Magic
Darkness Wins
Praelia Nox

Or visit
www.tjkellybooks.com/books
for information about the complete Armageddon's Ward
series and various short stories on her blog. Sign up for
the newsletter to receive notices of upcoming books and
exclusive content.

You can follow T.J. (@AuthorTJKelly) on:

Facebook
Giveaway announcements, book updates, and fun!

T.J. Kelly's Select Readers Group on Facebook
Join in the discussion! Interact with T.J. and other readers,
ask questions, and have fun! Offer your opinion on
upcoming novels and participate in special readers group
giveaways.

Blog at www.tjkellybooks.com
News and short stories.

Instagram
Pictures of projects and swag for sale and giveaways.

Twitter
Occasional news and retweets of awesome books.

www.tjkellybooks.com
List of books in the works and publish dates.

Amazon Author Page
www.amazon.com/author/tjkelly
Follow my page to stay informed about new book releases.

BookBub
Help build a following and stay informed.

Reviews
The number one thing readers check before purchasing a book are the reviews! If you enjoyed this book, would you be kind enough to leave a review? Amazon, Goodreads - wherever you prefer. It would be greatly appreciated!

About the Author

T.J. Kelly writes Young Adult, Fantasy, Paranormal, and Sci-fi novels. Destiny called on her thirteenth birthday when her mother asked the local bookstore owner to choose thirteen books a girl her age might like. The resulting pile of sci-fi and fantasy novels was her first love. When she can tear herself away from reading and writing, T.J. watches movies, asks countless questions, and bakes treats. Originally from California, T.J. now lives in Texas where she's hard at work on the companion series novels to the Armageddon's Ward series and the concluding novels to the Gateway Jumpers series.

www.tjkellybooks.com